DANTE

STONE SOCIETY BOOK 3

BY FAITH GIBSON

Copyright © 2015 by Faith Gibson
Published by Faith Gibson
Editor: Jagged Rose Wordsmithing
First e-book edition: May 2015
First print edition: May 2015
Cover design by KPG, photos from iStock
ISBN: 978-0692435243

This book is intended for mature audiences only.

Dedication

To the kids who enrich our lives. For me, the boy and the girl make it all worth it.

As always, to the man for indulging me and loving me, unconditionally.

Acknowledgements

My writing posse: Kendall, Jen, and Nikki – thank you for having my back, day in and day out

My beta readers: Alex B, Sharon B, Shannon P, Candy R, Tanya R, and Lita T

KPG – all I can say is WOW

The ladies at TaSTy WordGasms, thank you for always being there for me

Cherri-Anne Boitson, what a fabulous cheerleader you are, and your reviews make my heart sing!

Prologue

Greece, 2041

ISABELLE SARANTOS WAS seasick. The normally calm waters off the shore of Zakynthos were choppy and angry, matching the mood of her husband, Alexi. Her new husband. What was supposed to be the happiest time of her life was quickly turning into one of the worst. The honeymoon was definitely over. If she were honest with herself, it ended before it even started. Alexi's family had pushed for a quick wedding, but she had insisted on having a several months' long engagement.

Now that Alexi had his ring on her finger, he no longer felt the need to wine and dine her. Or kiss her. Or make love to her. Sure, they had sex, but it had turned as rough as her husband. While they were engaged, Alexi casually brought up discussions of her father, Jonas Montague. Her father, the world-famous doctor and scientist who successfully created the first cloned human. Once they were married, Alexi was no longer casual. When Isabelle couldn't convince him she had no dealings with her father, whom she assumed was dead, nor his research, Alexi turned cold and callous.

The yacht tipped and lurched, as did Isabelle's stomach. She tried talking to him. That angered him. She tried staying away from him. That angered him more. She asked to go back to their villa when the

1

weather turned dark. He slapped her, causing blood to pool in the corner of her mouth. The marina was no longer in sight; the yacht was in the middle of the ravaging sea. Still, Isabelle stood on deck, holding on to the railing.

"What are you doing out here? Get your ass inside!" Alexi had caught up with her. There were only so many places you could go on a boat, even one the size of *The Magdalena*. Isabelle thought for one brief second about jumping overboard. The man standing before her was not the man she fell in love with. The charm had been removed by the words *"I do."* Alexi caught her looking over the railing. "Do you want to go into the water? Is that what you're contemplating? Answer me!"

Alexi grabbed Isabelle and pushed her face over the railing toward the water. What happened next was a blur. Adrenaline must have set in, because Isabelle knew in that instant she did not want to go into the Ionian Sea. Rain drizzled, slicking the polished wood deck. She and Alexi fought. He slapped her, and she kneed him in the balls. When he recovered, he came at her. Somehow, the momentum of Alexi charging and the way Isabelle twisted had her husband flying over the railing into the tempestuous waters.

Isabelle heard a shrill noise, one that wouldn't stop. When one of the yacht crewmen grabbed her arms, she realized it was her. She was screaming for help. Panic erupted with everyone involved. Isabelle knew enough about the Sarantos family to know the shit had just hit the fan for her. It wouldn't matter that Alexi struck her, or she had been defending herself. They would blame her for what happened. Her life was ruined. She was ruined. Isabelle would have to leave Greece, return to the States, and start life over.

The next few hours were a nightmare. The harbor patrol was called to *The Magdalena* where Isabelle was grilled relentlessly. Had the bruise on her face and the swelling of her bloody lip not been indications she was telling the truth, she probably would have been hauled to jail for murder. When Stavros Sarantos, Alexi's father, heard the news, to say he was distraught was an understatement. He wanted Isabelle charged with manslaughter.

The next few days turned into weeks. Those were worse than the day Alexi went overboard. The weather broke, and the waters calmed; still, his body was never found. The authorities questioned all the crew members. Even though some had seen the way Alexi treated her, none would speak up against him. Isabelle was given an around-the-clock guard at her and Alexi's home. Stavros did his best to have Isabelle removed from the house, but a judge had ordered him to stand down. He must have been the one judge in all of Greece the Sarantos patriarch didn't have in his pocket.

Isabelle truly feared for her life. She didn't leave the house. She called the hospital administrator and asked for a leave of absence. This was granted considering she had lost her husband. A permanent leave was granted when Stavros strong-armed the chief of staff. Not only did Isabelle lose her husband, she lost her job. Her father-in-law called her daily, threatening her. Isabelle finally stopped answering the phone. She was in a country with no family, no friends, and no means of support. Luckily, she had put what she received from her salary at the hospital into a separate

3

account. Having signed a pre-nuptial agreement in the event of Alexi's death, Isabelle got a small settlement paid in cash. All property would go back to the family. She was thankful she and Alexi didn't have children. Stavros had mentioned more than once how he would have a hand in raising his grandchildren.

Almost a month to the date of the incident, the police found no evidence of foul play on Isabelle's part, and she was declared innocent. The policeman who stood guard outside her home drove her to the bank and then the airport. She withdrew all her money, putting it in a carry-on suitcase. It might be crazy to walk around toting that much cash, but she didn't trust its safety any other way. With one suitcase full of money and one full of clothes and jewelry, Isabelle left Greece and never looked back.

Isabelle returned to the one place where she had felt loved: Tennessee. Even though Maria and Rico were more like a foster family in the beginning, they had taken her in and cared for her when her own parents abandoned her. It took a couple of weeks, but Isabelle finally settled into a rental apartment. She bought a small, energy-efficient car and began applying for jobs. She pawned every piece of jewelry Alexi had ever given her. When her nausea continued, she finally convinced herself to take a pregnancy test. Isabelle hadn't left all of the Sarantos family behind. She had the newest member growing in her belly.

Chapter One

Dante Di Pietro pulled into the well-lit driveway but didn't cut the engine. His knuckles were white as he clutched the leather-wrapped steering wheel of his silver Aston Martin Vanquish. He was five hundred sixty-three years old and had been with countless women over the centuries. Never had taking one to a restaurant made him nauseous. Until now. Isabelle Sarantos was his mate. He should be ecstatic. Over the moon. Riding the high his brothers were. He wasn't. He had lived his many years without the hope of ever finding the one. The one who was meant to be by his side for all eternity. The one who would be the mother to his children. Now, he had found the one, and she wasn't sure she wanted him.

Isabelle's life had not been an easy one. Had not been one filled with the type of love that would encourage her to pursue a relationship with Dante, even if they weren't fated to be together. She had experienced love and loss at the hands of someone who used her, a man she had given her heart to who didn't offer his in return. Why wouldn't she be hesitant to be in another permanent relationship? Especially one where her partner was chosen for her.

Before a few weeks ago, Isabelle had been a physician, a mere human who had no idea Gargoyles existed or that she herself was half Gargoyle. She had lived her life without the knowledge of who and what she was. Now, she was still that physician, but she was also more. She was his mate.

Dante had given her an out, offering to part ways as friends. He also suggested taking things slow, a trial run of sorts. Isabelle had agreed to the second option, proceeding as if they were a normal, human couple. The last few weeks had been pure hell. Being in her presence and not touching her was the worst kind of torture. His beast fought him every time he was around her. Fought to get out, claim what was rightfully theirs.

Tonight was their first date, and Dante was nervous. What if she changed her mind? What if she didn't find him desirable? What if…? He could sit here all night and drive himself crazy with what ifs, or he could get his Gargoyle ass out of the car and knock on the door.

Surprisingly, Isabelle had been the one to ask Dante for a date. Wanting to impress her, he had suggested Chez Vaison, the fanciest restaurant in New Atlanta. Rarely did Dante have the opportunity to dress up. Being the city's medical examiner, his daily attire consisted of khakis and a lab coat. Isabelle was the current physician at the New Atlanta Penitentiary. She had accepted the position when the former doctor lost his life in the midst of the Unholy. Over the past couple of weeks, Dante and Isabelle had been in close proximity to one another, but it was more of a professional capacity than a personal one. They had spoken a little of personal matters, but their main focus had been the inmates they were treating. He was looking forward to seeing her in something dressier than her casual clothes, in a setting more conducive to getting to know one another.

Dante made his way up the front porch steps and stopped just short of knocking on the door. He smoothed his tie before sliding his hands down his thighs. It was more a nervous gesture than actually wiping sweat off his hands. Gargoyles didn't sweat easily. He calmed his breathing and reached out with his senses to get a feel of Isabelle's mood. His mate was moving around the house, pacing. She was talking. Listening closer, he ascertained she was on the telephone. It was rude to eavesdrop, but he couldn't help himself.

"Something has happened, and we really need to talk. I should be able to get away this weekend. I can't wait to see you, too. I need to go now, but I will call you back when I am more certain of my plans. You, too. Goodbye." Isabelle was now silent, but her footsteps continued. It wasn't lost on him she was making plans to go see someone. A man perhaps? His fists opened and closed, the jealousy tugging at his gut. Why hadn't he listened more closely to the other voice on the line?

Not wanting to give Isabelle any more time to think about whomever she had been talking to, he knocked on the door. Her footsteps halted before starting up again. The door opened, and Dante sucked in a breath. He always found Isabelle to be beautiful, but the creature standing before him was mesmerizing. A black dress hugged her every curve. Sparkly silver heels added to her frame, bringing her closer to Dante's height of six-four. Her hair was twisted up somehow in the back, exposing the pale skin of her neck. Dante's fangs were itching to burst forth and sink into her flesh.

Isabelle found her voice first. "Dante, please come in." She stepped back, allowing him entrance into her home. Once she closed the door, she complimented his attire. "You look very handsome this evening."

"And you are even more beautiful…" Dante had never been at a loss for words, but the woman standing before him had transformed herself from pretty to exquisite. Remembering the gift he'd brought for her, he pulled a box from the inside pocket of his coat and presented it to his mate. Isabelle stared at the box without reaching for it.

"I saw this, and it reminded me of your eyes," Dante said, hoping she didn't feel he was being too forward. "Please, Isabelle, it's just a small token of my appreciation." He felt self-conscious, holding the gift in the air.

Her eyes left the box and settled on his. "Your appreciation? I'm not sure what you would be thanking me for." She tentatively accepted the box. Taking care with the ribbon, she removed the lid, and a barely audible gasp escaped from between her lips. "Dante, it's beautiful, but you shouldn't have."

The chocolate diamond bracelet sparkled with the same intensity as her brown eyes. Dante took the bracelet and clasped it around her small wrist. Isabelle twisted her arm so the light caught the diamonds, causing them to sparkle. She smiled briefly then slipped back into her serious face.

"I appreciate the fact you are taking small steps toward a relationship. At least, I hope this is what we are doing. I apologize if the bracelet isn't to your liking.

We are new to one another yet, and I do not know what your preferences are. If you wish, you can exchange it."

"It's not that I don't like it. I just wasn't expecting it, that's all. We should probably get going. Our reservation is for seven." Isabelle reached for her purse, dropping her cell phone inside. She grabbed her coat off the rack and draped it over her arm.

Dante opened the front door and escorted her to his car. Her reaction to the Aston was much like the one to the bracelet. It was not what he expected. Most women at least smiled when they saw the expensive sports car. Some even oohed and aahed. Instead, Isabelle frowned. Maybe she didn't like sports cars. He would have to remember to drive slowly and carefully. Once she was seated, he closed her door and rounded the vehicle, getting in the driver's seat. The engine roared to life, and soft classical music filled the air.

ISABELLE WASN'T NERVOUS; she was leery. When she opened the door for Dante, it was as if time rewound itself. His godlike stature, his handsome features, the suit that molded perfectly to his body, and the bracelet, all of those combined to remind her considerably of Alexi. He, too, had been handsome beyond compare and had captivated her with his fancy dress clothes and expensive cars. In the beginning, he lavished her with expensive jewelry. Everything had been perfect. She had to remind herself Dante was not Alexi. Dante was her mate.

9

What did that mean, exactly? Was she just supposed to put her heart in the hands of the fates, beings Isabelle wasn't certain she even believed in? She was a doctor, and she believed whole-heartedly in the sciences, in facts. She had been raised by parents who believed in the old ways: the gods and goddesses. And the fates. She herself wasn't a religious person, never had been. Textbooks had been her bible, a classroom her temple.

She and Dante had spent little time together outside the Pen. While they were working, they maintained a professional relationship, no matter how much the mate bond pulled at her. Other than the chaste kiss Isabelle had placed on Dante's lips a few weeks before, there had been no physical contact. True to his word, he was being a gentleman, and it was driving her crazy. The need to touch him was becoming unbearable. Being so close in proximity in her tiny office while they pored over the inmate files was too much for her to handle. Either Dante had an extraordinary amount of self-control, or the bond didn't affect him as it did her. Pretty soon, she was going to own stock in a battery company.

In her home, there had been breathing room. Now that they were in his car, the nearness was stifling. She cracked the window, needing fresh air.

"Are you hot?" Dante asked.

"Yes, I'm…" She didn't finish. How did she tell him she was suffocating? That she was more confused than she'd ever been in her life. Isabelle had been the one to request they take things slowly, and now she wanted anything but slow. She turned and looked out the window so he couldn't see the indecision on her face. His large hand settled over both of hers. The classical music flowed through the speakers, keeping the silence from being so awkward.

Isabelle rarely ventured farther than her home and work. The drive downtown allowed her to get a glimpse of the bustling city landscape. At their destination, Dante pulled into the valet lane and angled out of the car. He made his way to her door, which the valet had opened. Dante moved in closer to assist Isabelle in getting out. Once she was by his side, they stepped up on the sidewalk where the valet gave Dante a parking stub. He secured it in his coat pocket before placing his hand on the small of Isabelle's back, walking close beside her to the entrance of the restaurant.

They were seated right away. Their table was one of the best in the house, out of the way of other patrons. Before the maître d' could pull Isabelle's seat out, Dante was there. He reminded her so much of Alexi in the early days that she really didn't know how to feel. On one hand, she was flattered. It had been a long time since she had been on a date that included dressing up and going to dinner at a fancy restaurant. On the other hand, she was guarded and wary.

The waiter asking for her drink order brought her attention to the here and now, back to the man in front of her. Make that the Gargoyle in front of her. He may look like a man, yet he was anything but. Having seen one of her brothers transform right before her eyes, she knew what Dante would look like when he phased. Would he ever phase in front of her? Did the mate bond create such a pull that during sex the beast inside would take over? The thought excited her. While she

11

was uncertain about a lifelong relationship, she was looking forward to getting physical. She couldn't help but admire how striking Dante looked in his charcoal gray suit. The bright blue tie against the stark white of his shirt kept grabbing her attention. Thoughts of Dante removing the tie from around his neck and using it for something much more wicked, such as tying her up or possibly blindfolding her, had her body humming. She caught the flare of Dante's nostrils. Dammit, she forgot his senses were so much more perceptive than a human's. He knew she was aroused.

To take his mind off her body, she told Dante, "I will have whatever wine you are having." He nodded and told the waiter to bring a bottle of Richebourg Grand Cru. Isabelle had never heard of the name brand nor the type of wine. She was pretty sure this bottle wouldn't have a screw off cap. She was about to ask what type of wine a Grand Cru was when she heard laughter coming from the other side of the room. A laugh she remembered after all this time: her mother's.

Chapter Two

ISABELLE STIFFENED WITH the knowledge her mother was close by. Her claws threatened to escape from her skin, her fangs from her gums. When she came face to face with Caroline about a month ago, all the heartache and abandonment issues came rushing back. Caroline tried to reach out and explain why she left Isabelle with Jonas all those years ago, but Isabelle wouldn't hear it. Her own mother had left her. Now that she had time to think on it, hadn't she done the same thing to her own son? Caroline had given most of her children up for adoption to protect them. Isabelle felt she had placed Connor in another home for his protection as well. So what was the difference? This war raged on inside Isabelle daily.

"Isabelle, what is wrong? And please don't tell me nothing. I saw you tense up prior to you getting lost in yourself. I would like to know what has you so on edge." Dante reached across the table and placed his hand on hers. A calm came over Isabelle. Was that the mate bond, or did Dante have some magical power? Her body no longer felt the need to phase.

"My mother is here." Isabelle didn't need to elaborate. During their time together at the Pen, going over the inmate files, she had told Dante all about seeing Caroline for the first time in twenty years.

"We can leave if you wish. I do not want our dinner to be tainted for any reason." Dante's thumb was rubbing softly over her wrist, touching the bracelet he had placed there earlier. The look on his face was sincere. He was thinking of her. If she asked him to leave, he would.

"No, I will be fine. It's just…" If her mother was here and laughing, did that mean her father was here as well? Isabelle's heart skipped a beat.

"Isabelle, if seeing your parents will ruin this night for you, I'd rather we go somewhere else."

How could he have known what she was thinking? "Dante, can you read my thoughts? Tell me the truth. Is there some type of connection through our bond that allows you to know what I'm thinking? Or are you psychic? Because you really freak me out sometimes." If he wanted honesty, there it was.

Dante's grip on her hand tightened slightly. "Since we are not truly mated, I can no more read your thoughts than I can anyone else's. I do have special abilities which allow me to know what someone is feeling. I can sense when people are near by the energy they put off. All Gargoyles can sense emotions; my ability is extraordinary."

The waiter appeared with the wine Dante ordered, presenting the bottle to him. Dante nodded, and the waiter uncorked the bottle. He placed the cork on the table to Dante's right before pouring a small sample in his glass. Dante lifted the glass and sniffed the liquid before taking a small sip. Isabelle was entranced at the show before her. At home, she poured her wine and drank it. When Dante approved, the waiter filled their glasses. He placed the bottle in the middle of the table and asked if they were ready to order. Isabelle's appetite was all but diminished by the thoughts of her parents. Dante took the liberty of ordering for both of

14

them.

When they were alone again, Dante said, "I need to tell you something. I should have told you sooner, but I wanted the time to be right. I am afraid there won't ever be a right time, so now will have to suffice. And I apologize in advance if this further ruins your appetite." He took a sip of wine before continuing. *Oh crap.* If he was drinking wine, she probably needed to as well. She sniffed the wine like Dante had before taking a sip. She found it to be delicious. She took another sip, a larger one this time, hoping it would steel her resolve for whatever Dante was going to tell her.

Dante loosened his tie just a fraction before continuing, "Isabelle, how well do you know Dr. Mooneyham?"

This was not what she had been expecting. "He hired me at New Atlanta Hospital and then helped me start my own practice. I don't know him personally. Not really."

"Please do not take offense at what I am going to ask you next, but did you not find it odd he would suggest you open your own practice so soon after you began at the hospital?"

Isabelle jerked her hand from his grip. "You find me incompetent? That's why you're at the Pen, helping with the inmates, isn't it?" Her eyes were prickling. Dammit, she would not give him the satisfaction of seeing tears. Why did no one believe in her abilities?

"That is definitely not what I'm saying. I told you not to take offense, but that is precisely what you did. Isabelle, you are a capable physician, much more so

15

than anyone else I know with the exception of Joseph." He paused and switched seats so he was sitting next to her instead of across from her. He took her hand in his once again. "This is not the way I wanted you to find out. I am going to be blunt, and you are not going to like what I have to say. Before you find out from someone else, I want you to know Joseph Mooneyham's true identity. Isabelle, Joseph is really your father."

Isabelle tried to pull her hand from Dante's, but he tightened his grip. "You're wrong. I think I would know my own father." She drained her glass of wine and reached to pour herself another with her free hand. If she were honest with herself, she probably wouldn't know him. She had thought the man dead, and besides, he was a master at disguise.

"When Tessa was in her coma, she could hear everything going on around her. She figured it out. When she woke up, she asked Gregor where Jonas was. She heard his voice while he was working to repair her injuries. Gregor also said there had been recognition between Tamian and Joseph as well. When Gregor called Joseph to schedule Tessa's after care, he confronted him. Joseph, *Jonas*, didn't deny it. He admitted to being in New Atlanta for the last ten years and didn't apologize for it."

"You're shitting me. You are *shitting* me." Isabelle had definitely been hanging around Tessa too much lately, because her cousin's foul language was taking root. Right now, she didn't care. She jerked her hand away from Dante and stood.

"Isabelle, please. I didn't tell you so you would confront him. I told you in order for you to be

16

prepared," Dante's tone was pleading.

"Prepared for what exactly?" Isabelle was garnering attention from the other patrons, so she lowered her voice. "The man has been in my life for the last six years and didn't bother to let on he's my father."

Isabelle didn't wait for Dante to stop her. She followed the laughter across the room. This part of the restaurant was set up so the tables were few and far between, allowing for a semblance of privacy. She passed several tables before she reached them. There they were. Her parents. *Both* her parents were laughing, enjoying themselves. She stalked up to them and braced her hands on their table. "Hello, Caroline. Hello, *Joseph*. So good to see you again. Imagine my surprise at finding you both here, together. What would my father think?" Caroline placed her hand over her mouth. Jonas opened his mouth to respond, but Isabelle didn't give him the chance. "Save it. I have spent the majority of my life without my parents, so here's a news flash; you are both dead to me. As of this moment, I have no parents."

"Isabelle, wait." Jonas reached for her arm. She heard Caroline's gasp as she jerked away and strode back to the table where Dante was watching her, his face guarded. She sat back down, placed her linen napkin in her lap, and drained the wine from her glass. Dante refilled it without asking. If she kept this pace up, she'd be good and drunk in about one point five more glasses.

DANTE WANTED TO shield Isabelle from the world, including her parents. He should have waited to tell her about Jonas, but since he was in the restaurant, Dante couldn't take the chance Isabelle would see him and be blindsided. Was blurting the news out the way he had any less hurtful? No, probably not. So he sat and watched his woman confront the two people in the world who should have always been there for her. Dante vowed then and there he would never abandon Isabelle. Mate or not, he would be there for her whether she accepted the bite or she decided she wanted a friendship.

Having had a father who loved him and his brothers more than life itself, Dante couldn't imagine being duped by the one who had brought you into the world. His own mother had left the States after their father was slain, but he had been over three hundred years old when that happened. A couple of centuries had passed, and the pain was no longer there. Rafael's housekeeper, Priscilla, had stepped into the role of mother over the last thirty years. Dante's own housekeeper, Oksana, came by twice a week. She had been with Dante for almost twenty years and still treated him like the royalty he was. Being the King's brother had its perks, but he would rather have someone more like Priscilla.

"Did you really mean what you told them?" Dante asked Isabelle after the waiter brought their entrees. He was certain she would pick at her food, appetite forsaken by the confrontation with her parents. Instead, Isabelle was digging into her food as if she hadn't eaten in days.

18

"Yes, why wouldn't I mean it? I haven't had a mother in twenty years. My father has been hiding himself from me for at least ten. If they were so concerned about a relationship with me, they wouldn't keep themselves away."

Dante began eating his own food while keeping an eye on Isabelle. Her vitals were stable; her mood was surprisingly calm. A soft buzzing sounded. If Isabelle heard it, she chose to ignore it. "Aren't you going to get that?" he asked, nodding in the direction of her purse.

"No, I will look at it later. I find it very rude when people pay more attention to electronics than the person they are with. If it's an emergency, whoever it is would have called, not sent a message." Isabelle placed another bite of food in her mouth and chewed slowly.

Dante couldn't take his eyes off her mouth. Her full lips weren't as red as they had been when he picked her up. The lipstick was fading with each sip of wine she drank, each bite of food that passed through her lips. He remembered their softness the one time she had pressed them to his own. That night he had dreamed of her pressing them somewhere else on his body. She had made the first move, and he wondered if that was a prelude of things to come. He hoped so.

When her phone vibrated again, he reached out with his mind. "You should probably take that." His mind was also alerted to Caroline and Jonas making plans to confront Isabelle. He would not let that happen. While Isabelle handled the frantic caller, he would handle her parents. "Will you excuse me?" Dante asked Isabelle. He stood, not waiting on an answer.

Dante strode to the table his mate had visited

earlier. If Jonas was surprised to see him, he didn't show it. Caroline, however, looked up at his tall frame, eyes wide. He wanted them to know how serious he was. "Joseph, if Isabelle wasn't clear earlier, let me reiterate what she said. She is serious about you not being in her life, and as her partner, I will abide by her wishes. What this means is I will do everything in my power to make her happy, and if you think for one second I will allow you close to her in this restaurant, on the street, at her place of employment, anywhere, you are sadly mistaken.

"While I may or may not agree with her decision, I suggest you leave her alone. She is going through a lot and does not need the extra burden of you harassing her. Do I make myself clear?" Dante knew he was stepping over the line as far as Jonas was concerned, but he would protect his mate at all costs.

"You do realize I am an Original, do you not?" Jonas whispered, knowing Dante would hear him.

Dante lowered his own voice even further. "Yes, one who was ostracized by the other Originals. One who has been hiding out for the last thirty-odd years, playing god with people's lives. One who abandoned his child when she needed him the most. One who has no authority in the States. That honor belongs to my brother. If you haven't heard, there's a war brewing. A war you started over two hundred years ago. If you don't want to get caught in the middle, I suggest you realize who *I* am." Dante didn't wait for acknowledgement. He had kept Isabelle waiting long enough.

He returned to their table, only to find the plates had been removed and replaced with dessert. She obviously hadn't taken the call, because Isabelle was smiling at him. "I hope you like chocolate."

Chapter Three

MARIA SANCHEZ PACED the living room of her home. Her husband was late. Enrico was never late. The money Isabelle gave them each month to watch over her son, Connor, was more than adequate to live off of. Rico kept his job as a welder so no one would be suspicious of two people living a modest life with no plausible income. Connor was sitting on the floor between the sofa and the coffee table, drawing pictures. He was advanced intellectually for his age, and his artistic skills were phenomenal. Most of the artwork that adorned their home had been created by the six-year-old.

Even though she had spoken to her on the phone earlier, Maria called Isabelle, only to have voicemail answer. She left a message, trying not to sound frantic, especially in front of Connor. Maria had yet to hear from her. She was worried and didn't know who else to talk to. Each call to Rico's phone had gone straight to voicemail. She couldn't call the police since he wasn't technically missing. She just felt in her soul something wasn't right. Maria and Enrico had been together since they were both fifteen years old. They were high school sweethearts who got married the day after graduation. Rico's welding job provided enough money that Maria could stay home and take care of future children. Having had several pregnancies end in miscarriages, they gave up the hope of having children of their own.

One day, Maria and Rico were contacted by an old

friend of Maria's family. Jonas Montague had a young daughter whom he needed a home for. Someone who would raise the girl as their own, protect her with their lives, all while keeping his secret. Even though they had wanted a baby, they were more than happy to take in the girl. Isabelle had been a blessing to them. They raised her and loved her until she left for college.

Isabelle kept in touch throughout college and medical school. Afterwards, when she decided to move to Greece, Maria's heart was broken. She had Rico, but the nest was again empty. Then one day, with no heads up, Isabelle returned. The once quiet, easy-going girl was now a quiet, withdrawn woman. A woman who had suffered at the hands of a wealthy family. A woman who was pregnant with a child whose biological grandfather vowed to raise him. After much persuasion, Maria and Rico agreed to take in Isabelle's child and love him as if he were their own grandchild. In a way, he was.

Isabelle visited often, with Connor knowing his mother loved him. That had been Maria's stipulation in taking the baby. He would know from day one his biological mother loved him and hadn't abandoned him. Rico had taken to the baby as if he were truly his flesh and blood. The two of them were inseparable when Rico was home. As Maria picked up the phone to try Rico once more, the front door opened.

"Oh, Rico, I was so worried. Where have you been, Papi?" Maria covered the distance between them quickly, smothering her husband with kisses to his face, not giving him the chance to answer. Even after all their years together, they were as in love now as they had been when they first met.

"I'm okay, I'm okay. I promise. Connor? Where's Connor?" Rico looked around frantically. Her normally calm husband was scaring Maria.

"Here, Papi." Connor walked up, carrying a drawing in one hand. He wrapped his free arm around his grandfather's legs. "You are very late, Papi. Is everything okay?" Maria and Rico could never hide anything from Connor. He was too astute, even at six years old.

"Yes, my boy. Everything is fine. I just had a little car trouble is all. Now, how about supper? I'm starving." Maria knew by the look in her husband's eyes there was more to his being late than he would talk about in front of the boy. They would wait until after Connor was in bed to discuss it.

"Of course. Connor, go wash up, and we'll eat," Maria said as she unwrapped herself from her husband. She didn't have to tell her grandson twice; he always did as he was told. He placed the picture on the coffee table as he went to wash his hands. While waiting, Maria sent Isabelle a quick text letting her know everything was fine, and Rico was home safe. When she saw the drawing Connor had abandoned, she sucked in a breath.

When Connor returned from the bathroom, Maria asked, "Connor, who are these people in your drawing?" Maria was holding the picture up for Rico to see as well. Their eyes met over the boy's head. It was evident by the skill of his artwork that two of the people were him and Isabelle. The man however…

"That's me, Momma, and my father. He saves us," Connor said matter-of-factly.

"Saves you from who?" Rico asked the boy,

frowning. Connor knew Alexi was dead; they had never hidden that from him. He must have conjured an image in his mind of what the man had looked like. Maria and Rico had never seen a photo of Isabelle's dead husband.

"The bad man. I'm hungry. May we eat now?" Connor didn't wait for them to respond. He sat down at his place at the kitchen table.

After the dishes were washed and Connor was tucked safely in his bed, Maria and Rico retired to their bedroom and went through their own nightly routine. When they were snuggled in, Rico didn't make his wife wait any longer. "I wasn't lying when I said I had car trouble. I don't want to worry you, Querida, but I am pretty sure my tire was slashed on purpose. To what end, I do not know. I didn't call you in case someone was close by, listening. I didn't want to appear suspicious. I sent a quick text to Isabelle, but when I didn't hear back from her right away, I let it go. I don't want to worry her either, but she needs to know there is a slight chance we have been found out."

"But how, Papi? We've been careful. This was an isolated incident, was it not? Please, Enrico. Has something else happened I don't know about? And what about Con's drawing?" Maria's whole body was shaking, and Rico pulled her into his arms, tucking her head under his chin.

"Yes, we've been careful, but we have always known the danger. It may be nothing other than a teenager pulling a prank. I just want to be cautious. As for the drawing, it's nothing more than a child's vivid imagination. Now, try to put it out of your mind."

"I will try. I spoke to Isabelle earlier, and she is

going to visit this weekend. We can talk to her about this when she gets here." Maria settled into her husband as he began singing softly to his wife. She knew it was to ease her fears and lull her into sleep. Normally, it worked. Her husband had a voice that would put any of the award winners to shame. This night, however, it would not work. The fear of someone finding out about Connor, the possibility of losing him, was forever at the back of her mind. This night, it was front and center and would remain embedded there.

ISABELLE WAS GLAD to see Dante enjoying the chocolate dessert. She had no idea what he liked, so she chose her favorite. While the soft moans emanating from his throat were for his appreciation of the mousse, she couldn't help but enjoy the sinful sound. Her body was hyper aware of his, and she was ready to be alone with him. When he excused himself earlier, Isabelle had followed him with her mind, reached out with her new, enhanced shifter senses. As she listened to Dante standing up to her father on her behalf, something inside cracked. Alexi had been loyal to himself and his family, but never her. Maybe the similarities between her former husband and her mate ended at the fancy car and extravagant gifts. She truly hoped so, because once they were back at her house, she was starting down a path she hoped was filled with sunshine and contentment, not storms and trepidation.

When Dante held his hand out to her, she took it

and stood from the table. Instead of letting go, Isabelle laced their fingers together. She couldn't help but notice the women staring at Dante. All the Gargoyles she'd met were handsome, some more than others or in different ways. But her mate, he was beyond handsome. Why he thought she would find him lacking was a mystery. She was proud to be seen on his arm. Jonas must have taken Dante's talk to heart. Neither he nor Caroline attempted to speak to Isabelle on her way out of the restaurant.

The valet quickly brought the Aston Martin around, and Dante opened the passenger door, helping her get in. Now that she wasn't as nervous as she'd been before dinner, she was excited to be in such an elegant car. She might not be the adrenaline junky her cousin Tessa was, but she loved this vehicle. It reminded her of all the old James Bond movies. Having no friends, Isabelle spent her spare time reading romance novels and watching action flicks. She often dreamed of being the heroine in an action movie and being rescued by the handsome hero.

Once Dante was seated, she admired his profile. As if sensing her staring, he looked at her before pulling out of the parking lot. "Is something wrong?"

She really wished he wouldn't frown so often. He had the most beautiful smile. "Absolutely nothing. Even my parents couldn't taint such a lovely dinner. Thank you." She took a chance and placed her hand on Dante's thigh. She felt the muscles bunch under her fingers. His green eyes darkened. Good, she affected him, too.

"You are most welcome. I hope it was the first of many nights on the town for us." Dante lifted her hand from his leg and softly kissed her knuckles. The humming she had been feeling turned into an electric zing as his lips brushed her skin. If he felt it, he didn't let on. He placed her hand back on his thigh and pulled the car out onto the road.

"Can I ask you something?" She felt really stupid, but there was no way to learn about her mate other than to ask questions, even those less than important.

"Of course. You may ask me anything." Dante glanced at her when he answered.

"Do you like James Bond? I mean, you do have his car, and well… I just…" Isabelle hated rambling, and she had a tendency to do so around Dante.

"Are you asking because of the Aston, or because you think I look like a devilishly handsome spy in my suit?" Dante kept his eyes on where they were going, but she could see just a hint of a smile at the corner of his mouth. Her oh-so-serious mate might be loosening up a bit.

"Both. I've already told you how handsome you look, and I love the movies and this car. This car is, as Tessa would say, the shit."

Dante actually laughed aloud. This was the first time she had heard the sound come from him, and she wanted to hear much more of it. His laugh, like his voice, was low and intoxicating. When his laughter faded to a smile, he responded, "I do like the movies. Most of them anyway. There was the one actor, that Dalton guy, who ruined the franchise. Now, may I ask you a question?"

"Of course. This is one of the ways we get to know one another better." Isabelle knew the hard questions would come up, but they had to be truthful if they

28

were going to build a relationship.

"When I picked you up, you did not appear happy with either the bracelet or the car. Would you care to tell me why?" Dante placed his large hand on hers that was still resting on his thigh. He laced their fingers together, something Alexi had never done.

Isabelle allowed their joined hands to give her comfort and strength. Dante knew about Alexi, just not the sordid details. "Honestly, I was comparing you to my late husband. I know that isn't fair, but in the beginning of our relationship, he would bring me gifts, trying to bribe me into marrying him sooner rather than later. I promise I will try to refrain from that in the future. You have to understand, while I had relationships in college, they were trivial. Just someone to pass the time with. I knew I would be going on to medical school, and I vowed to not tie myself to anyone. I graduated college and med school in fewer years than most.

"When I finished medical school, I wanted a break from the rigorous schedules I had set for myself. I decided to take a short vacation to Greece before I started an internship. I had seen pictures of the beautiful architecture and those crystal blue waters. So I went. Thinking back, it's as if Alexi targeted me straightaway. I no sooner got off the airplane than he appeared out of nowhere. It was like he was expecting me. He pursued me relentlessly with jewelry, clothing, weekends on the family yacht. By the time I figured out he and his family were only after my father's knowledge, it was too late. I was already married and miserable. Then the accident happened." Isabelle paused, allowing Dante to weigh in. She was being truthful, even if the truth wasn't what he wanted to hear.

"I will admit, it is suspect. Were they looking to get into the clone business? Or is it possible they were aware of him being a Gargoyle?" Dante asked, musing aloud.

"I believe the cloning. They never mentioned anything about shifters. If they had, I wouldn't have been so surprised when Tessa shared that knowledge with me."

"Speaking of Tessa, have you talked to her? Gregor says she is healing nicely, but she is getting stir crazy at the cabin."

Isabelle and her wild-spirited cousin had never really been close. When Tessa sprung the news of being a shifter on her, Isabelle had been beyond surprised. When she found out Tessa knew Jonas was still alive, and Tessa had spent time with both him and Caroline, Isabelle had been hurt. She had assumed her father was dead. Her mother walked out of her life when she was young. Why could she spend time with Tessa over the years but not reach out to her own daughter? Even though it had been explained, it still didn't make the hurt any less.

"I talked to her this morning. She is trying to convince Gregor to go with her to Egypt. Sophia is in over her head. Until he agrees, she wants to at least come to work with him and help me look over the files of the inmates. In other words, she's bored."

"I have a feeling Gregor will be giving in to the trip. As for Tessa helping with the files, it's not a bad idea. It will free me up to focus on the morgue and allow you time to work on the antidote. You and I have made a huge dent in finding all the inmates who were being injected with Unholy blood. If Tessa can continue looking at the files, it will make the process go faster." She and Dante had been like passing strangers the last couple of weeks. She would work at the Pen during the day, and he would relieve her after his shift at the hospital was over. They would spend about an hour together, and Isabelle would go home. Even though he was a Gargoyle, the double duty had to be wearing on him.

"I agree. I'm not sure how much of Tessa I can stand, though. If Gregor doesn't object, I will have Tessa look through the files while I continue working at my own office. If an inmate needs care, I can be there in a short amount of time." Her cousin was a firecracker, a redheaded biker who played by her own rules. Where Isabelle tried to be a little more refined, it was as if Tessa tried hard to be anything but. The motion of the car ceased, and Isabelle noticed they had arrived at her home. Enough about work and her cousin. Isabelle was ready to get Dante inside and get to know him better, on a different level.

Chapter Four

DANTE HELPED ISABELLE out of the low car and offered his arm as they walked together to her front door. She pulled her key out of her purse and asked, "Would you like to come inside?" If she had to label the look on his face, it would be nervous.

"I think it's probably best if I tell you goodnight now. Even with the small interruption of your parents, this has been one of the most enjoyable evenings I have ever had. As I said before, I hope this is the beginning of a beautiful relationship."

Even though his words were encouraging, his unwillingness to stay left Isabelle wanting. She had such hopes for the rest of the evening. "I understand," she told Dante, even though she didn't. Dante hesitantly leaned forward and placed a soft kiss on her lips.

"Goodnight, Isabelle. I will see you tomorrow."

"Goodnight, Dante." Isabelle was disappointed. And frustrated. Maybe he was just old-fashioned; he was from a different era, after all. Or maybe the mess with her parents had changed his mind about wanting her for a mate. As she inserted the key in the lock, she turned to watch him as he walked to his car. Sighing, she let herself into her home.

Needing another drink, she headed to the kitchen. Remembering her text messages, she pulled her phone from her purse. Isabelle poured a large glass of wine, taking a long sip before reading the first message.

Scrolling through, she noticed she'd missed several messages as well as a call from Maria. This was odd considering she had spoken to Maria earlier in the evening. She read all texts and listened to the voice message. A chill ran down her spine. Even though the last message from Maria was to set her mind at ease by letting her know Rico was home, Isabelle was anything but relieved. Thinking back to the restaurant, Dante had told her she needed to check her messages. His sixth sense seemed to be more powerful than he alluded to. Surely if he knew something was wrong, he would have been more adamant about her checking her phone, wouldn't he? Maybe he didn't know it was important. He could possibly have wanted to distract her while he spoke to Jonas.

Dammit! Would the lies with her parents ever cease? Why did they feel the need to hide the truth from her, their own daughter? Isabelle still didn't understand how they abandoned her yet included Tessa in all their affairs. It had taken her a while, but she finally came to the conclusion this was on her parents and not her cousin. Tessa wasn't to blame for her parents' deceit. Tessa had been a teenager when the lies began. No, this was definitely on them. She planned to spend more time with Tessa. She had brothers and sisters out there she was ready to get to know.

Isabelle thought back to what Dante said with regards to *Joseph* hiring her and setting her up in her own practice. It didn't surprise her when she was hired to work at the hospital. After all, she was top in her class, having graduated Summa Cum Laude. Okay, so maybe she had been a little surprised when he suggested she start her own practice. She should have been suspicious when Tessa showed up with boxes of Jonas' old journals and notebooks. Her cousin explained she had kept his entire collection of information safe until such a time as Isabelle could use it. Had Tessa really appropriated the journals? Or had Jonas given them to her to pass on to Isabelle?

Jonas had been ostracized from his family for mating with her mother, a human. Dante's uncle, Alistair, was the man behind the ousting. Alistair Giannopoulos was of the Original Gargoyle bloodline, as was Jonas. Where Jonas had no problem with humans, Alistair was a purist. Tessa said Jonas and Caroline only wanted to protect Isabelle and her siblings, but at what cost? Isabelle now knew she had sixteen brothers and sisters somewhere in the world. She had met Dane, watched him go through his transition. Tessa had recently visited a sister, Lilly. If her parents had been having children since they mated, the other fourteen could be anywhere in the world.

Less than two months ago, the biggest problem Isabelle had was making time to go visit her son. Now her list had grown exponentially. Sighing, she finished her wine and readied for bed. Alone. She removed her dress and the sexy underwear she had bought just for tonight. Even if Dante had come in, would they have gotten to the point of removing their clothes? Isabelle would have settled for a kiss, one that involved more than just a brief touch of the lips. She chose one of her toys to relieve the ache. She was already conjuring an image of Dante and his Aston, one where he was James Bond and she was the heroine he bent over the hood of his car as he took her from behind.

DANTE FELT LIKE a fool. A horny, unsatisfied fool. He could smell the arousal on Isabelle as they stood on her porch. Her heart had been racing as she waited for him to come inside. Instead of going in and possibly having an excellent end to a nice evening, he had to ruin it by being the coward he was. His beast had been demanding all night for Dante to remove Isabelle from the public place and drag her to the nearest dark corner. That just wasn't Dante's style. He was much more passive. Before, it hadn't been a problem. There were plenty of dominant women in the world. Women who relished taking control. He wasn't into the BDSM lifestyle; he just preferred to let the female lead in the bedroom.

While he wasn't certain Isabelle was as submissive as he was, he only assumed by her demure manner she would expect him to be in charge. Trying to get the image of her disappointed face out of his mind, he took to the freeway so he could allow the Aston a little freedom. After an hour of driving like he was above the law, Dante turned toward his home on the east side of town. Like his Clan, Dante's home was away from the city, his estate boasting a couple hundred acres. The property was surrounded with trees for privacy, but for the most part, it was open, spacious grounds. Like Rafael's home, Dante's house could also be described as a manor. The architecture was different, but the size was just as impressive as the design. Rafael had built it to Dante's specifications, full of stark angles and windows. Like his Clan, Dante built his home large in the hope it would one day be filled with a family.

He had an indoor/outdoor swimming pool that he utilized almost daily. Each of the Gargoyles worked out in their own capacity. Julian was the runner, while Gregor and Frey were boxers and martial artists. Rafael preferred lifting weights. Dante hated running but loved gliding through the water. It was like a balm to his soul, even if he was getting a strenuous workout. Dante was already planning on hitting the pool, hoping to relieve some pent-up tension. As he was pulling into his garage, his cell phone rang. Seeing it was Jasper, he truly hoped it was not a crime scene. His heart couldn't stand seeing an innocent body tonight. "Hello, Jasper."

"Dante, I hope I didn't catch you in the middle of something. I'm on patrol, and you are the closest one to me. I could use your assistance with some Unholy." The newest member of their Clan had been settling in really well since he transferred from the West Coast.

"Give me your location, and I'll be right there." Dante could use a little action, release a little tension of the Isabelle kind. He got the location from Jasper and quickly changed out of his suit into the customary black fatigues the Society wore to fight in. Not bothering to put on a shirt, he ran up the stairs to his rooftop balcony and phased, launching himself into the sky.

The Unholy had been restless these last few weeks. When Tessa had been chased by a serial killer, Gordon Flanagan had been involved. He had been in a helicopter, attempting to get Tessa to pull over. The man had been after Tessa ever since her mother disappeared with her when she was an infant. Geoffrey had ended up in an air assault with the other chopper and blown them out of the sky. As of now, Flanagan's body had not been recovered. One body had come across Dante's slab. Dental records confirmed the identity was that of the pilot, not Gordon Flanagan. If the man was still alive, he was no doubt in hiding, recovering from burn wounds.

His absence was lending to the madness of the Unholy. Obviously, whoever was second in command had no control over the army of monsters. Or maybe, Flanagan was alive, in charge, and pissed he had come so close to his daughter, only to watch her car flip and her life nearly end. It was not beyond the realm of possibility he was alive and knew Tessa was as well. The man had more money than the gods, so it only made sense he had eyes and ears everywhere.

The fighting was close to the hospital. It took a couple of hours, but with Mason, Urijah, and Lorenzo fighting with them, they eventually corralled most of the Unholy. The others offered to take the captives to the Pen where Deacon was waiting for them. With it being so late, Dante suggested he and Jasper clean up in the morgue.

Dante walked into the lower level of the hospital with Jasper on his heels. They didn't need enhanced shifter senses to hear the music coming from behind the closed door. Even though it was late, it was apparent Trevor was still working. The boy had no life. Dante entered the room to find Trevor bent over a cadaver. All of the required safety equipment – face shield, gloves, and plastic apron – were in place. Trevor was sawing into the chest as he nodded his head in time to the music. Dante used the remote to lower the volume on the stereo. Trevor looked up, startled.

"What in the gods' name was that?" Dante asked his assistant, shaking his head.

"Cyanide Sweetness," Trevor and Jasper answered at the same time.

"Dude!" Trevor looked at Jasper as though someone told him he had won the lottery.

"I know, right?" Jasper was grinning at Trevor.

Dante was thinking they'd both lost their minds. The hard rock Gregor made him endure when they rode together was bad enough. Why anyone would want to listen to someone screaming instead of singing was beyond him. Trevor raised the shield to rest on top of his head and pointed at both of them with his saw. "Why are you here at this time of night looking like you've been in a slasher flick? And where are your shirts?"

Thinking the morgue would be unattended, Dante had not counted on being seen with blood all over him. He hated lying to Trevor. One day, he was going to sit him down and tell him the truth.

"We ran into a little trouble taking down a perp, and we came in here to clean up," Jasper told him. It was basically the truth, except for the trouble part. They had no trouble with the Unholy. "Listen, Trevor, I have tickets to see Cyanide Sweetness in a couple of months. You wanna go with?" Jasper was washing the blood off his face, chest, and arms at the sink while talking. Dante didn't miss the look on Trevor's face. It was somewhere between *are you really talking to me* and *holy shit, I've died and gone to metal heaven.*

Dante didn't interrupt. Whether Jasper was using

38

this as a diversion or if he truly wanted Trevor to go to the concert with him, Dante wanted to see how this played out. When Trevor didn't respond, Jasper turned and looked at him with raised eyebrows. "So, you wanna go?"

"Are you asking me to a concert?" Trevor's voice was barely above a whisper. Dante felt a knife through his heart. How could he have missed the loneliness in his assistant? Jasper was giving him the world with this one conversation.

"Yeah. I mean, it's not like a date or anything. You're the only one I know besides Sixx who likes metal music." Jasper finished rinsing then grabbed the towel Dante handed him. Dante noticed Trevor's eyes were having a hard time focusing on Jasper's face. He didn't know Trevor's sexual preference; he had always assumed the younger man liked women. Now, he wasn't so sure.

"Yeah, sure, thanks." Trevor was blushing, his eyes now focused on the corpse.

Dante grabbed two clean T-shirts out of his locker, throwing one to Jasper. They would have to settle for wearing bloody pants. At least they were both wearing dark fatigues. If Trevor thought their similar attire odd, he didn't mention it.

"Okay, we'll talk more about it later. Right now, I have to get out of here. I'm feeling a little nauseous. Dante, I'll talk to you tomorrow. Trevor, take it easy." Jasper grinned at them and breezed out the door.

Trevor didn't move; he continued holding onto the saw, staring at the body on the table in front of him. "Are you okay?" Dante asked, thinking Trevor would be happy someone had asked him out, even if it wasn't

39

a date as Jasper had stated.

"Did you tell him to ask me out?" Trevor's voice was still low, his eyes still focused on the body he was working on.

"Trevor, I assure you, I do not meddle in the affairs of others. Jasper is his own man who happens to like the same music as you, if you can call that noise music. He is new to town and probably hasn't made many friends yet. The two of you have something in common. He knows you from the crime scenes, and you are a friendly face to him. If I'm not mistaken, he also likes video games, something else you have in common. You might want to reach out to him, you know, as a friend."

Dante hoped like hell Trevor didn't ask how he knew Jasper was into video games. He wasn't ready to spill all the Clan's secrets. Not yet. Soon, though. He had a feeling it wouldn't be long before he confided in his assistant as to the Gargoyles. He just needed to run it by Rafael first.

Trevor lowered the clear shield back down over his face. "I'll give it some thought." The saw came to life. Obviously, the discussion was over. Dante left him to the cadaver on the slab. His mind returned to his mate and the way he left her earlier. It had taken everything within him to walk away. Obviously, she had been expecting more, or she wouldn't have invited him in. Was it too late to go back? See what would happen between them? His mind was warring with his libido. He had promised to take things slow, but his body wanted anything but slow. The beast inside was urging him to take her, make her his own. Heading out of the hospital, Dante had a decision to make.

Chapter Five

"GO AWAY," ISABELLE mumbled in her sleep. Someone was knocking on her door in the middle of the night. The pounding got louder, so she sat up and yelled, "Hold on, I'm coming." Who the heck would be visiting so late? She slid her feet in her slippers and padded to the living room. Peeking through the peep hole, her breath hitched. She unlocked the door and pulled it open. Before she could say anything, Dante grabbed her and threw her over his shoulder.

"Dante, what are you doing?" Isabelle was mortified. Not because he had come back, but because she was in her flannel sleep pants and a ratty T-shirt.

"What I should have done hours ago. I'm claiming you." He strode to the Aston and placed her on her feet, spinning her around. "Lean over the car." Dante's hand pressed between her shoulder blades, pushing her forward. He ripped her pants down the back, tossing the shredded material to the ground. The sound of a zipper being lowered filled the air. "Spread your legs for me," he commanded her from behind. When Isabelle complied, Dante's hard length was between her legs, rocking back and forth. He was using her slickness as lube. Without warning, he pushed himself into her heat. The hand that was on her back slid into her hair, grabbing a fistful. The other hand held onto her hip, pulling her body to his with each thrust.

How had Dante known this was her fantasy? "You

really can read my mind," she whispered as her Gargoyle continued his assault. The warmth of the hood was nothing compared to the fire burning in her core, bringing her closer to climax. "Dante... I'm... god Dante... I'm close..." Her breathing was coming in gasps as she tried to hold on. He tightened his grip on her side, as he leaned over her back, his breath now in her ear.

"I'm going to mark you, Isabelle. I'm going to claim you now." Dante grunted with each thrust as his wings wrapped around her. She tried to reach out and touch one, but fangs appeared in her line of sight. She knew what was coming. He was going to bite her, seal the deal. Her core tightened around his shaft. Each stroke had him hitting her special spot, blinding her to reality. Was he really going to do it? Was she ready? Dante didn't give her time to decide. When her pussy clamped down on his cock with her release, Dante roared into the night before sinking his teeth into her neck. The pleasure overrode the pain causing her orgasm to intensify.

"Momma, what are you doing?" Connor was standing on the other side of the car, watching as she and Dante sealed the bond.

"Oh, my god! Dante, get off me... Get off me!"

Isabelle sat up, yelling. Her breath was coming in gasps as she became aware of the soft glow of the moon filtering into her bedroom. "Well, crap." She flopped back down onto her bed, swiping her sweaty hair off her forehead. *Of course it was a dream, you idiot.* She lay there, replaying the scene in her mind. At her request, they had agreed to take things slow, but if he were dominant with her, would she give in? Her body was so revved up, sleep at this point was futile.

She got out of bed and tried to read. When she read the same page five times, she gave up. While her coffee was brewing, she took a shower. Images of a half-naked Dante bending her over his car ran through her mind as she skimmed her hands along her flat stomach, reaching between her legs. Fingering herself wasn't nearly as satisfying as his cock would be, but she needed the release.

A short while later, Isabelle arrived at the Pen, bright-eyed and bushy-tailed. *Not.* While her appearance might be normal, her mood was somber. She started her day at work as she did every day, with a visit to see Vincent. Deacon had made it clear she was never to go to the lower levels unescorted. During the last few weeks, the two of them had gotten into a routine. She would put her purse in her office, and Deacon would take her to see Vincent. The first couple of days, Isabelle had to call for Deacon. On the third day he appeared at her door and asked if she was ready. She enjoyed his company. For a badass Gargoyle, Deacon was really sweet. It didn't hurt that he was absolutely gorgeous, too. He wasn't handsome like Dante. Deacon was dark-skinned and cute, like the boy next door.

They said good morning and made their way to the lower level. Isabelle was working on getting Gregor to let Vincent outside at least once a week. Rarely did the shifter speak to her except to ask for a cigarette. She had prescribed a pill to help with his addiction, but so far it wasn't helping. There had been no more outbursts from him since the day she interviewed him, trying to find out the whereabouts of Gordon

Flanagan.

Deacon stayed out of sight. Vincent grew agitated when the guards were around Isabelle. Today, she was going to try something different. She knew he was aware of her as soon as she reached his door. Most days he ignored her. Today, she was going to poke the bear. "Good morning, Vincent." He didn't move, just continued to lie on his back, staring at the ceiling. She tried again. "It's me, Izzy."

Slowly, Vincent turned his head toward the door, eyes boring into hers. Doing an ab curl, he sat up and swung his legs over the side of his cot. Isabelle waited, saying nothing else. "Izzy?" Vincent stood and made his way to the door, placing his hand on the window. Isabelle mirrored the gesture, her smaller hand pressed against the glass.

When Vincent had called her Izzy during her interview, she'd had a flashback to when she was a toddler. At least it felt like a flashback. She wasn't prone to visions or random memories, but his nickname for her had taken her back to another lifetime. Isabelle had dreamed of an older boy holding her. She wanted to know if she was actually remembering being a toddler. She could ask her mother, but she'd rather not. The look of confusion on Vincent's face bothered Isabelle. She wanted to help the shifter. Yes, he had killed a lot of people and had attempted to murder Kaya, Rafael's mate, now Queen. Obviously, he was troubled, and Isabelle wanted to help him.

"Vincent, tell me about Izzy." If she was remembering a time long ago, she wanted to know if he was the same man holding her.

"Not Vincent, Gabriel." He removed his hand and stepped away from the door.

"Who is Gabriel?" Damn, that name sounded familiar.

"Gabriel took Izzy, took Rebekah." Vincent went back to his bed and lay down. Isabelle didn't bother trying to get him to talk further. The name Gabriel was bothering her. She needed to talk to Tessa and find out if she recognized the name. It was time Isabelle became familiar with all things Gargoyle. She turned away from the door, and she and Deacon headed back upstairs.

DANTE SIPPED HIS coffee while he waited for the other Gargoyles to join the video chat. The Clan met on Sundays at Rafe's for what the King had dubbed as Family Day, but that was more casual, less business. The Goyles ate a huge breakfast prepared by Priscilla before spending the rest of the day shooting pool, playing video games, or just hanging out. Family Day wasn't mandatory, but most of the Clan joined in unless they were busy. The video chats were mandatory, off-premises meetings to bring everyone up to speed on any business needing to be discussed.

After his swim the night before, Dante had trouble getting to sleep. Between thinking he had royally fucked up with Isabelle and worrying about Trevor, he pretty much just stared at the ceiling all night. Now he was trying to get a jolt from the strong java in his cup.

"Good morning, my brothers. Thank you for

joining a call so early. I have decided to meet with the Clan heads. I will begin traveling next week to inform everyone of human mating possibilities, as well as the ramifications of such. It has been a long time since we had to think about a war, but now that we're at risk, I feel we need to polish up on our sword techniques. Frey offered to close the dojo early, but that would be too public. We don't know who is watching. I suggest we train at Dante's, if he has no objection."

"I have none." Dante knew his property was the most conducive to outdoor training as it had the most open land.

"Thank you, Brother. We will train in shifts, in case anyone is watching. We want to appear as though we are going about our daily affairs. Frey and Urijah will gather the necessary equipment from the armory, and Frey will set up a schedule.

"Nikolas has been keeping Julian informed regarding his quest to locate Sophia. As of now, he has had no luck in locating his mate. Even though Nikolas has not asked for assistance, I believe it is time we got involved. Given the fact that Tessa has already planned on going after her cousin, it makes sense Gregor be the one to aid in the search. Tessa's injuries have healed, and they will be leaving in the next few days. Deacon, Gregor assures me you can handle the Pen. Just know we are all here to assist in any way you need."

Dante wasn't surprised at the news of Gregor and Tessa traveling. He and his brother still talked nightly, even if Tessa was now fully entrenched in his brother's life. He and Gregor had a bond that couldn't be broken by anything or anyone. Theirs was a closeness much like Rafael and Sinclair had. Those two were more like twins than even Tessa and Tamian with their clone bond.

"Julian is getting closer to the identity of Bartholomew Cromwell. Jules, I'll let you explain."

"Until yesterday, there was no digital footprint I could follow. I set up algorithms in a program that would constantly monitor the I.P. address. It finally got a hit, and that hit came from New Atlanta, not Greece. In my gut, I believe we are being watched by Alistair, and he's using someone close by to do it. I will not stop until I know for certain." Dante could sense the unease in his cousin. Julian had to be missing Nikolas. They were two peas in a pod, and now that pod was split open with one of the peas on the other side of the globe. Dante would feel the same way when Gregor left for Egypt.

"I have one more announcement, but it will have to wait until Sunday when we are all together. Normally, Family Day isn't mandatory, but this week it is. Please make arrangements to be there. Is there anything else?" When no one else had business to discuss, Rafael ended the call. "Be well, my brothers."

"And you, our King." The automatic chorus of deep voices was getting louder with the addition of Dane Abbott. Kaya's lead detective was the newest member of their Clan. He was also the first half-blood. Rafael had a chat with Dane when he first transitioned, welcoming him to the family. Rafe made it clear he didn't care if Dane was full-blood or not. He was a Brother.

With the meeting out of the way, Dante could focus on the task at hand: Isabelle. He had confided in Gregor about the previous night. Gregor, knowing

Dante's passive tendencies, suggested another date. If Isabelle was frustrated at Dante's lack of aggression, she would readily accept another night out. If she turned him down, he would have to keep trying. Gregor suggested having her over for dinner so there would be no room for interruptions. Dante wanted the night to be perfect, and since he didn't trust Tessa's judgment when it came to a romantic evening, Dante reached out to the one woman he did trust: his Queen.

Dante phoned the manor, hoping Kaya hadn't left for the precinct. Before Rafael met Kaya, he conducted his video chats from the office. Now that Kaya was in his life, he lingered at home as long as he could. Kaya was keeping later home hours herself. Jonathan, Rafael's right hand man and Priscilla's brother, answered the phone, "Stone Manor."

The tone of his voice was less than his usual chipper self. Dante reached out with his senses as he spoke to the older man. "Good morning, Jonathan. Dante here. How are you?"

"Very well, Dante. How may I help you this morning?" Jonathan's voice was strained, as if he were in pain.

"I am calling to speak with Kaya, if she's available." Dante would not jump to conclusions, but he would speak to Rafael. If his senses were correct, Jonathan was sick. Very sick.

"You are in luck; our Queen is in the kitchen with Priscilla. Hold please." Dante listened as Jonathan made his way to take the phone to Kaya.

"Hello, Dante." Kaya sounded surprised. She more than likely thought he was calling on official police business.

"Kaya, my Queen, I am in need of a favor." Dante knew Kaya was still getting used to the whole "queen" business. The few times she had needed to step into the role, she had done so spectacularly.

"Okay, what do you need?"

"This is of a personal nature. One I am truly embarrassed to bring to your attention, but as a woman, you are the only one I can speak with. I took Isabelle out to dinner last night. Let's just say things were strained, and the night didn't end as either of us hoped it would. I want to ask her over to my place for another date, to make up for last night. I need help in making it romantic. Tessa's out of the question, because her idea of romance is jumping off a mountain without a parachute." Dante stopped talking when he realized he was rambling and Kaya was laughing.

"You are not wrong there. I've never met anyone like Tessa. I would be glad to help. How about lunch today at Anderson's?"

"That is perfect. I really appreciate this."

"No problem. I will see you soon."

Dante disconnected and sat back in his chair. Now, as a courtesy, he needed to let Rafael know he would be having lunch with Kaya. Before he met with his Queen, he wanted to gauge Isabelle's mood. He had a plan on how to do just that.

Chapter Six

STILL FRUSTRATED FROM lack of contact with Dante the previous night, Isabelle was in a fairly foul mood when she sat at her desk, attempting to look over files. Thinking of her Gargoyle had Isabelle daydreaming about him. She wanted to loosen his tie and unbutton his shirt. She wanted to know what he looked like underneath his clothing. Did he have a six pack with a hot V that ran along his hipbones? What about a happy trail of hair that started below his navel and disappeared below his underwear? Was Dante a boxers or briefs kind of Gargoyle? Did he even wear underwear? Was his chest smooth or was it hairy? Did he work out with weights or was he a runner? Did he look as sexy in real life as she imagined in her dream? Her thoughts were running amok with images of a naked Dante calling her name.

"Isabelle, is everything okay? You are flushed." A very real Dante stood by her desk, looking concerned.

"I'm fine. What are you doing here?" Dammit, she hadn't meant to sound so rude, but his surprise appearance while she was thinking naughty thoughts was a little embarrassing.

"I brought you breakfast." Dante was holding a bakery bag and a tray containing two coffee cups. "I was hoping we could share some time together this morning.

"I would like that, thank you." Isabelle cleared off the corner of her desk, making room for their food.

"Please, put it down here."

Dante was dressed in his usual button up shirt and khakis. "Do you wear blue jeans?" Probably a silly question, but she knew so little about the male who was supposed to be her mate.

He cocked an eyebrow and responded, "Of course. When I'm working, I wear khakis. When I'm home, I prefer to wear sweatpants or shorts. Since it's just me most of the time, there's no need not to be comfortable. But if I'm going out somewhere casual, I put on jeans. Do *you* wear blue jeans?" Dante waited for her answer while he arranged the food on her desk. First, he pulled a couple of small paper plates from the white take-out bag. Next, he removed a couple of bagels and cream cheese, placing one on each plate. Her coffee was already fixed with cream, no sugar. She appreciated the fact that Dante listened when she talked and remembered the little things she said. Like how she fixed her coffee. His own coffee would be black.

"I do, actually. I might not be the biker chick Tessa is, but I love my jeans and sweatshirts. What's your favorite dessert?" As long as Dante was being forthcoming, Isabelle was going to take advantage and learn little things about her intended.

"Chocolate. Anything chocolate. And yours?" Dante took a bite of his bagel, still giving her his undivided attention as he chewed. They spent the next half hour asking simple questions and answering honestly. When his time was up, Dante took Isabelle's hand in his and softy kissed her knuckles. "The morgue is calling. It's been a pleasure."

Isabelle was pleasantly surprised at his showing up unannounced. After he left, she was once again daydreaming of her Gargoyle and wondering how long he was going to be a gentleman. Tessa's voice from somewhere down the hall had her closing her eyes. She knew Tessa wanted to come help, but she really hadn't expected to have to deal with her this early in the morning. Tessa was a spitfire, wide-open throttle, twenty-four seven. The near fatal wreck that broke several bones and put Tessa in a coma hadn't slowed her down. If anything, it made her more appreciative of being alive, and now she was making up for lost time.

"Belle! You're looking like someone kicked your puppy this morning. What the hell?" Tessa plopped down in the chair Dante had occupied only minutes before. The cane was gone, and Tessa was looking as fit as she had before the wreck. "I just passed Dante. Please don't tell me you two are arguing already."

Instead of telling her cousin she was the reason for the mood, she could deflect the conversation to Dante. Did she really want to get into this with Tessa? Would her cousin take her seriously, or would she offer some smart-ass commentary? Sighing, she relented, "Dante and I had our first date."

"And?" Tessa sat up in her chair, expecting the juicy details, of which there were none.

"And, it was a disaster. I began the evening comparing him to Alexi. I confronted Caroline and Jonas, letting them know they are dead to me. Dante dropped me off and gave me a nice kiss before saying goodbye." There. Now she would see which part Tessa picked up and ran with.

"The only part I consider a disaster is I heard nothing about hot monkey sex." Tessa removed her leather jacket and settled in.

"There was no sex, not that I truly expected it on the first date. But there were no fireworks either. Don't get me wrong. The mate bond was there, pulling at me. If I'm not mistaken, Dante was feeling it as well, but either he was being a gentleman, or he isn't interested. He brought me breakfast this morning, and we talked, but still… nothing."

"You said there was a nice kiss. Did you grab his ears and pull him closer to you and lick the seam of his lips? That nice kiss could have turned into a *nice* kiss that could have turned into wild monkey sex." Tessa's eyebrows were raised. She was serious.

"No, I didn't grab his ears. I'm not comfortable being aggressive with someone so…" Isabelle couldn't finish her sentence. Dante was so what? Large? Intimidating? Absolutely gorgeous?

Tessa leaned to the side and placed her arm on Isabelle's desk, finishing the thought for her. "Someone so passive? Sometimes a man needs a little nudging, you know? Just because he's a badass Gargoyle doesn't mean he's the take-charge type in the bedroom. If you want it, go for it. I guarantee the mate bond will kick in if you take the Gargoyle by the wings, so to speak. Now, hand me one of those folders."

Isabelle handed the next file in the stack to her cousin. Could it be that simple? What if Dante was submissive? That would put a whole new spin on their relationship, if they ever got to the relationship level. She would definitely test Tessa's theory next time they were alone together. For now, she had an antidote to formulate. For the next few hours, the two women worked side by side, comparing notes on the folders

53

they studied. When they finally came up for a break, Isabelle asked about Sophia. Tessa hadn't heard from the girl, and she was getting really worried. Tessa was planning a trip to go search for her.

"How does Gregor feel about you heading off to Egypt?" Isabelle thought about Tessa traveling all over the world, watching over the half-bloods who had yet to transition. When she thought of her own adventure in Greece, she cringed. Connor was the only good that came from visiting a foreign country.

"He's ready to go with me. He says Deacon's got the Pen under control. Besides, he wants to help Nikolas search for Sophia just as much as he wants to watch my back. From what he's learned, Nikolas is ready to tear the sands apart. It's been weeks now with no sign of his woman, and he's freaking out. I have to admit, I'm sort of freaking out too. Not only did her parents disappear, now Sophia has as well. As a matter of fact, we're leaving Sunday."

Isabelle could understand how Sophia felt. If something were to happen to Connor, she would not stop until she found him, no matter how far she had to travel.

"I know you'll be glad to get out and do something… adventurous. I hope you find her and her parents. When you get back, I want to meet them. I want to know about all my siblings, and I want to meet those who have already transitioned and know about the family."

"We can do that," Tessa said, smiling softly. Tessa had apologized more than once for keeping her family a secret from her.

"I'm going to head over to my clinic. Do you need

anything before I go?" Isabelle stood, stretching her back. Her stomach growled, and she realized how much time had passed.

"No, Gregor is taking me to lunch, but thanks," Tessa told her as she stood and stretched as well.

"I probably won't see you before you leave, so have a good trip." Isabelle didn't bother telling her cousin she had her own trip to take. Hers wasn't out of the country, but it was important. She needed to see her son.

Tessa looked at her questioningly, but didn't ask whatever was on her mind.

Isabelle grabbed her purse and headed to the Pen's clinic. She finally had a good idea of what would be needed to create an antidote. Luckily, Henshaw had not used all the Unholy blood on the inmates. She was going to need some to create the serum. She removed the vials of blood she had found hidden in the back of the refrigerator and placed them in a small cooler. On her way out, Isabelle stopped in Gregor's office. Before Tessa's wreck, Isabelle had been intimidated by her boss. Now that he was practically family, she was much more comfortable around him. She knocked on his door before entering.

"Good afternoon, Isabelle. How's my mate faring? Is she driving you crazy yet?" Gregor was grinning, knowing just how high-strung Tessa could be.

"No. Actually, she's been pretty subdued today. We have a good grasp on the inmates who need an antidote. I'm going to my clinic now to work on it. The reason I stopped by is to let you know I'll be out of town this weekend. Will that be a problem?"

"Not that I can see. If anything arises, we can call

in Dante, or worst case scenario, Joseph."

Isabelle flinched at the mention of her father. "Excellent. Thank you, Gregor. I'll see you later."

Gregor clasped his hands together over his flat stomach. "Take care of yourself. Oh, and Isabelle? Be patient with Dante."

She gave Gregor a faint smile and turned to leave. She knew he and Dante were close, and with his comment, she wondered if Dante had shared the events of their date with his brother. She also wondered if her father had helped out at the Pen before now. How often had he been mixed up in their lives with no one realizing who he was?

As she drove across town, her thoughts turned to Sophia. Technically, the younger woman was Isabelle's niece. Sophia's father, Sam, was one of Isabelle's siblings. One of many she had yet to meet. Having no prior knowledge of her brothers and sisters, Isabelle didn't worry about them as she would someone she was close to, like Maria and Rico. Even though Maria's last text had been to assure Isabelle they were okay, she was still a little worried.

Two people in the world besides Isabelle knew who Connor really was. Even though he had started school, he was too young to discuss his personal life with any of the other kids. Isabelle had explained the importance of keeping her identity a secret. She often wondered if it was too much responsibility for one so young. Was that how Tessa and Tamian had been raised? Sure, they had been older, but they were trusted with the knowledge that not only Jonas was alive, but both their mother and Caroline were never going to age. Did Jonas not have enough faith in

Isabelle to keep the family secrets?

The ache in her heart was still present when she thought of her parents. At least she visited Connor as often as possible, ensuring he knew she loved him and wanted to be part of his life. She trusted him to keep her secret. If he slipped, she would deal with the fallout when and if it happened. She would never abandon her son completely, no matter what.

Rico had texted last night as per their agreement. Anything out of the ordinary was to be communicated immediately, no matter how small or insignificant. She might be considered paranoid, but she knew in her heart if Stavros ever found out Alexi had an heir, one of two things would happen. Either he would make sure no child of hers lived to see his father's inheritance, or the man would do his damndest to take Connor away from her. Either way, she would lose her son. She couldn't let that happen.

Before she transitioned, Isabelle felt truly alone, as though she had no family other than the three people in Tennessee. Now, she had Tessa back in her life, and by proxy, Gregor. She had Dane, sort of. She needed to reach out to her brother. If she were to agree to the mate bond, she would have Dante. If she had Dante, she would have the entire Clan at her back. Was her being scared of losing her son reason enough to mate with the Gargoyle? No, it wasn't. She had to wonder, though, what would it feel like to have a huge family? One who immediately accepted you, loved you.

Arriving at the clinic, Isabelle parked in her reserved spot and turned off the motor. Walking to the door, a chill ran over her spine. Hurriedly, she grabbed the mail out of the box before letting herself into the building and locking the door behind her. Only then did she look around the area. "Geez, paranoid much?" Isabelle chastised herself. She needed to put the bad thoughts out of her head and focus on the task at hand.

Isabelle placed the Unholy blood in her refrigerator for safe keeping. Before she started working, she made herself a sandwich so she would be able to focus better. As she sat at her desk eating, she unlocked the bottom left drawer, pressed her index finger to the hidden lock, and unlatched a secret compartment. She pulled out a stack of her father's journals. A picture of her and Connor from the last time she had visited him was nestled between the pages of the first book. Her heart skipped a beat thinking of how much she loved her little boy. If she mated with Dante, would he accept another man's child? Love him as his own? Or would he turn his back on them both?

She returned the picture to its hiding place and replaced all of the journals except one. This one she would need to reference when formulating the serum. She grabbed the stack of mail to read while finishing her sandwich. Most of the envelopes contained bills of some sort. One was an official notification from the FDA. She ripped the flap open and pulled the paper from inside. Her pulse sped up as she read the contents. "Yes! YES!" Isabelle pumped her fist in the air. Her pain medicine had received official approval and would be marketed soon.

One more envelope was left. There was no postage, no return address. Her name was written in bold, red block letters. *That's odd.* She shoved the envelope in her purse to look at later.

Chapter Seven

As Isabelle set up her supplies, her mind drifted to her son as it often did. She was looking forward to the weekend and spending time with the boy. Connor never ceased to amaze her with his artistic talent. She hadn't been around a lot of kids, but she knew he was brilliant. There was something else about him she knew was different, she just hadn't figured out what. Most of the time, speaking to Connor was like talking to an adult. Every now and then he would let loose and act like the six-year-old he was. Usually, he was quiet and contemplative.

Isabelle busied herself with the formula, checking over her father's notes on prior serums he had created. Somewhere along the way, Jonas must have come across a similar situation. Now that Isabelle was aware of Gargoyles, the notations made sense. In the past, she hadn't understood what he was trying to accomplish. Isabelle was able to take one of his formulas and tweak it fairly easily. It would need to be tested, of course. That was the only drawback; she would have to experiment on an inmate. Isabelle secured the antidote, getting it ready to deliver to the Pen. Before she left, she called Dante to let him in on her progress. He would want to be there when she administered the serum.

Reluctantly, she dialed his number. "Hello?" His rich, deep voice sent a shiver through her body. The sound of a woman laughing in the background quickly squelched any amorous thought. "Hello? Isabelle?"

"Dante, I have the antidote complete. I will deliver it to the Pen and administer a trial dose to one of the inmates. I just thought you would want to know." Isabelle hung up. Aggggh! She was so stupid to think he would actually wait around on her. After he brought her breakfast, she'd felt hopeful. How many women did he have lined up? Pretty women who weren't plain Janes. Whatever. Her phone immediately rang, and she answered without looking at the caller I.D.

"Hello?"

"Isabelle, why did you hang up on me?" Dante's voice was guarded, and the noise level in the background was much less than before. He must have stepped outside.

"Because I wouldn't want to interrupt your date." God, what was she, fifteen?

"I am not on a date, Isabelle. I am having lunch with my Queen."

"Oh. Well, you do not have to explain yourself. We are not mates."

"Not by my choosing, if you recall," he responded, his voice as clipped as hers.

Sighing, she responded, "I thought you would like to know I have the antidote. I am on my way back to the Pen to administer the first dose. I will speak with you later." She hung up, thinking about why he would be having lunch with Kaya. Isabelle liked the woman well enough. She had been helpful during Tessa's ordeal. She realized how relieved she was his lunch partner was Kaya. Wow. Was the mate bond causing the jealousy? Hearing another woman's laughter had

60

clearly caused her to become upset. She needed to think about that, analyze her feelings. However, that would have to wait.

She packed up the serum and drove across town. She didn't expect to see Dante there so soon, but he was waiting by the back entrance when she arrived. He opened her car door for her and offered his hand. She took it, allowing him to help her out of the small vehicle. She probably should apologize for being short with him on the phone. Instead, she removed her hand from his, and rather than walking around the car, she bent over the driver's seat to reach for the small cooler she used to transport the antidote. If Tessa was correct, she needed to up her game in making Dante want her. If he was submissive, she was going to have to do the seducing.

Isabelle heard Dante groan when she bent over. She knew he was close. Close enough that when she backed out of the car, she bumped into him. Dante's hands grabbed her hips as she looked up over her shoulder, "Oh, I'm sorry." Dante didn't release his grip, and Isabelle didn't step away. Instead, she leaned into his body. If the erection pressed to her back was any indication, he was definitely affected by her. She kept her eyes locked on his and licked her lips. He closed his eyes and released his grip.

"No apology necessary. I am proud of you for creating the formula so quickly," Dante said as he took the bag from her hand. She didn't miss the fact that he strategically placed it in front of his crotch.

"I can't take all the credit. I just tweaked one of Jonas's formulas." Isabelle shut the car door and locked it. She proceeded to the door of the prison with Dante

61

following behind. "It was strange, seeing a formula so close to the one I needed. It makes me wonder if he was already working on the same type of serum, and if so, why."

As Isabelle passed the door to Gregor's office, Dante reached out and took hold of her hand to stop her. "Hang on a second. I want to tell Gregor what we're doing." Instead of dropping her hand, Dante held it as they walked through the waiting area to the warden's door. "Hey, Brother. Isabelle's back with the formula."

"That was quick. Great work, Isabelle." Gregor stood from his desk and motioned for them to lead the way. Isabelle felt odd holding hands with Dante at work. He obviously felt it was appropriate as he threaded their fingers together. For some reason, that felt more intimate.

"Where's Tessa?" Isabelle asked Gregor as they reached the clinic.

"I dropped her off at home after we had lunch. She has to check on some of your siblings before we leave for Egypt."

Isabelle was glad her cousin wasn't there as a distraction. She was getting used to Tessa's high energy, but she didn't need her around when she was administering the antidote. After going over the inmate files for weeks, Isabelle had finally discerned who had been given the most Unholy blood. She had a list of inmate names in order of urgency. She gave Gregor a copy of the list so he would know who to call up first. Gregor radioed for the inmate, Teddy Johnson, to be brought to the clinic.

The inmates on the list had been monitored closely

for the last few weeks. Their tempers were higher and their aggression increased. Most had been moved to solitary until they could receive the antidote. When the guards brought the first inmate to the clinic, he was uncooperative. Once Isabelle explained she was hoping to counteract what the other doctor had been trying to accomplish, he calmed down. What she didn't explain to the man was exactly what Henshaw had injected him with. Half an hour later, the inmate was back in his cell, and Isabelle was ready to call it a night. "I'll draw blood from him tomorrow for testing. All we can do now is wait."

Gregor turned for the door once they were finished with the inmate. "Excellent work, Isabelle. I will leave you and Dante to do whatever it is you need to do. I'm headed home. I will see you both tomorrow. Good night." They both told Gregor goodnight.

Even though there had been two shifter guards along with Dante standing sentry, Gregor had stayed with them. She didn't feel as if she were being scrutinized. If she were in charge of all the inmates' well-being, she would want to be present, too. Actually, she was in charge of their well-being, just not to the extent Gregor was. Before that moment, she hadn't thought of what a huge responsibility Gregor had.

Isabelle walked to her office where she secured the rest of the antidote in the small refrigerator. She had left a small amount of the serum at her own clinic just in case something were to happen to the supply she brought to the Pen. As she locked her office door, Dante told her, "I'll walk you to your car." He took Isabelle's hand in his. He might not be aggressive, but he was affectionate.

Isabelle unlocked her car and tossed her purse onto the passenger seat. When she turned to face Dante, he squeezed her hand and asked, "Isabelle, would you please have dinner with me?"

"Tonight?" Isabelle was thrilled he wanted to see her again, but she was tired. The day had worn on her mentally.

"How about tomorrow night? I'd like for you to come to my home so I can cook for you." Dante was rubbing his thumb across the back of her hand.

Isabelle took a step closer, mentally willing him to kiss her. "I'd really like that." And she meant it. She wanted to see where he lived, wondering if his house was as anything like Gregor's.

"Excellent. I will pick you up at your house around six, if that is acceptable."

"It is. I will see you tomorrow then?" She hadn't meant for it to come out as a question, but her mind was on the nearness of his body.

Dante raised her hand to his mouth and brushed his lips softly across her knuckles. That was nice, but she wanted more than nice. Before he could walk away, Isabelle closed the distance between them, placing her hands on his chest, feeling his heartbeat beneath her fingertips. She ran her hands down his arms slowly, allowing herself to feel. Feel the lean muscle under the cotton material. Feel the strength of his shifter body. Feel herself getting wet from such a simple touch. She looked into his eyes to make sure she wasn't making a big mistake. When she saw longing there, she knew what to do. She didn't grab his ears as Tessa suggested, but she did place her hands on either side of his head, pulling him down so she could press their lips together. Dante's hands finally found her hips, pulling her closer to him.

The kiss was soft, unassuming, but Isabelle wanted more. She tentatively touched her tongue to the side of his mouth, and he opened for her. She didn't hesitate. Her tongue sought his, dancing, teasing, testing, learning. One hand clutched his hair tighter, the other sank into his bicep. The kiss deepened and became more heated, desperate. Dante's cock came to life, growing harder and longer against her stomach. Isabelle hated breaking the connection, but she needed to come up for air. Both of them were breathing heavily. If Isabelle didn't leave now, she was going to do something she hadn't done since college. There were too many guards who could walk out of the building and see Isabelle on her knees. Dante growled, low in his throat. He probably didn't know what she was thinking, but he could smell her arousal. Damn shifter senses.

Dante leaned his forehead against hers and whispered, "I will see you tomorrow." He touched her lips with his finger tip then strode to his van. Isabelle wanted to sit in her car and think about what she'd done, but Dante would probably worry when she didn't leave. Instead, she started her hybrid and headed for home. While driving, she began formulating a plan. A seduction of sorts that had tomorrow night ending the way she wanted it to. One where they wouldn't be ending the night unsatisfied. She was going to take Tessa's advice and grab her Gargoyle by the wings.

WITH A GLASS of Scotch in hand, Dante relaxed on the sofa, classical music softly floating through the air. Speakers were strategically placed around his home, allowing the music from the stereo and television to sound better than if Thomas Dolby had installed them himself. He thought back to his lunch meeting with Kaya. She had several ideas to offer when it came to a romantic night in with Isabelle.

When he and Kaya had finished eating and were ready to leave, Kaya told him, "Be patient, Dante. I know what it's like to be told you have a mate. When you live in a human world where you can choose your life partner, then are told that person has been chosen for you, it's a lot to swallow. I think I accepted it more readily because I hadn't been loved before. From what you've told me, Isabelle has already experienced love and loss. Some people don't want to risk the hurt again. I honestly think she'll come around. Just don't push."

After the phone call with his mate, he was pretty sure the dinner plans were moot, until he met up with her at the Pen. When she bent over to retrieve the cooler from her car, her slacks tugged at her perfectly round ass. The seam of her pants slid between her cheeks, giving the illusion she was either wearing a thong or no panties at all. The thought of her bare ass caused his dick to twitch. When she backed into him, her ass raised a little higher in the air, and he about lost it. And later, when she kissed him? His dick was ready to burst through the zipper. He had been harder than he could remember ever getting, all because his mate was flush against his body. With clothes on. He couldn't imagine how it would be when they were finally skin to skin.

Just thinking of his mate and their scorching kiss had his dick pressing against the shorts he had changed into. Dante pulled the elastic band down, freeing his cock from the restraint. He closed his eyes and imagined Isabelle on her knees between his opened thighs. He gripped his dick and began stroking, using the liquid seeping from the tip as lube. He thought of Isabelle's lips sliding over the head and down the shaft, taking him as far as she could. His cock was thick and long. He would have to be careful should Isabelle ever decide to give him a blowjob. Brown hair bobbing up and down the length, chocolate eyes focused on him as she savored his taste, had Dante gasping. Moans humming in her throat spurred his orgasm. Dante's hips pumped faster into his hand as he chased his release. With a final thrust, Dante roared out Isabelle's name as white streams of ejaculate shot onto his chest.

Chapter Eight

ISABELLE GRABBED A biscuit at a drive-thru and ate it on the way to the Pen. She was lucky to have shifter metabolism, or all the junk food she ate would take its toll on her body. She didn't plan on staying long, just long enough to look in on Vincent and take the blood samples from the inmate.

Isabelle stood at Vincent's door, watching the shifter sleep. At least he appeared to be asleep. He was lying on his bed with his back turned to her. She softly called his name, but he didn't move. This was the first time in recent days he didn't acknowledge her presence. After about five minutes, she was ready to give up when he rolled over and looked at her. "I don't want to talk." He rolled back over, giving her his back again. Isabelle couldn't imagine being confined to a small room day in and day out. She left him to his thoughts and headed to her office. She was going to draw blood from the inmate she had given the antidote and take it to her clinic for testing. Deacon escorted her back upstairs before setting out to secure the inmate.

Once the inmate was seated and strapped down, Isabelle checked Teddy's vitals. His heart rate was slower, and his pupils less dilated. The serum was having a positive effect already. As Isabelle was drawing the two vials of blood, the inmate spoke for the first time. "Thank you."

Isabelle was shocked, but she tried not to show it. "For what exactly, Mr. Johnson?"

"I know I've done bad things, or I wouldn't be here. But I don't want to become a monster. I kinda figured out what Doc Henshaw was doing to me. He never said anything, and it took me a while to get it. He told me he needed my healthy blood, but he was injecting me too. If I was healthy, why would he be injecting me with anything? Then after a few times of him sticking me, I felt my body changing and my mood getting foul. I wanted to punch something. I'm in here for robbing a bank, not because I killed someone. Whatever you gave me last night must've worked, 'cause I don't feel like that anymore. So, thank you."

"You're welcome. I'm taking your blood to see if one dose was enough to counteract what was previously given to you. Don't hesitate to let one of the guards know if you feel the antidote wearing off. We want to make sure to get all of the previous injections out of your system." Isabelle placed a Band-Aid on the withdrawal point and released him to the guards. How many of the other inmates had figured out what Henshaw had been up to? How many of those were like Johnson and didn't want the accelerated aggression? Whether they were aware of what was happening to their bodies or not, Isabelle was going to undo all the damage the previous doctor had caused.

Isabelle arrived at her clinic thinking about her dinner date later that evening. She would stay at work long enough to test Teddy's blood and then she would put her plan in motion. She was going to have a manicure and pedicure, as well as get a wax job. She didn't know if Dante preferred a bare mound or a more natural look. She would find out tonight.

Thinking of her mate, she absentmindedly placed her purse on the edge of her desk. It fell to the floor, spilling the contents. "Crap!" She bent over and picked up the miscellanea, shoving it back in. She grabbed the envelope without the return address, having forgotten all about it. She stood and placed her purse safely in the middle of the table before plucking the letter opener out of the pen holder. Carefully, she sliced open the top of the envelope. She pulled out a single sheet of paper and read five typed words:

We Know About The Boy

Isabelle barely made it over the trash can before she threw up the biscuit she had eaten earlier. When there was nothing left on her stomach and she was dry heaving, she grabbed a water bottle, rinsing her mouth. She picked up the letter and read it again. Five words. Those five words just turned her world on its axis. "Shit, Shit! Oh god, oh my god!" Isabelle paced the room as she called Rico's cell phone. He would already be at work, but she would leave him a message. One that would let him know they had been compromised.

When the three of them agreed on Maria and Rico raising Connor, Isabelle confided in them about Alexi's family. She did not tell them what the Sarantos family had been after. As far as Rico and Maria knew, her father was just another man, not the world-famous scientist who caused the near apocalypse thirty-three years prior. She did tell them if Stavros Sarantos ever found out he had a grandchild, he would be hell bent on taking him from Isabelle. He would have no legal ground to stand on, so he would take him any way he could.

Rico's voice mail picked up. "I'm calling about your cleaning services. Please return my call as soon as possible." If anyone were tapping into his phone, hopefully they would think it was a wrong number since Rico was a welder. If they had already tapped into Isabelle's phones and knew her number, they were well and truly screwed. Next, she called Maria. If Rico didn't get the message soon enough, Maria could lose valuable time. If they were being watched, they were fucked anyway.

When Maria didn't answer, Isabelle left the same message she left for Rico. Now all she could do was wait. She thought about calling Dante. If they had completed the mate bond, he would have no choice but to help her. Since she had put a limit on the relationship, she didn't feel like she could call him. There was no way she was calling her parents. If only she had family to help her. Wait, she did. Dane was a detective. Even though they hadn't known each other long, surely he would help her. She would call him if things went south. Well, farther south than they were at the moment.

Dammit! Isabelle hated the waiting, the not knowing. While she waited on Rico to call, she went about testing the inmate's blood sample. She tried to keep her focus on the specimen she was studying. Her son's safety was out of her hands. As much as she hated to admit it, she was helpless. If she concentrated, she could have the results and prepare more of the antidote if the samples proved to be successful. Rico would call her when they were on the road.

The blood samples were clean. There was no trace

71

of Unholy blood visible. Isabelle sat at her desk and put her head in her hands. Too much time had passed with no call from either Rico or Maria. She placed a call to both their phones. Immediate voice mail. This was getting to be too much. There was no way they would not answer and keep her waiting unless something was wrong. She didn't have Dane's number in her phone, so she pulled up his patient file in her computer. Finding his cell number, she called him.

"Abbott." His voice came through along with some background music. He was driving.

"Dane, I'm sorry to bother you at work. This is Isabelle, and I need your help." She was pacing the small space of her office.

"Isabelle, you sound like you're about to go off the ledge. What's up?"

"This is something private, and you're going to have a lot of questions. I promise I will give you the answers. I'd rather do this in person. Can you meet me? I know I'm asking a lot when you don't really know me, but I have no one else to turn to."

"This sounds ominous. Of course I'll help you. We're family, after all." The music was gone.

Family. That sounded so good to Isabelle. Other than Maria and Rico, she never felt like she had family to lean on. "Can you meet me at my clinic? I'm afraid to leave."

"Yeah, I'm not too far away. I'll be there within ten."

"Thank you, Dane. I'll see you soon." Isabelle disconnected. She continued to pace the floor, waiting on her brother. Wow, she had a brother. Actually, she had several, but until she met them, they wouldn't seem real. Smelling where she'd thrown up, she pulled the trash bag out of the garbage can, tying a knot in the top. Shifter noses were sensitive, and if she could smell where she'd gotten sick, she knew Dane would be able to as well. She took the bag to the back door and dropped it. She would deal with it later. She headed to the lobby to wait, cell phone in her hand. As soon as she saw Dane's car pull into the lot, she unlocked the door and held it open for him.

"Thank you so much for rushing over here. Like I said on the phone, I didn't know who else to call." Isabelle led Dane to her office.

Dane's appearance was casual, wearing the dress code of a detective. His stance was anything but. Before his transition, Isabelle had only seen Dane when he was sick. Now that he was a shifter, his demeanor had changed. He stood tall and alert. "You're welcome. But what about Dante? He's your mate, right?"

"Technically no, and what I'm about to tell you would probably change his mind about that anyway. Dane, how much do you know about me, about my past?"

"Not much, really. Why don't you tell me what this is about?" Dane sat in the chair next to her desk, giving her his undivided attention.

Isabelle sat down in her chair and, after showing him the letter, told her brother about her life. She didn't leave anything out. She began with her childhood, wanting Dane to know why she didn't feel she could call on Jonas or Caroline. She included her time spent with her foster family before she filled in everything after, leading up to now. "I'm really worried, Dane. It's been hours. They should have been

73

here by now. Every call goes straight to voice mail. I just know something has happened to Connor."

At some point in her story, Dane had taken her hand in his, offering comfort. He still didn't release it when he said, "I have a friend in New Nashville. That's pretty close to where they live, right?"

Isabelle nodded, and he continued, "Let me give him a call, see if he knows anyone in New Columbia. We'll start there. Write down everything you can think of. Address, phone numbers, make and model of their car." Isabelle did as instructed, then waited while Dane called his friend. She watched her brother as he did what he did best. She took in his features as he talked on the phone. Dane was handsome. She had noticed that immediately when he came to her as a patient. When she really studied his features, she saw a lot of Jonas in him. His hair was dirty blond, and his eyes were the most striking blue. She wondered how many of her siblings took after their father, and how many, like her, took after Caroline.

"Corey's calling a friend he knows in New Columbia. Since they haven't been missing twenty-four hours, we can't officially call in the authorities. But Corey knows as well as I do the importance of the first few hours when someone is missing. Can I ask you something?" Dane sat back down in the chair beside Isabelle's desk.

"Of course." Isabelle didn't sit, though. She couldn't. She offered Dane a bottle of water. When he took it, she paced the floor.

"Why are you reluctant to mate with Dante? I've met the guy on several occasions during investigations, and he's solid."

74

Seeing the empty garbage can, Isabelle pulled a new trash bag out of the cabinet and placed it in the can. "I told you about Alexi. I thought I was in love and that our marriage would last forever. I was wrong, on so many levels. I don't know if I trust myself to choose another life partner. Then again, I didn't actually choose Dante. From what everyone says, the fates choose our mates for us. Do you believe in that stuff? That there are these three mystical creatures out in the cosmos drawing names out of a hat, putting us with someone we are supposed to stay with forever? I don't doubt Dante is solid, as you put it. And I won't deny the mate pull is there, but we went on a date, and quite honestly, I'm not sure we're compatible."

Dane laughed at his sister's monologue. He took a sip of water and replaced the cap on the bottle. "I can find the fates conceivable. I mean, look at us; we're shifters. So if we're real, who's to say they aren't as real as we are? I get what you're saying though. You remind me of Tessa when she was denying her bond with Gregor. You're fighting to stay away from your mate while I'm fighting for mine. Julian is convinced Katherine is his mate, and I think she belongs to me. It's all crazy. But I do know this; Dante has already claimed you. He lost his shit when Deacon wanted you to interview the albino. Phased, wings and all, knocking breakfast dishes off the sideboard at the manor. Rafael had to order him to stand down. I've never seen anything like it."

"He did?" Isabelle knew from watching Gregor with Tessa how strong the bond could be, even before the mating was official.

"He did, indeed. And this thing with Connor? I can

75

promise you Dante is going to accept your son, because he's a part of you. It isn't like you turned your back on Dante for another man. You didn't know what you were back then. If you had known you were a shifter with a mate somewhere in the world, you probably wouldn't have married a man knowing he wasn't your mate. I can see why you told our parents what you did, but Dante is reasonable. He's not going to hold your past against you, nor turn his back on your son." Dane's phone rang, pausing their conversation.

"Abbott. Are you sure? Fuck. Okay, I'll call you back." Dane sighed, closing his eyes. When he finally looked at Isabelle, she could see the pain in his eyes. Pain for her. "I'm sorry, Isabelle. Rico's dead. Maria and Connor are gone."

Chapter Nine

STAVROS SARANTOS SAT behind the large mahogany desk in his home office, elbows resting on the arms of his overstuffed leather chair. His fingers were steepled under his chin as he thought about the proposals in front of him. Proposals that, if uncovered by the authorities, could have him sitting in prison. Being one of the wealthiest men in all of Greece afforded him the luxury of keeping those in positions of power on his payroll. Most of them, anyway. There were a few honest men left in the world who couldn't be bought, like the judge who let that bitch, Isabelle, go free when Alexi fell overboard.

His private line rang, and Stavros answered without pause. Only a handful of people had that number. The voice on the other end was one he hadn't heard in several years.

"Stavros, I have some information for you; news you will undoubtedly want to hear."

"And that would be?" Stavros was both wealthy and powerful. He was a peasant compared to this man.

"When Isabelle left the island, she took something of Alexi's with her."

"Impossible. There was a prenuptial agreement." There was no way that bitch was smart enough to steal from his family.

"Ah, but this wasn't included in the agreement. What she took, she carried for nine months, until which time she gave birth to a son. Alexi's son."

Stavros sputtered, "You're lying! That is not possible." How could the man know this?

"I assure you, I am being most forthright with you. I have people in place, watching."

"Why would you do that? What does this have to do with you?" He already knew the answer. The man wanted something. He wanted something from the Sarantos family. Again. They failed him last time when Isabelle refused to cooperate and give up information on her father.

"All in due time, my friend. Just know that for now, I have set events in motion that will bring your grandson back to you."

The line went dead. "Fuck. Fuck!" Stavros yelled to an empty room.

The door to his office opened, and his son stuck his head in. "Is everything okay in here?"

Stavros looked at his child. It was like looking in a mirror twenty-five years earlier. Where Stavros now had gray around the temples, his son still had a head full of dark hair. He was handsome. Stavros could see why the ladies flocked to the younger man. His once bright eyes, however, had dimmed over the last few years. The naïve boy had turned into a shrewd business man, following closely in his father's footsteps. He had no qualms about turning the family business over to his son one day.

"I'm not sure. I just received some information, and I need to process it. Now, have a seat. I received some new proposals and would like your input."

DANTE GOT OUT of his car and walked toward the hospital. The weather was cold for a Georgia November, and the brisk breeze felt good against his skin. His thoughts were on his mate as they had been since he found out she belonged to him. He couldn't stop thinking about the kiss. About the way she had pulled him into her body. He wanted tonight to be really special. He was headed toward the morgue when he felt a sharp pain in his chest. He didn't have to reach far into his mind to know it was Isabelle. Something was causing her a great deal of torment, and he wanted to help her.

Dante turned around and headed back to his car. He called Isabelle's number, but she didn't answer. He phoned Trevor to let him know he wouldn't be in this morning. He then tried calling Isabelle's office line and got no answer there either. Arriving at the prison, he didn't see Isabelle's car, so he hurried inside to Gregor's office. Laughter from inside reached his ears, so he listened to the conversation between his brother and Tessa, making sure he wasn't interrupting them. "You can come on in," Gregor said to him. He entered the office, fully expecting to see Tessa in Gregor's lap. Instead, she was sitting in one of the visitor's chairs. "Hello, Brother. What brings you here?"

He didn't want them to know he was panicking. If Gregor paid close attention, he'd know anyway. "I'm here to assist Isabelle." *And find out what's wrong with my woman.* "I thought she'd be here by now." Dante looked at his watch. What if she had already come and gone. What if she had been in a wreck? Could that be the pain he felt earlier? He pulled his phone out of his pocket. "I'm just going to call her again." He left his brother's office for the privacy of the hallway. His call went to voicemail. Again. Godsdamnit! He had a bad feeling. "Isabelle, it's Dante. Please call me when you get this." After disconnecting, he dialed the landline number at her clinic where the answering machine picked up. Again.

Gregor, now behind him in the hall, placed a hand on his arm, attempting to calm him. "She was here earlier. She drove over to her clinic to test Johnson's blood."

Okay, calm yourself. You're getting worked up over nothing.

Gregor moved his hand to Dante's shoulder and squeezed. "You want to tell me what's going on?"

"I'm being dramatic. Isabelle isn't answering her phone. I had a feeling something was wrong, and now she's not answering. Maybe she just doesn't want to talk to me."

"Why wouldn't she want to talk to you? Hang on. Tessa, come here please." When Tessa peered around the corner, Gregor told her, "Please call Isabelle and see where she is." When Tessa disappeared back into Gregor's office, he asked again, "Why wouldn't she want to talk to you?"

"I don't know. You know I'm no good at dealing with women."

Tessa came back and announced, "She's at her clinic." Dante didn't miss the look Tessa gave Gregor.

"And?" both men asked at the same time.

Tessa looked to Gregor. What the fuck? Gregor pulled his mate into his arms, whispering, but loud enough for Dante to hear, "Red, please. What did

80

Isabelle say? Is she all right?"

"I didn't actually talk to Belle. Dane answered. He said it wasn't a good time. When I asked him what he meant, he wouldn't elaborate."

"Why would Dane be at the clinic? It isn't like he can get sick now." Dante was talking more to himself than the others.

"All he would say was Isabelle had some type of emergency and called him. Said he couldn't tell me anymore and hung up." Tessa nestled herself closer to Gregor, as if Dante was going to shoot the messenger.

"None of this makes sense. I'm going over there." Dante headed for the door. Gregor called after him, but he didn't stop. In his soul, he knew his woman needed him, and he was going to be there for her.

By the time Dante arrived at Isabelle's clinic, he was ready to rip Dane's throat out. Dante called the detective who told him the same thing he'd told Tessa. Pulling in the parking lot, he saw Isabelle's car but not Dane's cruiser. Knowing it was futile, Dante knocked on the door anyway. When he realized Isabelle was either hiding out inside and not answering, or she had left with her brother, Dante lost it. He let out a roar that shook the windows. Godsfuckingdamnit. This was killing him. What hurt most was the fact that Isabelle called her brother instead of him.

Dante was at a loss. At that moment, his cell phone pinged with an incoming text message. *"The antidote worked. I prepared more, and it's in the cooler in my office. Please administer the serum without me. 2 cc is sufficient."* Another message came through right behind the first one. *"The antidote should take effect almost immediately. The code to the clinic door is 432867. Feel free to use any of my equipment.*"

Dante texted her back, "*Isabelle, please let me help you.*" He waited but received no response. He called Dane's phone again, but he didn't answer. "I'm going to kill the half-blood." Dante did the only thing he knew. He called Rafael and told him the little information he had. He asked his brother, his King, to step in and get Kaya to find out what the fuck was going on. For now, he would have to wait.

ISABELLE STARED OUT the passenger window. She wanted to drive her own car, but Dane insisted she was in no condition to drive herself. He was right. She was barely holding it together. She couldn't control her fangs or her claws. She was a bloody mess. Her one fear in life had come true. Her son was gone. She had no idea who had taken him, where he was, if he was even alive. A sob escaped her throat as tears streamed down her face.

Dane reached over and took her hand, being careful of her claws. "Don't think the worst yet. You need to think positive and stay strong. If what you told me is true about Alexi's father, Connor is probably being well taken care of."

Dane's phone rang. Looking at the caller ID, he let out a sigh. "Abbott. Hey, Kaya. Can Jasper take this one? I'm handling some family business right now. I'd rather not elaborate. Great, thanks." He tossed his cell phone on the seat beside him, looking at Isabelle. "You know this isn't going to stay between us long. By now,

Dante has called Rafe. Rafe will be calling Kaya who will try to pull rank. Think about this; from what I've heard, Julian is a genius. If my son were missing, I'd want him to be helping me. I'd want all the Clan helping me."

They were pulling into Isabelle's driveway when her cell phone pinged. She looked at the message, and her breath caught. *"If you want to see your son again, get rid of the cop."*

"Oh, god. Oh shit!" Isabelle exclaimed as she read the text again. Before she could stop him, Dane grabbed the phone from her and read the message.

Dane handed it back to her and swore, "Fuck! Okay, listen to me. You have got to trust the Clan now. We are being watched. Here's what we're going to do. I'm going to continue talking to my friend in Tennessee, and you are going to call Dante."

Isabelle shook her head. "No! I can't. If they're watching, they'll see anyone coming and going. I can't risk it."

"Isabelle, you cannot take this on yourself. Listen to me. I'm a detective. I deal with this kind of thing all the time. I've been involved in several kidnapping cases. They are going to make demands. We really need Julian's help on this. I want you to go in the house, and I will drive off. Is there a back way onto your property? What's behind those trees?"

"Another row of houses. Dane, I don't like this. What if they catch you?" Isabelle wanted to trust his abilities, but she was scared. This was Connor's life they were talking about.

"They won't catch me. I know you don't know me that well, but I want you to trust me on this. Now go

83

on in the house and unlock the back door. I'll see you in a few minutes."

Isabelle didn't agree to his plan, but she did get out of the car and go inside. As soon as Dane's car was out of her driveway, she received another text. *"Good girl. Now call a taxi and have them drop you off at Jefferson Park. You will receive further instructions there."*

Shit! Someone had to be right outside! She didn't hesitate. She did a quick search on her phone and called the first cab company that popped up. She had to warn Dane. She didn't want to argue with him, so she sent him a quick message. *"Received another text, they are watching the house. It's not safe."*

She cleaned the blood off her hands and face before changing into clean clothes. Less than ten minutes later, Isabelle ran out the front door and got in the cab. "Jefferson Park, please."

DANE PARKED AND made his way between two houses that were heavily wooded. He looked around before dashing to Isabelle's back door. He turned the knob, but it was locked. He peered in the window and knocked. Seeing no movement inside, he pulled out his phone to call Isabelle, but saw the text she had sent. Dammit! As he dialed her phone, he reached out with his shifter senses. He didn't hear the phone ringing inside or his sister moving about. *Fuck! Isabelle, what have you done?* She would probably be pissed, but she left him no choice. Dane ran back through the woods to his car as he dialed Kaya.

"Kaya, Isabelle's in trouble. It's a long story, but I need you to call Rafael and have him get in touch with Dante and meet me at the lab. We're going to need Julian on this. Yeah, it's bad. Just get them all there. I'm calling Julian now." Dane called Julian to inform him he was going to have company.

Chapter Ten

JASPER FELT A small sense of pride when Kaya called and gave him lead on a case. A burned body had been found by some runners who were training for a triathlon. The path was mostly isolated, especially this late in the year. Jasper saw the M.E.'s van when he pulled up. CSU was on site as well. Several patrolmen were securing the area and speaking with the runners. Jasper made his way over to begin his investigation. He felt the unease rolling off the couple as he neared them.

Troy Quinn, one of the officers, was openly ogling the female runner while the male was giving his statement to Quinn's partner. Usually, Jasper tried to steer clear of the cop. Every time he was around Quinn, it left a bad taste in his mouth. The man was always putting down his wife for one thing or another. He openly flirted with every woman who came in the station. Jasper thought the guy was a real douche. Quinn didn't take his eyes off the woman's legs when he asked Jasper, "Where's the Doc? We got the weirdo."

Jasper looked to where Troy was thumbing to see Trevor waiting for the go ahead from CSU. Jasper grabbed Troy by the elbow and shuffled him away from the runners. He didn't hold back. "Dante is busy with another case. Trevor is not a weirdo, and if I ever hear you speak of him that way again, you and I will have trouble."

"What *the fuck*, Jenkins? You sweet on the geek?"

Troy sneered at Jasper as he jerked his arm from his grasp.

"He happens to be my friend, Quinn, so that's *what the fuck*." Jasper didn't waste any more time with the juvenile of a man. He was there to take on his first case, and his start was less than professional. When he looked over at Trevor, the kid had an odd look on his face. Gods, he was so endearing, *and* he had great taste in music. Jasper spent the next few minutes finishing up the interview with the couple. When he was done with them, he headed to where Trevor was now examining the body. Jasper squatted down next to him. Fuck! He felt light-headed. The stench from the body was overwhelming. It wasn't the first charred body he had ever seen considering he'd spent over thirty years as a firefighter.

"Hey, Buddy. What do we have?" Jasper asked as Trevor went through the same motions Dante would if he were there. When Trevor finally turned to answer, Jasper took in the beautiful green eyes staring back at him.

"We have a mess. I will have to get him back to the morgue, and we'll have to request dental records for an I.D. There's no usable tissue to test for DNA. By the amount of decay visible, I'd say he's been in the elements for approximately two to three weeks. There are no burn marks on the ground, but CSU is checking the area. My guess is he was torched somewhere else before being dumped here."

"I'm impressed. You sound just like Dante." Jasper grinned at Trevor who had yet to smile. When he just stared at Jasper, he asked the kid, "What's wrong?"

"Do you like video games?" Trevor blushed before

the question left his lips. His dimpled cheeks actually turned pink. How fucking cute.

"I do. As a matter of fact, I have a brand-new system I haven't had time to check out." Jasper looked around the area to make sure all CSU personnel were out of earshot. "Would you like to come over later and help me christen it?"

Trevor's cheeks pinkened up even more. If Jasper had to guess, Trevor wasn't gay, just shy. He'd have to tread lightly with his new friend. He stood, and Trevor did the same.

"I'd like that very much. Let me finish up here, get the body back to the morgue, and check in with Dante. I'll need his input before we make the official request for the records. I should be able to get loose by around eight. Is that too late?"

"No, that's perfect. It'll give me time to get home and take a shower." Jasper pulled a business card out of his wallet. "Here's my cell. Call me when you're on your way, and I'll text you the address." When Trevor took the card, their fingers touched for just the briefest of moments. Jasper felt a tingle. *Damn, you need to get laid if the straight kid is cranking your motor.* He stepped back and watched Trevor work with the CSU unit as fluidly as Dante would. The young man would make a great M.E. one day.

DANTE INJECTED THE serum into the second inmate. He shouldn't be doing this; Isabelle should. She was the one who formulated the antidote. Dante was so proud of his mate, and he wanted her here with him. What the fuck happened to make her run? And with Abbott? The half-blood was her brother, but they weren't close. At least, he didn't think they were. Dante felt more than heard Gregor coming down the hall. His mood was off.

"What's wrong?" he asked his brother as soon as he stepped in the room.

"How much longer will you be?" Gregor's face was pinched; his vitals were all over the place.

"I'll ask you again, Brother, what's wrong?" Dante stood and got in Gregor's space. He placed his hands on his brother's shoulders. The tension was tangible. His touch did no good to relieve the stress flowing through Gregor.

"Rafael called. You are needed at the lab." Gregor wouldn't meet his eyes.

"Take him back to his cell," Dante told the guard who was assisting him. He stored the rest of the antidote in the refrigerator and locked the door to the clinic. He knew without further interrogation Gregor's mood had everything to do with Isabelle. If not, he would have told him what was going on. He didn't hesitate, didn't wait on Gregor to ask any questions about the antidote. Fuck the inmate. If Isabelle was in trouble, she came first. Whether she wanted to be his mate or not, she was his intended, and he would never abandon her.

The drive to the lab took forever. Dante hit every red light in the city. When he finally pulled in the parking lot, he saw not only Julian's Corvette, but also Rafael's Jag and two standard-issue police vehicles. Kaya's and probably Dane's, if he had to guess. If Dane was inside, hopefully Isabelle would be as well.

He found his assumption correct when Dane was the first person he saw, only Isabelle was not present. The detective was pacing back and forth like a caged animal. As soon as he saw Dante, his face paled. Rafael stepped between Dante and Dane, putting his hands on Dante's shoulders, much the same way Dante had Gregor earlier, only Rafael didn't have calming powers. Dante closed his eyes, willing his body to calm. "Tell me."

"Brother, you need to sit down. This isn't a quick story." Rafael didn't move his hands until Dante looked him in the eye and nodded. Kaya was chewing on her thumbnail, a nervous gesture Dante had seen more than once.

"Please, somebody, tell me what the fuck is going on." Dante looked at Dane when he spoke. Considering Isabelle had called her brother, he more than likely was the one who knew the story.

Dane opened his mouth to speak but was interrupted by the door opening. Gregor and Tessa hurried in. Gregor said, "You didn't think I'd let you do this alone, did you?" He cupped his brother's face, pulling their foreheads together.

Dante relaxed a fraction. When Gregor released him, he told Dane to proceed.

"This goes against everything I believe, telling Isabelle's story when she should be the one telling you herself. However, she isn't here, and I fear she is in mortal danger." Dane glanced at Julian whose back was to them as he focused on his computer. Dante knew his cousin wasn't missing a word as he worked.

Dane relayed the details as Isabelle had told them

to him. "Dante, she didn't call you for help because she was afraid you wouldn't want anything to do with another man's child, or her, after you found out."

Tessa couldn't contain herself. "I knew she had a kid! I asked her, point blank, and she lied." Gregor wrapped his arm around her shoulder, squeezing. She stopped talking.

Dante was shocked, to say the least. He had never considered his mate would already have a child, but when he thought about it, it didn't bother him. The child was part of Isabelle. He would have to think more on it later, when mother and child were both safe. "Let's get to the part where you lost her," Dante said to Dane.

"Technically I didn't lose her. I had a plan; she just didn't stick to it."

Julian turned briefly toward Dante and interjected, "Dane called me as soon as she gave him the slip. A taxi picked her up and took her to Jefferson Park. Mason and Lorenzo followed her there."

Dante didn't have to ask to know Julian had hacked Isabelle's phone. He didn't care what his cousin did, as long as they found his mate. Julian's desk phone rang. "Go ahead, Lorenzo. I have you on speaker."

"We have the taxi in sight; however, we cannot find another vehicle. Jules, there's a small drone in the area. At first, I thought someone was flying an RC plane, but it's following the cab. I'm pretty sure that's how they are tracking Isabelle."

Julian switched to another computer, bringing up several monitors. The room was quiet as he did his thing. "There, I have it. Sonofabitch, that's some advanced technology." Nobody said a word as Julian furiously tapped away at his keyboard. "I have a lock on the signal, now I just need to... There! The transmission is scrambled. Rafe, I think it's safe to bring Isabelle in."

"Even with the drone scrambled, whoever is pulling the strings will continue to contact her. Then what?" Tessa asked, now pacing the floor. "If you bring Belle in here, she's going to fuckin' freak! I know I would."

Rafael was still staring at the computer monitors when he spoke. "She may freak, but we are her best bet at a positive outcome."

"You know that, and the rest of us know that, but this is her child. None of us know what she is going through. I can't even begin to imagine how she must feel right now. I mean, not only is Connor missing, but so is Maria. And Rico, gods poor Belle. She sure has been dealt some shitty hands when it comes to dealing with family." Tessa went to Gregor, and he wrapped her in his arms. Kaya was subconsciously holding a protective hand over her stomach.

Julian was now turned facing everyone. "Dante, she's your mate. What do you want to do?"

"Can you transmit an anonymous text to Isabelle?" Dante needed to come up with a plan, but first he wanted Isabelle in his sights.

"Yes, what are you thinking?"

"Jefferson Park isn't far from the armory. Give her that address, and instruct her to get out of the taxi and send him on his way. Tell her a car will be waiting for her. Lorenzo, you and Mason head over there, and when she arrives, bring her back here. Remember, she's a shifter now, so she may put up a fight."

"We're on it." Lorenzo broke the connection. Julian turned back to the computer and did as Dante asked.

Dane rubbed his jaw. "We need a plan. Both Kaya and I have been involved in kidnapping cases. The window of opportunity is a short one in best case scenarios. I hate to say this, but I honestly hope the kidnappers turn out to be the Sarantos family. They will want Connor unharmed."

Dante leaned his head back, looking at the ceiling. He agreed with Dane, but before they could formulate a plan, they had to deal with Isabelle.

Chapter Eleven

ISABELLE WAS ANGRY, confused, worried, and basically pissed off. The taxi driver must have thought she was crazy. She explained she was on a scavenger hunt, but by the look he gave her in the rearview mirror, he didn't believe her. The first text sent her to Jefferson Park. Once she was there, she received another one, telling her to head to the airport, alone. Why had they sent her to the old industrial park only to tell her to go to the airport? Were they watching to see if she was being followed? She could see no other cars at the abandoned warehouse. Just as she was telling the driver to head for the airport, another message came in, telling her to go to a different address.

"Make up your freakin' mind," she mumbled to her phone.

"Did you say something?" the taxi driver asked her.

"Sorry. I need you to go to this address." Isabelle gave him the information from the last text, and they were on their way. She leaned her head back against the seat, her eyes filling with tears. How could she have been so careless? Rico was dead. That was going to tear Connor apart. They had been so close. Rico had taken her child in and loved him as his own. Would Dante feel the same way? Dante. He sounded so hurt on the phone earlier. If she had given in to the mate bond when she first found out she was his, would things be different? He swore to protect her above all.

Surely, he would protect her child as well.

"We're here." The taxi driver's voice brought her back to the present. The text said to get out of the cab and send the driver on his way. Isabelle glanced out the window looking for any sign of someone out there, watching, waiting. Again, she didn't see any cars in the vicinity, but that didn't mean there weren't any. She paid the driver and stepped out of the vehicle. The building reminded her of a smaller version of the Pen. It had the same stone architecture, only it was one story and wasn't surrounded by razor wire and armed guards. The November wind whipped through her hair, blinding her momentarily.

When she pushed her hair out of her face, two huge men were standing in front of her. Before she could scream, a large hand clamped over her mouth, gently. "Shh, Isabelle, it's me, Lorenzo. You remember Mason? Rafael sent us to protect you, bring you in." Isabelle cut her eyes to the younger man, remembering them both from when she interviewed Vincent. She nodded, and Lorenzo removed his hand. "I'm sorry if I scared you."

"What are you doing here? They are watching me!" Isabelle looked around, knowing she wouldn't see whomever had been sending her the texts.

"No, they aren't. We took care of their spy, but we have to hurry before they override Julian's override." Lorenzo gently grabbed her bicep, directing her toward the back of the building to a blacked-out SUV.

"Where are you taking me?" Isabelle asked as she climbed in.

"To Julian's lab. Rafael and Kaya are waiting for you," Lorenzo told her reflection in the mirror. "Try to relax, Isabelle. We know what's going on, and we're all here to help you get your son back. You're family now."

Isabelle's mouth opened then closed. What could she say to that? The ride was mostly quiet, with the exception of Lorenzo calling Rafael to confirm they had secured Isabelle. Thirty minutes later, they were pulling in the parking lot of a building that looked a lot like the one they'd just left. Mason opened her door and helped her out. Isabelle heard a growl and knew Dante was watching. She mentally rolled her eyes. If he was this protective now, she couldn't imagine what he'd be like if they ever officially bonded.

Dante held the door open but didn't say anything. He just walked quietly beside her until they were in the lab. Lorenzo had left out a few people when he said who was waiting on her. Tessa met her with a tight hug. "Belle, I'm so sorry about all this shit. We're gonna get your son back, I promise."

Rafael stepped forward and reiterated what Tessa said. "That we are. I know you're scared, but on my honor as your King, I vow to bring you and your son back together." He fisted his hand over his heart and bowed his head to her. The tears once again welled in her eyes, spilling down her cheeks.

She felt strong hands on her shoulders and knew they belonged to Dante. "Don't," she said to him over her shoulder.

Dante removed his hands and held them up in the defensive. "I apologize. I won't touch you again," he said with a defeated look.

"No, Dante, I meant don't do that calming thing you do. I don't want to be calm. I want to be angry. I

96

want to be pissed off. I want to scream at the top of my freakin' lungs!" Isabelle yelled. "You don't understand. None of you could possibly understand how I feel right now." Her voice lowered as she placed her tear-streaked face in her hands. She felt herself being engulfed in strong arms. This time, she allowed herself to be swallowed in the embrace of her Gargoyle.

"Isabelle, give me your cell." Isabelle handed her purse over, knowing Tessa would dig through it for the phone. She leaned farther into Dante's body as she listened to the voices all around her making plans. Her phone pinged with an incoming text, and she jerked, trying to get free.

Dante didn't let go. He did loosen his hold enough so she could turn in his arms, but he kept her back to his chest as she listened to Tessa read the message.

"You have one hour to get to the airport. A private jet will be waiting."

Everyone started talking at once, but it was Tessa who got their attention. She stuck her fingers in her mouth and let out a loud whistle. She must have learned that from Tamian.

"I have a plan. I am going in Belle's place." Gregor was shaking his head emphatically, and Tessa put her hand on his chest. "I'm trained for this; Belle isn't. Just hear me out. I have disguises at home as well as tracking devices and hidden microphones. I have just enough time to get home and change. Julian, I can give you all the info you need to track me and monitor all conversations. Gregor, you will follow in the family jet along with Dante and Isabelle."

"But what about Sophia? She needs your help, too." Isabelle hadn't forgotten her niece was missing.

97

"I've already called Zeke, and he's meeting up with Nikolas. They can handle a few more days without us." Tessa closed the gap between them. "I want to do this for you, Belle. I've let you down long enough." Isabelle was surprised at the tears shining in her cousin's eyes. She'd rarely ever seen Tessa cry.

"Still, I can't let you risk your life. This is my child. My past coming back to haunt me."

Dane's phone rang. He was staring at Isabelle as he spoke. "You did? Are you sure? Okay, I want round-the-clock protection outside her door. If you can't arrange that, I'll send my own man. Good, call me when she wakes up." He disconnected and offered a small smile. "That was Corey. Maria Sanchez was found a few miles from her home. She's in a coma, and for now, it's just wait and see."

Dante's arms tightened, and this time she didn't yell at him when she felt the calming effects of his touch. She closed her eyes and sent a message through the cosmos to whatever deity was listening for Maria to pull through.

Rafael asked Gregor, "Are you good with this? She's your mate." Rafael obviously didn't know Tessa that well. Once she had her mind made up, there was no changing it. Gregor, however, did know his mate.

"I trust Tessa and her abilities. I don't like it, but I'll go along with it." Gregor's voice was low, his heart was in each word.

"But what about the Pen?" Isabelle turned and looked up at Dante. "What about the morgue?"

"Trevor can handle the morgue, and Deacon's got the Pen. We've got this," Dante assured her. When Gregor nodded, she settled back into Dante's body.

"Good, now let's go. Time's wasting." Tessa slipped the cell phone back in Isabelle's purse and handed it to her. Tessa then headed for the door without looking back.

Rafael and Julian discussed the tracking capabilities, as well as some drone that had been following Isabelle. Dane spoke softly to Kaya about Maria and contacting some friends of theirs in Tennessee. Lorenzo and Mason stood off to the side of the room, talking quietly to each other.

Dante continued to hold Isabelle, placing soft kisses to her hair and temple. In that moment, Isabelle had perfect clarity. Lorenzo's words from earlier snuck back into her mind; *You're family now.* As she watched Dante's Clan making plans to get *her* son back, it hit her; they had already accepted her into the fold. They were her Clan, her family. Something she had longed for since she was a teenager.

Whether it was the mate bond or Dante's special touch weaving its way into her soul, a bright light was flipped on in her brain after having been shrouded in darkness for so long. She wanted this. She wanted Dante. She didn't know him as well as she would like, but what she did know warmed her heart. Somehow, she knew he would never turn his back on her and treat her the way Alexi had. Turning in Dante's arms, she pulled his head down to hers and melded their lips together. Sliding one hand up in his hair, she tugged him closer, licking across his full bottom lip, asking for entrance. If this kiss was all they ever had together, she was going to make it worth remembering.

He opened for her. Not caring who was watching, Isabelle slid her tongue into his mouth. Dante's hands came alive on her body, one hand fisting her hair as the other moved down her back, holding her firmly in place. Isabelle's other hand grabbed onto his hip, her fingers kneading into his side. Isabelle poured her heart and soul into their mouths, allowing the kiss to say what she could not. She wanted him… permanently. First, she had to get her son back safely. If she survived, only then would she think about the future.

After a few minutes of allowing herself to feel wanted, she pulled away from Dante. His gaze was filled with lust and longing, warmth and acceptance. His usual frown was gone, replaced with a beautiful smile. She couldn't return the smile; she was dying inside. Everything she could ever want was at her fingertips, with the exception of her son being there to enjoy it with her. Sighing, she placed her hand on his cheek, memorizing his face. Now, their moment was over. She hoped it was enough to carry them both through whatever happened next. "I need to use the restroom. Which way?"

Kaya, who was standing near, said, "I'll show you."

Dante ran his fingers through the tips of her hair. "I need to call Trevor and fill him in. You'll be okay?"

Isabelle gave a weak smile and nodded. "I'll be fine." She motioned for Kaya to lead the way. Once in the restroom, she rested against the wall, leaning her head back and closing her eyes.

"You're doing great, Isabelle. I am a veteran cop, and I'm not so sure I'd be doing as well as you are." Kaya was leaned against the sink, arms crossed over her breasts.

"To be honest, if it weren't for Dante's magic, I wouldn't be quite so calm. Do all the Gargoyles have powers?"

"Not that I know of. At least, he's the only one Rafael has mentioned as being special."

"I appreciate everyone wanting to help. I need you to promise me something." Isabelle pulled away from the wall and put her hand on Kaya's arm. "Promise me you'll take care of Maria. I want to be there for her, but that's going to be impossible now. Please, Kaya, promise me if she pulls through, you'll make sure she's safe."

Kaya placed her hand over Isabelle's. "You have my word."

"Thank you. Now, if you don't mind, I would like to be alone for a few minutes."

"Of course. I'll go wait with the men." Kaya patted her hand and left her to her thoughts.

Isabelle listened for Kaya's footsteps to retreat. When Kaya was far enough away, Isabelle pulled out her cell phone and called the same cab company as before, scheduling a pick-up at a convenience store down the street from where she was currently located. Her heart was full as she thought of all the people willing to put themselves in danger for her, but this was her son. This was something she needed to do herself.

Silently, Isabelle exited the building. She kept her body close to the outer wall then ducked between two of the vehicles. When the coast was clear, she sprinted across the parking lot and down the street. She slipped inside the store, waiting for the taxi. She grabbed a protein bar and bottle of water, not knowing when or if she would get to eat again. Her appetite was absent, but she needed strength for what was to come. When she spotted the taxi in the parking lot, she paid for her items, and with a heavy heart, headed to the airport.

Chapter Twelve

DANTE COULD FEEL the excitement coming from Trevor through the phone. His assistant gave him the details of the burned body, and Dante granted permission to proceed with the examination. He knew there was more to his enthusiasm than being put in charge of the body, but he wasn't going to pry. Without going into too much detail, he told Trevor to man the morgue while he was gone, and if he needed anything to reach out to Kaya. If Trevor thought Kaya being his point of contact was strange, he didn't let on. The kid was definitely preoccupied.

Isabelle and Gregor returned, with Isabelle looking around. "Where is she?"

The face was right, but the voice was all wrong. "Holy hell," Dante muttered as he looked at Tessa, disguised as Isabelle. "How in the gods' name did you do that?" He couldn't believe how much she looked like his mate.

"Prosthetics. Now, where is she? I need to get her voice programmed into the distorter."

Dante looked around. "She went to the restroom. Kaya, did you leave Isabelle alone?"

"Yes, she needed a minute. She should be…"

Dante didn't wait for the Queen to finish. He sprinted toward the restroom, reaching out with his senses. He didn't have to open the door to know Isabelle wasn't in there. He let out a roar. She was gone. His beautiful, stubborn woman was gone. He didn't wait to get back to the lab. Instead he yelled, "Julian, find Isabelle!" He ran outside, looking around, knowing she had a big head start. Why the fuck had he let her out of his sight?

"I've got her!" Julian yelled, bringing Dante back inside. "She's headed north towards the airport."

"Fuck. FUCK!" Dante kicked the nearest chair, sending it flying across the room, denting the sheetrock. Gregor made a move toward him, but Dante held his hands up. "Don't. Do not fucking touch me. Julian, I'm headed to the airport. Get every godsdamned flight plan there is and send them to me."

"Dante, I'm sorry." Kaya was holding her belly, tears running down her cheeks.

"It's not your fault, my Queen. Isabelle is my mate, my responsibility." He looked her in the eye, glanced at her stomach, and fisted his hand over his heart. Bowing quickly, he turned and sprinted from the building. Gregor and Tessa were hot on his heels as he headed to his car.

"Come on, Brother, I'll drive." Gregor and Tessa waited by the Hummer. Dante knew Gregor would get them there quickly and in one piece, whereas he would not. He climbed into the backseat, urging his brother to hurry. He called Julian, impatient for the information his cousin was searching for.

"Dante, I was just about to call you. I am sending all data to your phone now. There are several private planes set to take off within the hour. Just because they told her a jet was waiting doesn't necessarily mean they are putting her on a plane. I am working on tapping into the airport cameras now. I also sent my own text to Isabelle, begging her to let us help. She

104

hasn't responded," Julian said, while he tapped on the keyboard.

"She hasn't responded to any of the ones I've sent either. Please keep trying."

"Will do. Rafael is going with Kaya and Dane to Tennessee. They want to be there if Maria comes out of her coma."

"Thank you, Julian."

Dante was about to disconnect when Tessa said, "Let me talk to him." Tessa took Dante's phone. "Julian, remember those trackers I was talking about? I dropped a small transmitter into Isabelle's purse before I gave it back to her."

"Why did you do that?"

"Because I was afraid she might go off on her own, which she did. As long as they don't throw her purse out somewhere, you should be able to locate her. The tracker is new technology, and even if they jam the signal, you can still receive it. You just have to find the right frequency."

"Where did you get the transmitter? This technology is far more advanced than anything I've seen."

"Where I get all my toys – from Jonas."

"I'll get on it and keep you posted," Julian said and disconnected.

Tessa handed Dante's phone back to him.

"What made you think she'd take off on her own?" Gregor asked his mate as he reached for her hand.

"Because it's what I would have done in her place. She has lived most of her life without anyone having her back," Tessa told him, a hint of sadness in her voice.

Dante sent Isabelle another text. *"I understand why you are doing this, and I will do everything within my power to find you and bring you back to me."* While listening to his brother chat with his mate, he opened the document that contained all flights scheduled for the evening. He thought of Isabelle, feeling alone at a time like this. It hurt his heart that she didn't think she could trust him, or anyone, to help her out. He made a silent vow to not only get Isabelle back, but to bring Connor back safely as well. When that was accomplished, he would spend the rest of his long life earning her trust as well as her love.

"I want to know how the kidnappers knew Isabelle had a kid. I mean, I didn't even know, and I've been following her for years." Tessa was still in her disguise, and Dante found it a little unnerving.

"Obviously you aren't the only one who has been following her, but that doesn't matter now. What does matter is we get to the airport before she's put on a plane. There are seven private flights scheduled. Five of them are domestic. One is traveling to Italy, and one is going to Greece. Fuck! This can't be a coincidence." Dante had a bad feeling.

"I have to agree with you, Brother. Alistair's hatred for Jonas has been going on for centuries. What if he's had eyes on Jonas this whole time? He would have known about Isabelle and her foster family. I wouldn't doubt he put Alexi up to seducing a young Isabelle to gain any knowledge she had of her father's work." Gregor was confirming Dante's own thoughts.

Tessa told the men, "I'm calling my dad, see if he can give us a head's up on where Alistair lives." She pressed a button and waited. "Hey, Mom, is Dad

106

home? Shit. Did you know Isabelle has a kid? Yeah, well, I didn't either." Tessa told her mom all she knew about Connor, and what they were up to. "I will. Love you, too."

"Mom gives you both her love. Dad is in Italy, but she suggested you call your mom. Alistair is her brother, after all."

"I've already thought of that. I will call her as a last resort. Right now, I'm not so sure I trust her." Dante called Julian and relayed their conversation, asking him to find a way to delay the plane headed for Greece.

TREVOR'S MIND WOULDN'T slow down. *What the hell is going on?* First Jasper asked him to a concert, and not just any concert. It was Cyanide Sweetness! That shouldn't be such a big deal, but it was huge. Second, he asked him to come over and play video games. It had been a couple of years since he'd spent time with anyone. All his friends from college had either moved off or were married. The one time he had tried dating had been a disaster, so he hadn't tried again. Even though he talked to Travis on the phone at least once a week, he hadn't seen his brother in almost a year. Sadly, all his friends were bodies on a slab, and he was even more boring than they were.

On top of all that, Dante was turning the morgue over to him for the time being. What the fuck was up with that? Dante never went out of town. He had sounded really stressed on the phone, too.

Trevor knew Dante had his secrets, and he was okay with that. He had some of his own. It didn't mean he thought less of his boss. It just meant theirs wasn't a relationship solid enough to confide in each other. However, it felt as if things were changing. When Trevor told Dante he was a clone, Dante hadn't flinched. Then again, neither had the warden. Being a clone wasn't his biggest secret, but he wasn't ready to share the truth with anyone.

He pulled the business card out of his pocket and put it on the kitchen table. He wanted to shower before he hung out with Jasper. Not that he was trying to impress the guy. He just didn't want to smell like a burned corpse the rest of the night. *Yeah right.*

He was too nervous to call Jasper, so he sent him a text. *Leaving soon. Need your address.*

Jasper responded immediately, telling him where he lived. He followed up with: *Do you like pizza?*

Trevor: *Yes, anything but anchovies. Those are gross.*

Jasper: *Dude, you work in a morgue. How is anything gross to you?*

Trevor: *I have my limits. Do you need me to bring anything?* Trevor was enjoying the banter.

Jasper: *Nope, not unless you don't drink beer.*

Trevor: *I drink beer. See you soon.* Trevor didn't drink a lot of beer, but he would probably need some liquid courage tonight. He showered and dressed in record time. While he was brushing his teeth, he looked up Jasper's address on his phone. He knew the area; it was close to where the warden lived. With one last glance in the mirror, he was out the door of his apartment and on his way.

As he drove across town, he let the sounds of his

favorite band fill the car. Cyanide Sweetness was hardcore. It amazed him Jasper liked them. It didn't surprise him Dante didn't. His boss was more of a classical music lover. The closer he got to Jasper's, the more nervous he got. *Dude, chill the fuck out. It's not a date. It's just you and your new friend hanging out.* He continued to give himself a mental pep talk until he finally arrived at the address Jasper had given him. Trevor pulled in the driveway and looked around. This couldn't be right; the property was secure, much like Gregor's. He was just about to call Jasper and ask for the right address when the gate opened. His phone pinged with a message.

Jasper: *Are you just going to sit there? The pizza's getting cold.*

Huh. Trevor pulled down the long driveway that curved between stands of pine trees on either side of the paved drive. The home that came into view was impressive. It was like Gregor's house in that it was log and stone. However, this one was not a three-story monstrosity. Jasper was waiting on the front porch, leaning against one of the massive log posts, hands in the pockets of his jeans. Trevor turned the motor off and wiped his sweaty hands on his own jeans. *We're just friends. This is just two guys hanging out.* Steeling his nerves, he got out of his car and walked up the steps. When he saw the tight black T-shirt stretched over Jasper's chest, he laughed.

"What are you laughing at?" Jasper straightened up and looked down at his shirt. "What? You don't like Star Wars? You better 'fess up right now, because if you don't, you need to leave," Jasper teased him.

Trevor unbuttoned his long sleeve shirt, showing

109

Jasper the same black Darth Vader tee hidden underneath. They both laughed, and Jasper wrapped his arm around Trevor's shoulder. "I knew I liked you." Trevor had to make his body relax. The feel of Jasper's hand on his shoulder had his body zinging. Jasper led Trevor into his home, stopping in the huge family room. A large cedar chest topped with pizza served as a coffee table. The sofa was a leather sectional. A seventy-two inch TV hung over the mantle of the stone fireplace. Game controllers were scattered on the floor beside the sofa. Trevor had died and gone to geek heaven.

"Are you on the take?" he blurted out before his brain could stop his mouth. How could a cop, even a detective, afford a house this massive and all the luxuries that came with it? He hadn't seen the rest of the house, but he was certain it would be just as impressive.

"You mean like a dirty cop? What the fuck?" Jasper dropped his arm from around Trevor's shoulder and turned, facing Trevor with his arms crossed over his massive chest.

"I'm sorry. That slipped out. No, I don't think you're a dirty cop, but dude, how do you afford all this?" Trevor didn't want to ruin his friendship before it started.

"I have a really good investor. Now, do you want to eat pizza and play games, or piss me off some more?" Jasper replied, his face barely hiding a smirk.

Relief flooded Trevor. "Pizza, definitely. These don't look like delivery. Did you make 'em yourself?" He sat on the sofa, eyeing the delicious looking pies.

Jasper handed Trevor a beer before sitting down

next to him. "I did. It takes too long to get delivery out here. Besides, this way I know they're gonna be just the way I like them. Help yourself." Jasper handed Trevor a plate and napkin, then grabbed several slices of pizza and put them on his own plate. He turned the television on, muting the volume.

Jasper turned toward Trevor on the sofa. "So, tell me all about yourself."

The two men ate pizza, drank beer, and told each other small bits of info. Nothing really personal, not at first, since this was just two friends having a chat. Trevor talked about working in the morgue. Jasper told some stories of living on the West Coast and being a fireman. When the pizza was demolished and the plates cleared, Jasper asked, "Have you played Gods of Chaos Four?"

Trevor's heart skipped a beat. "You have Four? It's not even out yet. How the hell did you get your hands on it?"

Jasper grinned, his straight, white teeth shining. "I know someone who knows someone. Now, do you wanna play or what?"

Trevor really wanted to *or what*, but he wouldn't dare go there. Not with this man.

"Put it in." Trevor realized too late what he'd said. He felt his face blushing. Jasper winked at him and fired up the game. When he returned to the sofa, he sat next to Trevor. There was barely any space between their thighs as Jasper handed him a controller. The brief contact of their hands caused a stirring sensation in Trevor's body. He was going to lose before they began playing, because he couldn't keep his mind off the man sitting next to him.

Chapter Thirteen

ISABELLE PAID THE cab driver and got out of the car. The last text she received gave explicit instructions as to where she was to be dropped off and where she was to go to afterward. She was walking while chastising herself the whole time. Maybe now she understood why her father didn't trust her all those years ago; for someone so smart, she was stupid. Even Tessa didn't pull this kind of stunt. Well, she probably did, but this was the kind of thing Tessa lived for. She was prepared for this, whereas Isabelle was not.

The click of her shoes on the pavement tattooed a beat in sync with the double-time thumping of her heart. *Step, beat, beat. Step, beat, beat.* Now reality was setting in, and she realized, too late, she should have let Dante and the Clan find Connor. It wasn't that she didn't trust them. Just a few weeks ago, Isabelle watched the Clan rally around Tessa when she was being hunted by a serial killer. They would do the same for Isabelle, but she just didn't feel right putting all of them in danger when this was her problem. Dante's last text message made the panic a little more real. He was coming after her anyway.

Three small planes were lined up outside private hangars. The last one was her intended ride for the next however many hours it took to arrive wherever she was being taken. As she neared the jet, a woman about Isabelle's age appeared in the door and descended the stairs.

"Welcome, Isabelle. My name is Kallisto, and I will be escorting you." Kallisto could have been a fashion model with her long legs and flawless skin. Her blonde hair was pulled into a tight bun. Her blue pantsuit and mirrored sunglasses reminded Isabelle of an FBI agent. All she needed was the badge. Her accent hinted at Greek.

"Where are we going?" Isabelle asked as she ascended the stairs into the plane's cavity. She didn't expect an answer and was surprised when Kallisto responded.

"To see your son, of course. Please, make yourself comfortable. We have a long flight ahead of us." Kallisto motioned for Isabelle to have a seat in one of the plush leather captain's chairs along the left side of the plane. She had flown in the Sarantos jet, but it hadn't been nearly as opulent as this one. If circumstances were different, she might enjoy the flight. Considering she was headed off to an unknown destination, she doubted she would be comfortable, even in all this luxury.

Kallisto disappeared into the cockpit momentarily. When she returned, she pushed a button, retracting the stairs before closing and locking the door to the plane. She took a chair opposite Isabelle, her sunglasses now absent from her face. She buckled her seatbelt and told Isabelle to do the same. Isabelle tried not to stare at the woman sitting across the aisle from her, but it was difficult. She was drop-dead gorgeous with eyes such a pale blue, they were almost absent any pigment. She also had a certain air about her, one that said, "Don't fuck with me".

Isabelle had no problem admitting when a woman

113

was beautiful. If they had been in a different time and situation, a time before Dante, Isabelle might have given in to the attraction. Instead, she closed her eyes and tapped into her shifter senses. She was still learning how to control her breathing, calming herself. Tessa had told her what to expect with her body, how her strength and stamina would increase, and her senses would heighten.

The plane began moving, and within a few minutes, it was taxiing down the runway. Isabelle looked out the window as the plane rose into the Georgia sky. The sun had gone down, and the bright lights of the airport shone like beacons below. Isabelle felt a strange vibe, a sense of familiarity. Could Kallisto be a shifter too? Not wanting to be conspicuous, Isabelle kept her eyes closed, concentrating on slowing her heart rate. If Kallisto sensed her nervousness, it would give the woman an even greater advantage. When Isabelle heard movement, she cracked her eyes as her hostess unbuckled her seatbelt and strode to the back of the plane. Isabelle listened closely when she heard voices.

"He wishes to speak with you," a man's voice said.

Kallisto spoke softly. "Yes, sir. We have just taken off. Other than the drone going offline, we had no trouble. She has been compliant the entire time. I understand." After that, the voices were muffled, and Isabelle couldn't understand, even with her shifter hearing.

"Isabelle, are you hungry? Would you care for something to drink?" Kallisto asked from the rear of the plane.

"No, thank you." She didn't trust them not to drug

her. They had been fairly hospitable so far, for kidnappers. Technically, they hadn't abducted her; she'd come of her own free will.

"Where is my son?" Isabelle asked when the blonde sat back down.

"Somewhere safe." Kallisto didn't look at Isabelle when she answered.

"Who hired you?" Isabelle twisted in the plush leather seat.

"You'll find out soon enough. Now, no more questions. This is going to be a long flight. We have magazines, books, and movies available. If you change your mind about food or drink, do not hesitate to let me know. And, no, we are not going to drug you. Our intentions are not to hurt you, Isabelle, only to reunite you with your child." Kallisto settled into her own chair, opening a folder and scanning the documents contained therein.

Isabelle didn't want reading material, nor did she want to watch a movie. What she wanted was Connor, and if the woman sitting across from her was being truthful, Isabelle would see him soon.

JULIAN CALLED AHEAD so the Stone Society jet was on standby, fueled up and ready to go. Dante, Gregor, and Tessa arrived at the airport minutes after the private jet had taken off for Greece. Julian confirmed he was able to track Isabelle, amazed at the technology Jonas had created. He knew the man was a genius, having knowledge of his past accomplishments. This new technology was even more impressive. He wanted to spend time with the doctor, pick his brain. Julian himself had an IQ that was off the charts, but he had a feeling he could learn so much from Isabelle's father.

Julian was feeling restless. He knew his job within the Clan was important, but at that moment, it didn't seem enough. Nikolas was somewhere in Egypt, searching for Sophia. Dante was off to Greece, going to rescue Isabelle. Rafael was headed to Tennessee with Kaya and Dane to check on Maria. He was sitting at a bank of computers, watching. He thought of his own mate, Katherine, wondering what she was doing. Was she off on an adventure of her own, searching for the next big story? Was she getting ready for a date? Dane was under the impression Katherine was his mate. His impression was wrong.

The door opened, and Frey walked in. "Hey, Little Brother, what the fuck is going on? I went by the manor to talk to Kaya, and nobody was home. I called Rafe, and he asked me to rearrange all the patrol schedules. Said you'd fill me in on what's going down." He sat down in Nikolas's chair, leaning back with his hands clasped behind his head.

Julian told his brother everything that had transpired that day.

"What a cluster fuck. Why can't one of us find a mate who doesn't have a target on their back? Speaking of women, what's going on with yours?"

"Nothing is going on with mine. I am too busy trying to keep everyone else's alive." Julian wasn't bitter, just honest.

"Truth, Brother. Truth. So Isabelle has a kid. How did Dante take the news?"

116

"The same way we all did. He was shocked at first, but we all realized we don't know her. Why would we have known she has a kid? I know nothing about Katherine I haven't read in a file online. I'm sure she has secrets like the rest of us. Dante has already accepted Isabelle, and he's ready for a family. He will do the honorable thing and accept Connor without hesitation. Wouldn't you?"

"Of course I would. We all have pasts, good and bad. We cannot judge others without judging ourselves. I, for one, would hate to have stones cast my way for the shit I've done. Besides, I'm ready for a rugrat or ten myself."

Even though they were brothers, Julian only knew snippets of Frey's life. He was the most guarded of the Gargoyles and definitely had secrets of his own he refused to share with the Clan. They didn't push. He had seen combat more than once in his long life, having joined the military several times. Geoffrey was a born soldier. It was only recently he'd hung up the dog tags and settled on opening the dojo. It sounded as if he was ready for another type of settling as well.

"I had set a training schedule, but now that Gregor and Dante are heading out of the country, I will need to revise it. Rafe doesn't want me to postpone working with the rest of the Clan. I am meeting Uri in the morning at the armory, and we will proceed as planned. Dante has already spoken to Oksana and given her an extended vacation. Even though she is in the know about us being Goyles, I don't want her around when we're all half naked and swinging swords. I'd hate to give the old girl a heart attack." Frey wiggled his eyebrows.

Julian barked out a laugh. "Hell, you're enough to give someone a heart attack just by walking into a room. Have you seen yourself?" Frey was the largest Gargoyle in the Clan. He had a dangerous air about him, and his presence alone commanded a room. Even though he was devastatingly handsome, most women took one look at the huge Goyle and shied away. Men refused to look him in the eye. It was interesting to watch him train fighters at his gym. The first thing he taught them was to stare him down, or at least not look away. It was hard to stare someone down when they stood almost a foot taller than you.

"Heard anything from Nik?" Frey had wanted to go with his brother to help look for Sophia. Truth be told, they all had. Not that they didn't trust his abilities; they were just used to looking out for one another.

"I talked to him this morning to put him in touch with Ezekiel. Since they're both searching for Sophia, we figure it's better if they work together. Now that Gregor has gone to help Dante, his plan to help Nik has been delayed. Hopefully both outcomes will be positive, and we can get Nik home soon." Julian missed his brother.

"It's crazy how a few weeks ago we didn't know half-bloods existed, and now we're mating with them and working closely with them. Is Nikolas going to be adding them to our archives? Who keeps their information?"

"According to Tessa, Sophia is their archivist. Makes sense she and Nik would be mates. Rafe wants all the half-bloods rounded up so we can bring them into the fold, so to speak. The biggest headache is going

118

to be Jonas. He's been doing his own thing for so long now. Rafe's going to have a hard time convincing him he needs to join our Clan officially." Julian thought back to what Frey said when he arrived. "If you don't mind me asking, what did you want to speak to Kaya about?"

"One of her cops. Apparently he's a douchebag who likes to beat on his wife and her brother. I want more intel before I go to bat for the kid."

If there was a champion for someone being bullied, it was Frey. As big and scary as he looked, underneath he had a soft spot for the underdog.

"Why don't you just kick his ass and scare the shit out of him?"

"I wish it were that simple. This is something I've got to tread carefully with. Now, I will leave you to your monitors. I've got to hit the skies. Maybe I'll get to kick some Unholy ass instead." Frey pulled a cigar out of his pocket and bit the end off. Pointing the unlit stick at his brother, he said, "Call me if you need me. I'll be here."

Julian nodded and turned back to the screens. If this was where he was needed, he would sit here and make sure he kept his family as safe as he possibly could.

Chapter Fourteen

DANTE HADN'T FLOWN in an airplane in quite some time. Ten years to be exact. He and Gregor had taken a trip to one of the many Clan properties, just to get away. They had spent a couple of weeks at the seaside resort, soaking up the sun, fishing, drinking, just basically enjoying life. Both Goyles had enjoyed the company of women, Gregor more so than Dante. Being passive made it hard for him to find a suitable partner for sex. Most women were used to the man taking over, or just going along with whatever happened. He wanted to be dominated, told what to do, when to do it. He wasn't into any type of pain or bondage. He just didn't want to be in control of what happened in the bedroom. When he found a female who dominated him, it would rile his beast, and the sex was good.

Isabelle had kissed him. Twice. That didn't mean she was dominant in the bedroom. Had the fates chosen a submissive mate for him, and if so, why? Was Isabelle truly submissive, or was she also wading through the waters of a new sexual relationship? Dante understood the first few times were awkward, at least for him. It took a while to figure out what the other partner liked, what turned them on, what set them on fire. Maybe that was it, and she was figuring him out. She had kissed him after all. It hadn't been a soft, chaste kiss either. Her tongue had begged entrance to his mouth, and he gladly obliged. His mate knew how to use her tongue. He was ready to see what else she could do with her mouth. Before he let his thoughts get too far out of control and his cock too hard, he returned his attention to the trip they were embarking on. With any luck, he would save the damsel as well as her child, and have plenty of time to explore the sexual side of their relationship later.

The Clan jet was in the air. Gregor and Tessa were settling in for the long flight. Dante pulled a bottle of Scotch out of the liquor cabinet and poured himself a tall glass. He didn't bother with ice. It just watered down the expensive whiskey. He sank back into his seat, sipping the fine liquid.

The worst part of this rescue mission was they had no idea where they were going or who they were up against. They assumed Stavros was behind the kidnapping since he was Connor's grandfather. Then again, Alistair could be the mastermind, wanting to punish Dante's family. Was his uncle aware Isabelle was his mate? It wouldn't be hard to find out they spent time together, especially if he had spies in and around New Atlanta. What if one of the guards had turned traitor? Dante hated to become suspicious without probable cause, but anything was possible. Even though the Gargoyles didn't want for money, there were those beings, even Goyles, who never had enough.

Tessa sat on the long sofa with her legs curled under her. "I hope they're taking Isabelle to Zakynthos. At least there she will have some familiarity, even if we don't."

Once they were at a safe altitude, Dante contacted Julian, inquiring into the Stone Society's properties. Jules pulled up the list of properties in and around

Greece. "Atokos Island is closest to Zakynthos. I'll have to get with Sixx and find out if it's currently occupied. If it is, you can always stop off at Rafael's villa. Speaking of Rafe, he and Kaya should be in Tennessee by now. As soon as I hear something, I'll let you know."

"Thanks, Jules. I would prefer to stay on Atokos since it's closer. Hopefully being off season, the villa will be vacant." There wasn't really such a thing as off season in Greece. The islands were beautiful no matter what time of year it was.

The unknown was their biggest foe at this point. They were going to have to rely on Julian's assistance from thousands of miles away. With Alistair being King of Greece, they couldn't ask for help from other Clans. As a last resort, they would call Dante's mother and ask for her assistance. If Dante had his way, Isabelle would be his true mate, and Connor would become his son. Athena would have her first grandchild, even if he wasn't by blood.

"What if whoever has Isabelle isn't the one who took Connor? What do we do then?" Tessa was tapping her fingers on her legs. Gregor placed his hand over hers to stop her fidgeting.

"One thing at a time, Red. That is a possibility, but we need to focus on Isabelle since we have a bead on her. We have to assume whoever took Connor will be in touch with Isabelle. We need to track her and get her to safety." Gregor put his arm around his mate and pulled her into his lap.

"What if taking her from her abductors puts Connor in more danger than he's already in?" Tessa asked with her head on Gregor's shoulder.

"We have to pray it doesn't." Gregor kissed the top of her head, running his hand along her arm. The soft caress lulled Tessa into an unusual state – quietness.

Dante was ready for the closeness Gregor and Tessa possessed. He may not pull Isabelle onto his lap, but he would definitely put his arm around her and lavish her with affection. He had to wonder if her kiss back at the lab had been out of need or if she was saying goodbye. He swirled the Scotch in his glass as he thought of Connor. It would be to their advantage if the boy looked like Isabelle. He was formulating a plan in his mind, going through scenarios of rescue. Not knowing where Connor had been taken was making it difficult to come up with anything useful. He downed the rest of the liquid, setting the glass aside. He leaned his chair back and closed his eyes, sending positive thoughts through the airwaves to his woman. "Hang on, Beautiful. I'm coming to get you."

STAVROS SAT ON the patio overlooking the water. His breakfast was set before him, his coffee poured. The linen napkin unfolded and placed in his lap. His servant did everything but cut his food and feed it to him. That task he reserved for one of his girls. Since he was at the main villa and not one of the smaller ones, he would have to feed himself. It was risky keeping women around who he was actually training to be slaves.

When he first got into the market of kidnapping women, he had made sure they were destitute. He only took the ones who had no family who would miss them. He didn't just kidnap women and sell them. First, he brought them in, cleaned them up, fed them, clothed them. Made them feel wanted. Rarely did they realize they were actually being abducted. When he had their loyalty, he would *suggest* he had a friend who was in need of a companion. One who would take care of the woman as long as she would let him. What he neglected to tell the woman was he was being paid handsomely for this service he provided. After all, he was making sure the women were healthy and cooperative. Once the woman was placed with the buyer, it was out of his hands what happened.

He did have several clients who were repeat customers. Once the woman reached a certain age, the buyer would trade her in for a younger girl. Stavros had no idea what happened when one was replaced. He didn't want to know.

Lately, he had branched out to tourists, young college-age girls on spring break who were bored with their families and wanted a little adventure. That was where his son came in. The handsome young man could seduce even the prudest woman away from what she thought was right or wrong. It now appeared he and his son would be branching out even more. The proposals they looked over the night before had been specific in their requests. The purchasers were looking for a certain type of girl, younger than most Stavros dealt with. He and his son might not be upstanding citizens, but their moral compass did point closer to north most of the time. The age of these girls had the arrow pointing south. Way south. The risk was great, but the money was greater. His son hadn't batted an eyelash when Stavros showed him what the buyers were looking for. "It's not like we'll be fucking them," he said as he slid the folders back across the desk to his father.

It was decided they would accept the proposals. The younger girls, however, would not be trained by Stavros or his son. He would draw the line there. The girls would be found, per the buyers' specifications, but would be immediately turned over with no lag time. Once they agreed to the new parameters, his son had left to do whatever or whomever he did at night, leaving Stavros to think about the news of having a grandson. He had yet to mention this little tidbit to his son, as he didn't know how the news would be received. Even though his old acquaintance had put things into motion, Stavros would have to tread carefully with the boy's life. He just needed to come up with a plan to keep his grandson hidden for a while.

As Stavros was finishing his coffee, his son came out to the patio. "I'm going to get started on our newest acquisitions. I will be traveling to Athens for the day, possibly spending the night."

"Very well. I have business I need to tend to as well. I will see you later." Stavros didn't elaborate on what type of business. He and his son were both grown men with lives of their own. Their business arrangement had them working closely most days, but when they needed their private space, neither one asked any questions. As soon as he finished eating breakfast, Stavros gave instructions to his butler he was not to be disturbed under any circumstances. He left the main villa for one of the smaller houses where he was going to meet his grandson.

CONNOR'S ARMS CRAMPED, and he needed to pee. He was trying his best to be brave so his momma would be proud of him, but he was scared. Somehow, he had known bad things were going to happen. He dreamed of finding Papi and Mimi on the ground, covered in blood. He dreamed of his momma and some huge man fighting the bad guys together. He could see the man clearly in his mind. He wasn't his father, but he was important. His father was dead. So who was this man who came to rescue him in his dream?

He had never been on an airplane before, but he could feel the room he was in moving, bumping up and down. He could be in a big truck, but he didn't think so. He was pretty sure he was on an airplane.

The tape across his mouth kept him from doing more than grunting, but he really had to go pee. So he grunted and kicked the wall as hard as he could. Finally, one of the bad men opened the door. The light hurt his eyes, but he blinked the brightness away and grunted some more. The bad man ripped the tape off his face. "I need to pee, please." He would not forget his manners. Even if this man was bad, he had been taught you get more flies with honey. He couldn't imagine why you would want to draw the flies closer. They were nasty creatures.

The bad man cursed and grabbed Connor by the arm, pulling him off the floor. The man cut whatever ties had been keeping his arms together and pointed to a bucket in the corner. "Use that." The bad man didn't turn his head, just kept watching as Connor eyed the bucket. Mimi had warned him about strangers and how there were some really bad people in the world. He knew in his heart this was one of those really bad men. Even as bad as he had to go, it took him a minute with the man watching. He used the bucket, keeping his back to the man. When he was finished, the man grabbed his arms and tied them up with another piece of plastic. Once again, the door was closed, leaving him in the dark.

Connor sat back down on the floor and rolled to his side. It was the only way he could lie down and not hurt his arms worse. He closed his eyes, wishing for sleep, because that's where his momma and the big man were.

Chapter Fifteen

THERE WAS NO change in Maria other than the guard placed at her door. Knowing the hospital wouldn't talk to anyone but family, Julian fabricated some documents stating Dane was Maria's brother. On the drive up to Tennessee, they agreed Dane would be the one to stay in town and keep an eye on things. Rafael didn't like being in public more than he had to, and Kaya and Jasper could cover the police work until Dane returned home.

Rafael called in a couple of Goyles who lived in the New Nashville area so Maria would have round-the-clock security by someone Rafe trusted. They would also be notified immediately if there was any change in her status. Normally, he would stay behind the scenes and allow his Clan to take care of business, but this was personal. In his gut, he knew Alistair was somewhere in Greece calling the shots.

Rafe, Kaya, and Dane met Corey and the New Columbia sheriff at Rico and Maria's home. The sun had long since set, but Corey and the sheriff had graciously agreed to meet them. CSU had finished going over the house. The sheriff hesitated in giving them any information until Corey pulled him aside, explaining the gravity of the situation and how Dane was the missing boy's uncle. New Columbia was a small town and didn't have as many resources as either New Nashville or New Atlanta. He eventually gave in to the help from the big city Detective and Chief.

Rafael stood back and let his mate and Dane do what they did best. Even though the crime lab had searched for clues, Dane and Kaya carefully went through the house, looking for anything that could have been missed.

Forced entry into the back door was evident; however, there were no signs of a struggle. Both Rico and Maria had been stabbed multiple times. The only room in the house that was disturbed was their bedroom, where the murder and attempted murder took place. Their bed was a bloody mess on both sides. While Rico had been found on the bed, Maria had been taken and dumped away from the house. A trail of blood led from the bedroom, down the hall, and out the front door. Maria's body had been dragged.

Connor's bedroom did not look like a typical six-year-old's room, not that Rafael would know what one looked like. He imagined it would be filled with toys and games, not books and art supplies. The desk in the corner was filled with various drawings and paintings.

"Take a look at this." Dane was holding up one of the drawings.

Rafael took the paper. "Holy hell, is that Dante?" The drawing wasn't a crayon stick figure family portrait. This was done with charcoals. The detail was stunning. "Surely the kid didn't draw this. I mean, how could he? He's never met Dante."

Kaya, looking around Rafe's arm, said, "There's no doubt it is Dante. Are we sure he's never seen him, though? We don't really know Isabelle. What if Connor has visited New Atlanta and happened to see them together?"

"I really don't think so. The way Isabelle explained

129

it to me, the kid never leaves New Columbia. She's very careful about visiting him here as well," Dane said, still staring at the drawing.

"I'm going to send this to Dante, get his take on it." Rafael took a picture of the drawing with his phone and forwarded it to his brother.

After about an hour, Kaya and Dane had searched every inch of the house, having found no evidence to help find whoever kidnapped Connor. They thanked the sheriff, and he left them to speak with Corey.

"So, Abbott, what's really going on here?" Corey asked, now that they were alone.

"It's a long story, but I'll make it as short as possible. Isabelle is my sister. I was put up for adoption as a baby, and she was sent to live with Rico and Maria when she was a kid. She moved to Greece and got married, but her husband fell overboard their boat and drowned. She moved back to the States after, pregnant with her late husband's kid. Her husband's family is beyond rich, and we're afraid they've found out about the boy and are behind the kidnapping."

"Whoa, that's some story. That would make sense why there has been no ransom demand."

"Exactly. All we have to go on at this point is the family lives on an island in Greece. Isabelle is on her way there now, as are her ma... uh man and his brother."

"Corey, thank you again for meeting us here. I want to head back to the hospital." Rafael wasn't in a hurry, he just wanted to have some privacy to speak freely. They said their goodbyes, with Dane and Corey promising to keep in touch. Once Corey had driven away, Rafe said, "I'll be right back." He let himself into

130

the house and made his way to Connor's bedroom. He straightened the stack of drawings on Connor's desk and picked them up. He wanted to study them more closely, hopefully to get a little insight into the mind of Isabelle's child.

When he reached the car, Kaya cocked an eyebrow and asked, "And just what are you doing with those?"

He grinned at his woman and kissed her. "Research."

TURBULENCE WOKE ISABELLE, surprised she had fallen asleep. When she asked about Connor, Kallisto assured her he was being well taken care of. Isabelle had vowed to never step foot in Greece again, but she would walk through the Christian's hell if it meant getting her son back.

Isabelle's rumbling stomach reminded her she hadn't eaten in hours. When Kallisto asked if she wanted breakfast, she gave in. She would have to chance them drugging her. They wouldn't be in the air much longer, and Isabelle needed strength for whatever she would find when they landed. If Kallisto was working for Stavros, things were going to be bad. Very bad. The man hated her when he thought she was responsible for Alexi's death. The rage he had directed her way was still alive in her mind, even six years later. She couldn't imagine anyone else being responsible.

Poor Connor. Her son was smart and brave. Even so, he was only six years old. What had he seen? Was he there when Rico was killed, when Maria was injured? Had he been drugged to keep him compliant? Was he already in Greece at the Sarantos villa, or was he being held in a dark room? Was he scared? Her own stomach rumbled again, and she felt guilty for eating when she didn't know if her child was hungry.

Kallisto's partner in crime, Sergei, rolled a breakfast cart down the aisle. Instead of separate plates of food, there were platters of eggs, bacon, toast, and bagels. It was obvious he prepared the meal this way for her benefit. If they all ate from the same platters, she would be assured they weren't drugging her. Guilt stabbed at her heart as Isabelle dished food onto a plate, assuring herself she was eating to keep her strength up. She poured herself a cup of coffee, adding cream to it.

Once breakfast was finished, Sergei piled their dishes on the cart, pushing it to the back of the plane. Instead of returning, he called out to Kallisto, "Phone for you." Kallisto headed to the rear compartment, closing the door behind her. Even with her shifter hearing, Isabelle could only make out a few words. None that gave any indication exactly where they were taking her. She leaned back against the seat and closed her eyes. All night her thoughts had ping-ponged between Dante and Connor. Was her son okay? Was he being taken care of? Was Dante in an airplane, flying toward her? Was he angry with her? Would he really save her and Connor as he said he would?

During the course of the flight, Isabelle watched and listened as her two hosts interacted. It was clear Kallisto was in charge, but she didn't treat Sergei as a lackey. There was an affection between them, more platonic than sexual, but it was evident they were fond of each other. When Kallisto gave Sergei an order, it was done with a please and thank you. Now, the two sat side by side in companionable silence. Neither tried to engage Isabelle in conversation, and for that she was grateful. When her own questions had gone unanswered, she clammed up and settled into herself. She picked up a book to have something to keep her hands still.

Sergei disappeared to the rear of the plane for a while. When he reappeared, he sat across from her and informed them both, "Buckle up. We will be landing soon."

Isabelle's stomach rolled, and nausea climbed her throat. She took a deep breath, calming herself. She would not show weakness in front of this woman. It was bad enough Kallisto looked as fresh now as she had when they first met. Isabelle had gone to the restroom a couple of hours ago and retightened her ponytail. Using a paper towel and water, she attempted to unsmudge the mascara under her eyes. Her clothes were wrinkled from sitting so long. Good thing for her she wasn't trying to impress anyone. Her stomach jerked again as the plane touched down. "Here goes nothing," she thought to herself as she waited for the jet to stop rolling.

When they were given the all clear, Kallisto told her, "Please follow me." As Isabelle stood, Kallisto handed her purse to her.

"Where are we?" she asked, not expecting an honest answer. At some point during the flight, they had stopped to refuel, but there was no indication as to where they landed. She had watched as the plane flew over the blue waters of the Mediterranean. The outline of Italy clued her in they were nearing the islands. There were so many small islands, it was impossible to know which one they landed on.

Kallisto's face was blank and her answer cryptic. "We're home."

Isabelle rose from her seat and followed. They descended the stairs, stepping out into the Greek sun. There were no other planes around, no workers securing the jet, no one coming to gather luggage. The hangar was deserted except for Isabelle, Kallisto, and Sergei. As they neared the building, Isabelle caught sight of a limo. Was Connor in there? Could she possibly see her son this soon? She received her answer when Sergei opened the back door, allowing the women to climb inside. The door closed behind them, and Sergei took his place in the driver's seat.

Isabelle's heart sank. "When do I get to see my son?"

Ignoring her question, Kallisto instead said, "I do apologize, Isabelle, but I'm going to need to blindfold you." She was holding a strip of black cloth in her hands, waiting for Isabelle to comply.

"Why? It's not like I know where I am anyway." Isabelle had a sinking feeling her life was about to go from bad to worse.

"I understand, and if it were up to me, I would allow you to enjoy the scenery. But I have my orders, so please…" Kallisto held out the blindfold, still waiting for Isabelle to turn around.

Sighing, Isabelle did as she was asked. When Kallisto had tied the material around her head, she slid her hands under Isabelle's hair, moving it over her shoulders. "There. That's not too tight, is it?"

Isabelle just shook her head. Her body shivered at the soft touch. She didn't want anyone touching her, only Dante.

"Do you want something to drink? We have water, juice, and champagne. I'm having a Mimosa. Would you care for one?"

Maybe a little alcohol wasn't such a bad idea. It would calm her nerves and give her a little courage. "Mimosa would be great, thanks."

The sound of the cork popping and the liquids being poured into the glasses filled Isabelle's ears. Kallisto placed her hand in Isabelle's, rubbing her thumb along her knuckles before placing the stem of the glass in her fingers. Not wanting to think about the goose bumps Kallisto's touch caused, Isabelle downed the entire glass of fruit juice and champagne. The bubbles from the alcohol caused gas in her throat, and Isabelle puffed out a burp. "Excuse me." The glass was taken from her hand.

A hand touched her cheek, fingers caressing her skin. "I'm really sorry, Isabelle."

"Sorry for what?" she asked, just before everything faded to black.

The first thing Isabelle noticed was the pounding inside her skull. She rubbed her temple with her fingertips, but the motion did nothing to alleviate the pain. Her stomach rolled. She was getting really tired of feeling nauseous. She parted her eyelids, allowing a little light to stream in. When she noticed very little light in the room, Isabelle opened her eyes all the way. She found herself lying on a bed, the duvet filled with down. The furnishings in the room were sparse yet elegant. No pictures or other accoutrements adorned the walls. There were no windows, only a door leading… Where was she? Last thing she remembered was getting in the limo with Kallisto. Ah, the Mimosa. The bitch drugged her after all.

Gingerly, she sat up, allowing her stomach a chance to calm down. The thudding in her brain would just have to wear off as the drug left her system. *Dammit. You stupid girl, you let your guard down. Now what have you gotten yourself into? I swear to all that's holy I will never, ever set foot in Greece again. This freakin' place is cursed!* Even her mental chastisement hurt her head. The tears slowly eased out of the corners of her eyes. Poor Connor. He had an idiot for a mother.

With no window or clock, Isabelle had no idea of the time or how long she had been unconscious. She looked around the room, spotting her purse on the only piece of furniture other than the bed. She padded over to the dresser and opened the bag. Of course they had taken her cell phone. You don't leave someone a way to communicate when you freaking kidnap them! She was surprised to find the rest of her personal belongings were still inside. Isabelle threw her purse on the bed and looked around. Knowing it was futile, she tried the doorknob. Locked.

Hating the unknown, Isabelle banged on the door. "Let me out of here!" She continued pounding and yelling until she heard a key being placed in the lock. She backed up, waiting to see who her captor was. Expecting Kallisto, she was surprised when a handsome man stood in the doorway. Tall, broad shoulders, late thirties, early forties at the latest. He was built much like one of the Gargoyles. This man was not Stavros.

"Hello, Isabelle. The yelling really isn't necessary. We locked you in for your own protection. Are you hungry, thirsty?" Even though he was pretending to be hospitable, his demeanor gave Isabelle the chills. This man might be off the charts handsome on the outside, but his insides were something else. She worked around inmates, criminals who had done heinous things. They at least had a small amount of humanity left in their gaze. This man had none. No, he was evil. She felt it seeping out of his pores.

"I am still recovering from the last drink I was offered, so if I decline, you'll have to understand."

"That, too, was for your safety. If you knew your final destination, let's just say some might be inclined to torture the information out of you."

"Who are you?" Isabelle stared at the man, studying his features as if they would give away his secrets.

"That depends. If you behave, I am your host until I have no further use for you. If you give me trouble, I will be the one to sell you to the highest bidder." His body was blocking the doorway; his stance was one of a man who relished a challenge.

"Where is my son? Where's Connor?" Isabelle was beginning to shake.

Smiling, the man said, "Right where he is supposed to be." The look on his face verified her earlier suspicion; she was an idiot, and she was never seeing her son again.

"Life as you know it is over, Isabelle. I suggest you get used to the idea." The door closed, the lock turned. She was a prisoner, and absolutely no one knew where she was.

Chapter Sixteen

GREGOR AND TESSA'S talking woke Dante. There was only one bedroom on the plane, and Dante had insisted they take it. The leather sofa was comfortable; still, his sleep had been dream-riddled and fitful. Usually, he didn't remember his dreams, but those he had during the night were as clear as if he were watching them on a television screen. One dream didn't bother him at all. It was a sexual romp with Isabelle after their date. Instead of walking her to her door, he bent her over the hood of his car. His hands slowly pulled her black dress up her legs, leaving her beautiful ass on display for him. She had on thigh highs attached to a garter, with no panties in sight. He had taken control, commanded the scene, dictated the moment. Being in control had been the most erotic moment of his life. Too bad he didn't feel that way when awake. The idea of over-the-hood sex, he assumed, stemmed from their James Bond conversation.

The other dream, the one that wouldn't let go of his attention, was causing his heart to ache. In this dream, a small boy with brown hair and chocolate eyes was calling to him. "Please come for me, Da" was on repeat in his head. Dante knew in his heart this was Isabelle's child; this was Connor. Was he calling out to Dante, or was he calling out for his real father who was dead?

"Hey, Brother, you okay?" Gregor was holding a cup of coffee out in front of Dante, looking concerned.

"Thanks, and yes, I'm fine. I just had a really weird

dream, and I can't shake it." He took the coffee from Gregor and sipped it, hoping the caffeine would kick in soon.

"You do work in a morgue around dead people. I would imagine you have lots of weird dreams," Tessa said, sitting in the chair across from him, pulling her legs underneath her, sipping her own coffee. Dante noticed Tessa sat that way all the time. Did Isabelle sit that way? Did she get comfortable wherever she was? Was she comfortable now? Or was she being drugged and tied up?

"Actually, I rarely remember my dreams. I have been a coroner for so long being around the dead has no effect on me whatsoever. It's the way they died I tend to contemplate on. The bodies brought into the morgue have more often than not been murdered. It's hard to comprehend how life is so meaningless to some."

"Says the man who hunts down Unholy and slaughters them." Tessa raised a challenging eyebrow.

Dante looked to his brother. "Have you not explained to her what it is we do?" Returning his gaze to Tessa, he said, "We do not hunt Unholy just to kill them. We gather them up and put them in the Basement. It is true some die in the fight, but those are the ones who are trying to kill us and give us no choice. Self-defense is always a valid excuse for killing."

"So, you're saying you've never once taken to the skies with the intent of taking out a few of the bad guys? Just to release some stress?" Tessa looked between Dante and Gregor. What could he say? Of course he had.

"What he's trying to say, Red, is there's a

difference in killing an innocent and ridding the world of a few monsters." Gregor leaned over and kissed her lips. Dante knew a diversion when he saw it.

"How close are we?" He was ready to be on the ground, putting some type of plan in motion.

"About thirty minutes. The villa is free, so we will set up base there. Also, Rafe called, wants you to look at your phone. He sent you a drawing."

Dante pulled out his phone and opened the attachment. "Did he say what kind of draw…" Dante's voice trailed off, stunned, as he examined the image. "Where did this come from?"

Gregor held his hand out, and Dante passed his phone over. Tessa leaned over to view the drawing with Gregor.

"Holy shit! Is this a family portrait? I didn't think you knew the kid, Dante," Tessa said as she zoomed in on the picture. "Where did Rafael get this?" she asked Gregor.

"Rafael said Connor's room was full of drawings, sketches, and paintings. All of them were this detailed. Some had been framed and hung on the walls. The boy is beyond talented. Rafe was asking the same question Tessa is. Dante, have you ever met Connor?" Gregor handed his phone back to him.

"Only in my mind." Dante told them of the dream he had during the night of a little boy, one who looked just like the one in the drawing, calling out for his *Da* to come save him.

"That is weird. What if the kid is psychic?" Tessa asked.

"Anything is possible. Dante has his own abilities, so it is very possible Connor could have as well. He does come from a strong line of shifters. Rafe wants you to call him, Brother. You need to tell him what you told us."

Dante did exactly that. "Hello, Rafe. Before you ask, no, I have never seen Connor before," Dante told his brother before he could ask the burning question on everyone's mind. "Unless Isabelle somehow has a picture of me she has shown the boy, I have no idea how he drew the likeness."

Rafael offered the same excuse Gregor and Tessa had. "Unless he has psychic abilities also. I'm going to tell you something I haven't told anyone else. Shortly after I met Kaya, I was in the garden meditating. My subconscious pulled me deep, and I met a small child. A boy. He called me Papa. Once I came out of my session, I didn't think anything about it. Not really. Not until it happened a second time. Kaya had been abducted by Alexander, and the boy told me to go get her. Brother, I honestly believe I was communicating with my child. If my unborn son could reach out to me, is it so far-fetched your mate's son could feel you? We don't know much about the half-bloods, but we do know they come from the Original line of shifters. That's some mighty powerful blood. So who's to say the children won't be powerful as well?"

"I have to say, I agree with you. I had a dream about Connor last night. When I woke, I didn't know it was him, just that he had the same features as Isabelle. Now that I have seen the drawing, I know without a doubt it was him." Dante was a believer in the unexplainable. He experienced it on a daily basis as part of his genetic makeup.

"Then use this to your advantage. Meditate. Tap

141

into your subconscious and reach out to the boy. He may be special in the same way you are, or you may only be connected through Isabelle. Either way, give it a try."

"I definitely will. And Rafe, thank you for sharing about your son."

"You're welcome. Listen, I wanted to let you know I'm calling Jonas. I'm giving him a heads up about Isabelle and ask if he has any idea where Alistair would be holed up."

"Things are a bit rough between Isabelle and her parents, but I agree they should be told, regardless of how she feels about them. Keep me posted." Dante told his brother they were landing soon and would speak again later.

Knowing about Connor eased the ache in Dante's chest. If the boy already thought of him as a parental figure, it would make the transition easier when they were all home safe. He would do everything in his power to make that a reality.

As soon as Dante hung up, Gregor relayed Julian's information. "Isabelle's phone went off grid about an hour ago. The good news is the tracker Tessa put in Isabelle's purse is still active, and he has a bead on her. The bad news is she was taken to Poros. It's a relatively small island, but one that is heavily guarded and private. It was bought by a private investor about thirty years ago. Jules is researching the owner now. Poros isn't close to Zakynthos, where we assumed she would be taken. We need to decide if we want to stay on Atokos or get closer to Poros."

"For now, let's proceed to Atokos. I would like to shower and change clothes. I am anxious to find her, but I don't want to run around half-cocked either. The more I think on the situation, the more I feel Alistair is behind all of this. If Stavros had known about Connor, he would have come after him before now. The timing is too coincidental."

Gregor instructed the pilot to land on their small island. Dante called Julian and told him of their plans. He asked his cousin to research the Stavros family and send everything he could find to the office computer at their villa. Every property the Society purchased looked like vacation villas on the outside. Each was luxurious and accommodating for the most frugal traveler. Hidden interior offices were set up with state-of-the-art computer equipment, satellite phones, medical equipment, extra clothes, and panic rooms. Each property could be used as a safe house.

Within an hour, Dante, Gregor, and Tessa were settling in at the villa. It was a beautiful home that had been transformed from a hotel. Tessa was entranced by the place, taking in the view of the beach from the floor-to-ceiling windows. She grinned at Gregor. "Maybe we can come back here sometime. You know, just the two of us?"

"Anything you want, Red." Gregor wrapped his arms around her as they took in the view together. Dante wasn't jealous. Not really. He was happy for his brother. He would be lying, though, if he said he didn't feel a longing to be just as content.

The family who took care of the property greeted them and asked what items they needed before leaving them to their privacy. Dante headed to one of the suites to take a quick shower. His mind was reeling from his worry for Isabelle and Connor. Now that he had dreamed of the boy, he felt a connection with him. He wanted to study the information Julian was sending, but before he did that, he was going to take Rafael's advice.

He stepped out of the shower and dried off. The clothes he had asked for were laid out on the bed. When he was dressed, Dante walked out onto the balcony of the suite, allowing the saltwater air to fill his senses. The sounds of the waves floated on the breeze. He sat in one of the chairs, closing his eyes. For a few moments, he thought of nothing but the waves rolling in and out. A random seagull cry echoed through his consciousness, harmonizing with the tinkling of wind chimes that were hanging on the balcony above his. He allowed his mind to envision Connor, the version of the boy as he'd drawn himself, holding onto Dante's hand, looking up at him as if he were a hero. Dante looked down at the child as he had been in the drawing, smiling back at Connor.

The small hand squeezed his, the smile disappearing. Connor floated away from Dante, the room growing dark. The boy was lying on his side, his hands tied. His mouth was covered in duct tape. Dante's heart squeezed tightly, aching as he looked around the dark room, searching for any type of clue as to where the boy was. Nothing. The walls were stark with no windows. One door led into and out of the small space. Connor was in a closet of sorts. Dante reached out for him, but his hand found only mist as it moved straight through to the other side of Connor's body. Of course Dante's non-corporeal body couldn't touch the boy's. *Connor. Connor, it's Dante, can you hear me?* Dante tried several times to speak to the boy.

When he was about to give up, chocolate eyes opened, looking around the room.

Connor, can you hear me? Connor continued to squint into the darkness. *Don't be afraid, Connor. I'm coming to get you. Just hang on.* The child squeezed his eyes shut, a small sigh escaping from his body.

Dante opened his eyes. "Hang on, Son. I'm coming to get you."

Even though it was heartbreaking, it had been the single most exhilarating experience of Dante's life. Knowing Rafe had made contact with his unborn son through meditation led Dante to believe what he just experienced had been real. While it could be wishful thinking on his part, he knew in his soul he had made contact with his future son. He blinked back the tears forming in his eyes.

Dante gave himself a few minutes to think about what just happened before making his way to the office. He was ready to see what information Julian had found on Isabelle's former family. When he looked at the monitors, files were already coming in. Most of the information was public knowledge: articles from newspapers, spotlights in magazines. The Stavros family was beyond wealthy. Dante began familiarizing himself with names, faces, known properties. The information he really wanted was the data Julian would have to hack into to retrieve. Gregor and Tessa, having also showered, came into the office carrying sandwiches and drinks. They would eat while going over the intel.

"So, that's what Alexi looked like," Tessa said, pointing to a computer screen. "Wow, he looks like a real douche."

145

Dante was surprised by her assessment. He looked at the man on the screen. A very handsome man. No wonder Isabelle had fallen for him. "What makes you think he was a douche?" Dante asked Tessa.

"Look at his eyes. They're flat. There's no emotion, almost evil looking." Tessa studied the article. "That can't be right. This newspaper is dated last year. Holy fucking hell. Isabelle's husband is alive."

Chapter Seventeen

ALEXI SAT AT a café table, the tilted umbrella shielding him from the Mediterranean sun. His khaki shorts and blue polo shirt were forgettable. A navy baseball cap covered his short hair. His sunglasses hid his eyes from passersby, making it impossible to see him watching. Searching. The port where the large cruise ships docked was overrun with tourists, families who were disembarking from the boat to enjoy the sights the large island offered. People looking for day excursions to break the monotony of being holed up on a boat. Sure, there were plenty of activities aboard the large vessel, but there was only so far you could go to get away from someone on a boat. He should know.

His thoughts drifted back several years when he had seduced and married a young girl. His duty to his family, his father told him. She had been pretty enough, if a little plain, but she wasn't his type. Alexi liked tall, leggy blondes with large breasts. Women who had been around the block a time or two, who knew how to give head like a prostitute. Some of his best fucks had been from whores. When his father insisted he marry the mousy doctor, Alexi had balked. Seducing her to get information was one thing, but tying himself down to the girl for good was asking a little much. His father insisted once they had the information they needed, he could divorce her and move on with his life. Things hadn't turned out quite like they planned. His pulse sped as he thought of the

147

fight they had that nearly killed him. The bitch was supposed to go over the side of the boat, not him. If he hadn't been such a strong swimmer, Alexi would have drowned that day.

The current dragged him through choppy waters as he swam for his life. At some point, he passed out. Instead of dying in the sea, his body washed up on the bank. The area had been mostly isolated with the exception of a run-down section of tenement houses. It was a part of the island he knew well. One of his favorite whores lived there. He pulled himself out of the water and made his way to her home.

Alexi had stayed hidden away from everyone, allowing his father, his wife, and the authorities to think he drowned in the sea. His whore nursed him back to health, hiding him away where no one would think to look for one of the wealthiest men on the island. Eventually, he tired of living in squalor. There was only so much a good fucking could accomplish. He had the prostitute gather information daily regarding the progress of the case against his little mousy wife. He almost felt sorry for her, being pitted against his father. Once it was known his wife was clear of the charges and had left the island, Alexi made his way back home after paying the whore a handsome fee.

A loud giggle returned Alexi's thoughts to the present. A young girl was chasing a lizard along the sidewalk. Just when she would reach out to grasp the slippery creature, it would dart the other way. He watched the girl for almost a minute before looking for her family. No one was traipsing along after her. No mother or father frantically searching for the wayward child. He rose from his seat and followed her, staying far enough away it didn't appear they were together. The farther she ran from the crowds, the better his odds were of luring her away completely.

Alexi joined in the chase, scooping the lizard into his hands. The little girl stopped and stared at him as if he had wrestled a bear to the ground. "Would you like to keep him as a pet?" he asked the girl, her bright blue eyes shining from her smile.

"Yes, please." She held her hands out, but he kept the lizard safe in his own grasp.

"I tell you what. How would you like to have a large container to put him in so he can't get away?" God, this was too easy. They were standing behind a row of vending machines, well hidden from prying eyes.

"Ooh, really?" Her blonde curls were bobbing up and down as she shook her head yes.

"Really. I have one in my car. Let's go see about it, yes?" Alexi cautiously looked around before stepping onto the pathway that led to the parking lot. Headed his direction was a local policeman. Alexi returned to the vending machines, pretending to purchase a soda. Once the officer had passed, he made his way to his vehicle.

Alexi didn't dare take the girl's hand, lest her parents see them from a distance. The way it looked now, he was walking away. The child just happened to be following him. He had parked his car in a spot where he made sure there were no security cameras. They arrived at his car, and he used the key fob to unlock the door. "Get in, and I'll let you hold him while I look for the container."

The trusting child climbed into the back seat, holding onto the lizard for dear life. Alexi walked to the front of the car and got in. The girl was so preoccupied with her new pet she didn't realize what was happening. Alexi smiled to himself as he headed for the villa where he would keep his temporary guest.

STAVROS COULDN'T MOVE, couldn't speak. The man who commanded politicians, policemen, judges, even his own son, was at a loss. Standing before him was his grandson. Okay, so he didn't look like Alexi. This child was the spitting image of his mother. Mousy brown hair and those light brown eyes offered no indication this child was his blood, but the man wouldn't lie. Not about something as important as blood. The woman standing in front of him was eyeing him with an arched brow. Her impatience was clear on her beautiful face. What was a woman who looked like a model doing in the kidnapping business?

"Mr. Sarantos, I would like to introduce you to Connor Sanchez."

"Sanchez? What the fuck kind of name is that?" He glanced from the kid back to the blonde.

"His foster name, I would assume. Now, if you don't mind, I have other matters to attend." The woman removed the tape from the child's mouth and cut the bindings from his hands. She pulled out her cell phone and said, "Smile!" She snapped a picture. Mussing the kid's hair, she walked out the door.

"Hello, Connor. How do you do?" Stavros had no

idea how to speak to a small child. When his own son was that age, he'd had nannies taking care of him.

Instead of responding, the child stood silently, rubbing his wrists where the plastic tie had previously held his arms captive.

"I am Stavros Sarantos, your grandfather. Are you hungry, thirsty? I assume you had a long trip. You must be tired. Let's get you settled so we can talk, yes?"

Again, the child just stood still, mute. He wouldn't meet his eyes. Instead he was looking around the villa. He placed his hand on the boy's shoulder and gently urged him toward the kitchen. He opened the refrigerator and pulled out a juice box. "Here you go. Is grape all right?" He had asked his housekeeper to stock the pantry full of things kids liked to eat and drink. It had been a long time since his son had been small.

"I don't drink those. They're full of sugar." Finally, the child spoke.

"What do you drink?" he asked his grandson.

"Milk or water, but I'm not thirsty. Why did you hurt my Mimi?" the boy asked, sounding more like an adult than a boy of six. What an odd name to call his mother. He was clearly upset, hands fisted at his side.

"I assure you, I did not hurt your mother. Let's sit and talk, shall we?" Stavros pointed to the living room, and Connor had a seat. "Your mother was married to my son, Alexi. When she left the islands, she was pregnant with you. Here, let me show you a picture." Stavros picked up a five by seven photo of him and Alexi and handed it to Connor. The boy studied the picture then handed it back.

151

"That man is not my father. My father is tall, and brave, and he's coming for me." Connor defiantly crossed his arms over his chest and looked away.

"You are as stubborn as your mother, this is true. I have no doubt you have been told nothing about your real father. You will meet him soon, and you will see. You belong here with us!" Stavros's raised voice startled the boy. He took a deep breath and said in a normal voice, "Let's get you settled into a room. Come with me." Stavros didn't wait to see if he followed. He knew this was going to be a testament to his patience. If this child was a true Sarantos, he would not be belittled or treated as if he were stupid. His father had shown early signs of high intelligence. There was no doubt Connor was just as special.

They were walking down the hall toward the bedrooms when the front door opened. Stavros stopped dead in his tracks as Alexi walked in with a little girl in tow. Fuck! What were the odds they would choose the same location for their private business?

"Father, what are you doing here? I thought you were—" Alexi stopped speaking. His eyes were trained behind his father. "When did we start peddling boys?"

"We didn't, and you might want to watch what you say." Stavros was staring at the pretty little blonde who was preoccupied with a jar.

She looked up and asked Connor, "What's your name?"

"Connor. What's yours?"

"I'm Alyssa. Did you get a lizard, too?"

"No, I got kidnapped," he said matter-of-factly.

Alexi's eyebrows shot up close to his hairline. He picked the little girl up and took her into the kitchen, placing her and her jar on the island. He looked at the juice box on the counter and held it out to the little girl. "Would you like some juice?" Blonde curls bouncing, she shook her head yes.

Stavros needed to diffuse the situation and quickly. "Connor, let's get you settled. I need to speak with my son privately for a moment." He directed Connor down the hall into one of the larger bedrooms that had been set up for his arrival. There were plenty of toys and coloring books in the room to keep the child occupied. "Please, help yourself to the toys or crayons. I have something I need to see to. I won't be long. Afterwards, you and I can go to the beach, if you like." He didn't give Connor time to respond. He closed the door and locked the child in.

When he returned to the kitchen, he noticed the little girl was nowhere to be seen. "Where is she?" he asked, looking around.

Alexi was leaning against the kitchen wall, drinking a beer. "She's passed out in the living room. Now, do you want to tell me why the fuck you have a boy here?" His eyes were narrowed at his father. Alexi had the wrong idea.

"I wanted this to be a surprise, but I guess the cat's out of the proverbial bag. Alexi, that boy is your son, Connor."

Alexi spewed the beer he had just poured in his mouth. "What the fuck? I don't have a kid."

"Did you look at him? Really look at him? He looks just like Isabelle, and he's six years old." Alexi slammed the beer down on the counter and stormed down the hall. Stavros watched as his son tried the doorknob. "Here, it's locked." He stepped around

153

Alexi, unlocking the door. He stood back as he watched his son and *his* son together.

"Hey, kid, look at me," Alexi told the boy as he squatted in front of him. When Connor looked up with those chocolate-colored eyes, Alexi gasped. Instead of the heartfelt homecoming Stavros hoped for, Alexi stormed out of the room. Stavros quickly locked the door and went in search of his son. "Alexi, wait."

His son was lifting the little girl from the sofa. "I don't know what shit you're trying to pull, but that kid is not mine. He looks nothing like me."

"Where are you going with her?"

"Unlike you and your games, one of us has a job to do. The contracts call for five girls. She is only one. Now, I need to obtain four more, or have you forgotten? I am going to put her in one of the spare rooms. If you do not want to babysit, I suggest you take your plaything and move to one of the other villas." Alexi strode down the hall, depositing the girl on the bed before locking her in.

It had been a long time since Stavros had seen his son this upset. Not since Isabelle had been in their lives. When Alexi showed up after a month of being presumed dead, he was a different person. He had always had a chip on his shoulder, but the ordeal had turned him hard and calloused. Why hadn't he realized Alexi might want nothing to do with his own son, especially if he was a product of Isabelle? He should never have agreed to Connor being taken from his home, no matter what the man wanted.

Chapter Eighteen

THE TUMBLER DANTE was holding shattered when his claws broke through the skin. Glass and water flew through the air, landing on the floor at his feet. Had he been human, the shards would have cut his hand. As it were, he'd just made a huge mess. "What did you say?" he asked Tessa, accusingly.

She pointed at one of the computer screens. "Look at the date of the newspaper. Unless he has a twin, Alexi Sarantos is alive."

Dante took a step closer to the monitor, crunching broken glass as he did. He couldn't believe it. Even though it was there in black and white, he couldn't wrap his head around the fact his mate was still married. His claws were still front and center, as were his fangs. He closed his eyes, calming his body. He phased back and let out a deep breath. Luckily, his outburst hadn't scared Tessa. Being a half-blood, she knew about shifting against your will. "I'm sorry."

Tessa waved her hand in the air, dismissing his outburst. Gregor had retrieved a broom and dustpan. Dante reached for the broom since he made the mess, and Gregor didn't hesitate in handing it over. He moved to stand beside his mate and look through the other information Jules had sent them. Once the mess was cleaned up, Dante returned to studying the data. At least he tried to. The fact that Isabelle was still married weighed on his heart. How could she not know this?

As if reading his mind, Tessa turned to him. "Dante, Isabelle thought he was dead. And after what went down, she will probably wish he still was once she finds out he isn't. Don't worry about this. She can get a divorce from the skeeze." Tessa stated what he knew, but still. They had a son together. Was that reason enough for Isabelle to want to stay married to the man? Surely she wouldn't want to subject her son to the type of man she had portrayed him to be.

Gregor pointed at his monitor. "Here, look at this. Julian just sent the info on Poros Island. Take a look at the owner – WSD Holdings. That can't be a coincidence."

Tessa asked, "Who is WSD Holdings?"

Gregor explained the strange email Rafael had received a while back. "Rafael received a bid request a couple of months ago from a Bartholomew Cromwell. It came from an anonymous email address, and that rarely happens. The firewalls happened to be down when it came through, but Julian did some digging anyway. He finally figured out the parent company to Cromwell, Inc. was WSD, Inc. The email originated from somewhere in Greece."

"So you think Alistair is behind WSD?" Tessa asked.

Gregor nodded. "It's looking that way. If he has been watching Jonas all these years, he would know about Isabelle, and in turn, Connor. Alistair pulling the strings makes more sense to me than Sarantos. Stavros or Alexi, now that we know he's alive, would have already gone after Connor."

"Unless they didn't know about the kid until now. But if it is Alistair, why wait all this time? Connor is

156

six. That's a long time to plot a kidnapping." Tessa turned back to the monitor. "We need more intel on Poros. If that's where Isabelle is being kept, we need to find a way onto the island without causing suspicion." Tessa began typing away at the keyboard. It surprised Dante at how comfortable Tessa looked in their current setting. He had been around his brother's mate quite a bit, but he'd never seen the serious side of her.

Gregor wasn't as adept at computers as Julian and Nikolas, but he was doing his own research on one of the laptops. Tessa, still typing, told Dante, "Please ask Julian to dig a little deeper into the Sarantos family. If what Isabelle said was true, they are corrupt. We may need to use that information against them to get Connor back. For now, we have to assume your uncle is the mastermind since we know Isabelle is on Poros. If we are going up against Alistair or his people, we'll have to tread carefully since he will know what you two look like. As for me, he won't see me coming."

"What are you thinking, Red?" Gregor asked his mate.

"I'm thinking another Isabelle walking the streets of Poros will probably get somebody's attention," Tessa replied, her usual playful mood gone. No wonder her family chose her to be a watcher. She was pretty good at the cloak and dagger stuff.

Dante was thankful his brother and Tessa were with him. Now, he needed to get his head out of his ass and help. Once he had called Julian, he studied the map. "I think we should move closer to Poros, probably Athens. There are plenty of tourists coming and going with the cruise ships. We would be less conspicuous in a busier city."

Tessa looked up and asked, "What about Connor? We don't know if he's on Zakynthos or not."

"No, but we do know where Isabelle is, so it's my opinion we need to start there. Once I have my mate back, I will worry about rescuing our son."

Tessa and Gregor both stared at him as if he'd sprouted a third eye. "What?" he asked them both, looking from one to the other.

Gregor's mouth turned up slightly in a grin, but it was Tessa who answered. "You said *our* son."

Dante frowned. He didn't tell them about the meditation or the feelings it stirred. "Yes, well, if I have anything to say about it, he will be mine."

ISABELLE'S EMOTIONS HAD run the gamut from scared to angry to sad to her current condition – pissed. She was pissed off at herself, at her father, at Kallisto, and at the evil man, but mostly at herself. Her claws and fangs had once again cut into her skin as she was pacing the small room. With no bathroom in which to clean herself up, she rummaged through the dresser to find random items of clothing. She removed a dark shirt from one of the drawers and, using her spit, removed the blood as well as she could. She folded the shirt and replaced it at the bottom of the stack.

It wasn't lost on her this room belonged to someone. Kallisto possibly? Highly doubtful. The woman was tall and curvy. The clothes Isabelle found would fit a much smaller woman. She thought back to her captor's cryptic message. If she behaved, she would stay where she was. If she misbehaved, she would be sold. He was a slave trader? How in all that was holy had she found herself in the clutches of a slaver? Had that been the plan all along? Lure her out by kidnapping her child? That didn't make sense.

Isabelle flopped down on the bed, staring at the ceiling. *Think, dammit. You're a doctor. You're smart,* and *you're a shifter.* She was still getting used to that aspect of her life. She reached out with her senses to listen. Noises throughout the house, she assumed she was in a house, were muffled. She calmed her heartbeat so she could concentrate further. Tessa had coached her on separating the noises. She let all the sounds infiltrate her senses, and one by one, she put them into boxes. The mundane sounds such as the air conditioner went in one box. The opening and closing of doors, another. Voices. There they were. How many? Two, no three. Three voices, all women. Hushed talking from down the hall. Isabelle strained to hear what they were whispering about.

"The Princess brought in another girl. She must have been drugged, because Sergei was carrying her," woman number one said. Princess, who the hell was the Princess?

"I wonder where they put her? Was she giving them trouble? Why would they lock her away?" woman number two asked. Was Isabelle the *her* who had been carried in?

"The choosing is in two days. She will not be ready by then." This was woman number three. What were they being chosen for? She listened closely again, but their voices were quiet. A door opened, and a fourth voice sounded.

159

"Eve, The King wishes for you to join him in the sitting room. Please follow Sergei."

A quiet response of "Yes, Princess" sounded. So Kallisto was a Princess? Did that make the evil man the King? These women obviously behaved. The sound of footsteps leading away from her door eventually quieted while a set leading toward her door got louder. Isabelle sat up as a key was turning in the lock. The door swung open, and Kallisto appeared, taking in the room as well as Isabelle's appearance. "Good, you're awake. We need to have a little chat."

Isabelle didn't want to have a chat. She wanted to scream and punch and kick. Her ire from earlier returned with a vengeance, but she was not a fighter. She knew nothing about the woman standing in front of her other than she was regarded as The Princess. Isabelle couldn't imagine true royalty would be involved in kidnapping, so she assumed it was just a moniker the woman used to make herself sound important. Kallisto could be a fighter, and Isabelle preferred to use her brains over her fists. For now, she would play along and work on a plan that would outsmart her captors.

Kallisto walked farther into the room and shut the door. "I apologize for drugging you, but the King has very specific rules about our guests knowing their exact location." Isabelle couldn't help the rude sound that escaped her throat. "Isabelle, you may not believe it, but you are a guest here. Are you here against your will? Yes, but we will not harm you. We hope you will eventually become comfortable in your new surroundings. I want to show you to your bedroom where you will be staying from now on. If you will

160

follow me please, I will tell you the rules as we walk."

Kallisto waited for Isabelle to grab her purse, then opened the door and turned right, away from where the other women were. "The rules are simple, really. You will speak to no one else in the house with the exception of me, Sergei, and the King. You will take all your meals in the main dining room. Your allotted times are seven a.m., one p.m., and seven p.m. You will have twenty minutes to eat. No matter where you go on the grounds, a guard will be present at all times. The library, the gym, and the swimming pool are for your use as long as no one else is using them. You may help yourself to anything in the kitchen at any time, as long as you dine at the previously mentioned times. Your job, while staying here, is to tend to any medical needs that are brought to your attention. Here we are."

Isabelle felt as if she were in a dream. She had willingly allowed herself to be held captive, and now she was expected to be compliant to the demands of the demented. Kallisto opened the door to a huge bedroom, this one much larger than the one she just left. The furnishings were opulent, as if she were in a home fit for royalty. The bed was a four-poster with swaths of silk hanging between each post. An open door showed a bathroom she imagined was as extravagant as the bedroom. A set of double doors led to a balcony that overlooked the swimming pool.

"Do you have any questions?" Kallisto asked from directly behind her.

"Where is my son?" Isabelle turned and was face to face with the woman. Too close, really, but the allure of her beauty had long been forgotten by the events of the day.

"Connor is safe. I do apologize for luring you to us using your son as bait. However, it was a necessary ruse to assure your compliance."

Isabelle fisted her hands and willed her claws to stay inside her skin. "And what about Rico and Maria? Murder wasn't necessary for my compliance."

"Casualties of war, I'm afraid," Kallisto stated as if they were discussing which color to paint her nails. Unbelievable.

"Now, I will give you time to get settled. Feel free to freshen up. Your closet and armoire are filled with clothes in your size. The bathroom is stocked with all the essential toiletries you should need. Your guard will be outside your door. Remember, lunch is at one, and you are expected to be on time. Once you are finished eating, you will be shown the grounds. Your assigned guard will take you on a tour, but you are not to speak to him," Kallisto said with a smile on her face. A smile! "Oh, I have something for you." Kallisto handed Isabelle an envelope.

Isabelle couldn't believe the nonchalance rolling off the blonde. The acts of kidnapping and murder were business as usual? What kind of people had she given herself over to? With the click of the door closing, Isabelle was left alone. If they thought she was going to be compliant and basically start a new life with them, they had another thing coming. She would play it cool, as cool as she could, given the circumstances. She would bide her time, find out where they had taken her son, and then she would get herself out of this mess.

She opened the envelope and pulled out a photo. Isabelle was staring at a picture of a surprised Stavros and a very scared Connor. Isabelle's heart stopped.

Chapter Nineteen

DANTE SLID THE plastic card in the reader, waiting for the light to turn green. He had traveled on ahead of Gregor and Tessa, securing the top floor at a posh condo in Athens. Eventually, they would be seen together, but for now, they wanted to be as inconspicuous as possible. Dante quickly unpacked the suitcase he had borrowed from the villa. Looking out the window of their suite, he scanned the surroundings. Several cruise ships were docked in the distance. He would prefer to be on a small island, but this gave them more cover to come and go freely.

Dante felt Gregor's presence in the building. His brother knew of his abilities, but he was the only one who knew just how powerful Dante was. All the Gargoyles could sense moods, and after hearing Rafe confide in him about his unborn child, he had to wonder if they all were even more special than each other realized. Maybe they all had gifts they didn't disclose with one another. He heard the elevator ding, so he opened the door to the suite, waiting on his family. Family. Their family was growing a little at a time. First there was Kaya, now Tessa. If Dante was lucky, Isabelle and Connor would be added to the list.

Tessa and Gregor headed to their own bedroom to unpack. Dante continued to look out the window and was surprised when Tessa made her way over to him, wrapping him in a hug. "We're going to get them back," she whispered. A low growl sounded behind them, and Tessa laughed. "Down, big boy," she told Gregor as she let go of Dante and went to soothe her mate's jealousy. Dante couldn't blame his brother. He wouldn't want Isabelle in someone else's arms either, even if it was Gregor.

Tessa placed her back to Gregor's front and wrapped his arms around her waist. She didn't look like someone who had been in a horrific car wreck weeks earlier. She leaned back into her mate as she told Dante, "I spoke to my dad before we left the island. Since you don't trust your mother, I decided to call Xavier. He agrees with our assessment that Alistair is behind all of this. He is calling on a few of his Clan who have ties to the Greeks. Alistair is not a popular King, and there are those who are willing to risk going up against him. It seems things aren't all rainbows and kittens where he is concerned. There is talk that some have been planning an uprising for some time. Dad is going to put us in contact with some of his men who know the setup and security on each of the islands. When we get our plan in place, he is willing to call a meeting of the Council to draw Alistair away from Greece, giving us time to go in and get Belle. He is also going to do some digging of his own on the Sarantos family."

Dante was glad to hear Xavier was willing to help. Having someone with inside knowledge would certainly make their mission easier. "I appreciate all the help we can get. I'm going to go for a walk, get a feel for the city. I'll be back later." He knew they had probably taken care of personal business before they left the island, but Gregor and Tessa's relationship was still new, and they probably relished any alone time

165

they could get. "Here's an extra room card. I'm going to find something to eat while I'm out, so I will see you in a couple of hours."

Dante took the stairs instead of the elevator. He would love to go for a swim in the hotel pool, but he wouldn't be able to get in laps with all the guests enjoying the water. He was going to miss being able to take to the skies as well. His wings were ready to unfurl and lift him up. There was no headier feeling than soaring above civilization, the wind in his face, the cold air burning his lungs as he rose higher and higher. Exiting through a side door, Dante walked through the parking lot that led to the busy street. He directed his feet to the Piraeus Port. Once the largest port in all of Europe, the gateway was considerably less traveled now than before the apocalypse. When the world fell apart thirty years prior, most modern travel ceased to move forward for many years.

With technology as advanced as it was, Dante would have expected space travel to be commonplace by now. Instead, all space exploration had stopped until recently. Automobiles were much the same now as they had been thirty years ago. Electronics were only now beginning to see advancements. The biggest difference Dante noticed was governments had reverted back to less democratic times. In most countries, Kings ruled in place of Presidents. Slave traders were on the rise, and the governments were having a hard time getting a handle on the situation.

The Gargoyles had seen all types of humanity over the years, and instead of moving forward, it appeared civilization was regressing. When he sat alone at night, contemplating the state of the world, he often

166

wondered about the extinction of the females of his kind. Were they better off if their species died out? His heart ached at the thought of his kind just slowly drifting away. Sure, the ones who were alive now would carry on indefinitely, but without a mate to keep you company, what was the point?

The fates must have seen how the Gargoyles were needed, now more than ever. Was this why they could bond with humans and have children? Isabelle already had a child, but he was human. Or was he? He did have strong shifter blood running through his veins, and Connor had his own special abilities. Dante was anxious to see if Connor would be a shifter as well. Thinking of the boy, Dante wanted to try reaching him again. Having arrived at the pier, he sought out a spot close to the water. An outdoor café proved to be the perfect place. He was directed to a seat overlooking the water. The waitress arrived, and he placed his food and drink order. Once his Scotch was delivered, he took a sip of the fiery liquid, allowing it to warm his throat.

Dante closed his eyes. The sounds of tourists talking and laughing filled his ears. The saltwater breeze floated around him. He shut out all the sounds, focusing on one small boy. He called Connor's name as he had before. Several minutes passed with no connection. He tried one last time, and a feeling of fear washed over him. Concentrating harder, Dante opened his senses further. He was looking at a drawing. This wasn't as artistic as before, but the crayon sketch was definitely being produced by the talented boy. In this drawing were four people – Connor, a little blonde-haired girl, and two men. The men favored each other, but the drawing was incomplete. All of a sudden, the paper was wadded up and thrown away. The connection was lost.

The waitress placing Dante's food on the table interrupted his thoughts as Connor slipped away. "Can I get you anything else?" the waitress asked.

"Another Scotch, please," Dante answered as he downed the rest of the first glass. The men in the drawing had to be Stavros and Alexi. But who was the little girl, and what did she have to do with them? Dante finished his meal as well as his drink and headed back to the hotel. He stepped out onto the busy sidewalk, lost in thought, and ran into someone walking down the street.

"Watch where the fuck you're going."

Dante opened his mouth to apologize to the irate pedestrian. Instead, he closed his mouth, unable to speak. He watched as the stranger strode away angrily. Dante couldn't move. He could only stare at the back of Isabelle's husband.

GODDAMN TOURISTS. ALEXI didn't care that he was the one who ran into the man just then. He was still reeling at his father. A kid! His fucking kid. Was his father crazy? No way in hell did he have a kid with Isabelle. He made sure he wore a condom every single time. Not once had he fucked her without... Fuck! How could he have been so stupid? Isabelle had been sick for about a week. He couldn't remember what she had, pneumonia or some shit. He took her to one of their villas, needing to get away from his father for a while.

Jacking off was getting boring, and his favorite whore had been out of town. One night, Isabelle finally came downstairs, and Alexi had been drinking. Not caring that she was tired, he bent her over the couch and fucked her. Bare. But she had been on the pill. Fuck!

His father could play *dad* to the kid all he wanted. Until he got a paternity test, he wasn't wasting his time on the brat. Hell, even if the kid was his, he wasn't wasting his time on him anyway. He had business to tend to, and right now, that business was walking about fifteen feet in front of him. A family was arguing about where to eat. The parents were trying to corral six kids without losing any of them. Three boys and three girls, a regular goddamn American Brady Bunch, were the perfect targets. He stopped on the sidewalk, pretending to look at his cellphone. The arguing continued as the boys wanted pizza, the older girls wanted hamburgers, and the little one, the one he needed, wanted ice cream. The parents were explaining they were in Greece and wanted the kids to try Greek cuisine.

After what seemed like an eternity, they decided on an open-air market with a food court that had mostly local options but also American basics. They each could get what they wanted. Pulling his ball cap lower on his forehead, Alexi followed at a safe distance. The food court was busy, and it wasn't hard to keep up with the family. They continued arguing about who was getting their food first. Why did they all have to stand in line together? Why couldn't they sit down and the parents get their food? Obviously exasperated, the father agreed to the kids sitting at the table while the parents divided and conquered the food orders. Stupid fucking sheep. Why have this many kids if you couldn't handle them? Why have kids at all? All they did was take up time better spent doing important things, like drinking and fishing. And fucking.

Alexi waited. The older kids were supposed to watch the little ones. However, typical of teenagers, the boys were watching for girls, and the girls were watching for boys. The younger boy was about the same age as his... as Connor. The little girl looked like his twin. She tapped one of her older sisters on the arm and told her she had to go pee. "Mom said we couldn't get up. Just hold it." The little girl squirmed. She whispered something to her sister who rolled her eyes and looked around. Spotting the restroom not too far away, she conceded to the little one.

The older girl stood outside the door while the little girl went in by herself. The teenager spotted a cute boy, and her attention turned from the door. Alexi had an idea. It was probably a stupid one, but it just might work. He quickly bought an ice cream cone and returned to his spot by the door. The older sister walked back to the table, whispering to the middle girl about the boy she saw. They were giggling and pointing. When the little girl came out of the restroom, Alexi took a big chance. Not seeing the parents, he *accidentally* spilled his ice cream cone. It dropped on the ground at the girl's feet with a splat. She looked up at him, wide-eyed.

"I'm so sorry! Did it get on your shoes?" Alexi asked as he bent over, brushing at the toes of her shoes. He took another look around. People glanced at him, but none paid enough attention to recall a strange man with a little girl. Stupid fuckers.

"It's okay," the little voice said as she gave him a tentative smile.

"Would you like some ice cream? I'm going to buy myself another one."

She looked around, obviously for her sister. He assured her, "I told your sister I'd watch out for you while she went back to the table. I have a little sister your age. I was getting the ice cream for her. Do you want someone to play with?"

"Okay…" She wasn't convincing, but he would go with it. Again, he walked in front of the child. If she followed, it wouldn't look like they were truly together. When they passed the ice cream stand, the girl pulled on his shirt. "There's the ice cream."

"But the stand down here has sprinkles. My sister always has to have sprinkles." He winked at her and continued walking. Eventually the crowded sidewalk swallowed them up, and he took a chance on picking her up. "My sister's name is Alyssa. She's pretty just like you, and she has a puppy. Do you like puppies?" The little girl forgot about ice cream and sprinkles and wanted to see the puppy. Alexi kept the kid occupied long enough to get out of sight. He heard a commotion from the food court and knew his time was up. Walking quickly, he made his way to his parked car and shoved the kid in the back seat. A police car pulled into the parking lot behind him.

171

Chapter Twenty

ISABELLE HAD TAKEN a shower and changed clothes. Most of what was hanging in the closet was more formal than she cared to wear and probably cost more than she had ever spent on clothes in her life. There were shoes from designers she'd heard of, and some she hadn't. She didn't even want to fathom how much those cost. Isabelle made a decent wage as a physician, but she never understood spending extravagantly on clothes. She preferred to be comfortable. It's not like she got to dress up anyway, except when Dante took her to dinner. Isabelle allowed herself a moment to remember how handsome Dante looked in his suit. If she ever got out of here, she was going to tear his suit off him.

After digging through the drawers of the armoire, she found clothing more suitable for being held prisoner. The clock on the wall reminded her it was almost time to escape her room. While in the shower, Isabelle had allowed herself a small pity party. Once that was over, she remembered the text Dante sent. *I'm coming for you, Beautiful.* She momentarily worried about the message but remembered Kallisto didn't have the password to unlock her phone. Hopefully, her captors weren't aware Isabelle had someone looking for her.

She allowed herself a moment to daydream of her tall Gargoyle. Of Dante storming the castle and rescuing the damsel. That made her sigh. Dante was no knight. He was more the secret spy type, infiltrating the evil scientist's laboratory quietly before subduing the bad guys with his shifter strength as he rescued the busty brunette. Isabelle couldn't wait to bury Dante's face in her bust.

The house was quiet. Even using her shifter hearing, Isabelle could detect no sounds other than the shuffling of her guard from one foot to the other. What a boring existence it must be for him, standing guard of her door, twenty-four seven. Was he a prisoner as well, or was he paid handsomely to keep tabs on Isabelle? She would ask him, but then she would get in trouble. Did her captors truly expect her to keep quiet at all times? It was a good thing Tessa wasn't the one who was being held against her will. She would be sold into slavery within the first half hour.

There was a quick knock on her door before it opened to a very tall, very built man motioning her forward. Was he not allowed to speak either? Isabelle followed like the meek little mouse they wanted her to be. Question was, who was she following? Another mouse, or the cat? Isabelle studied the man in front of her; taller than Dante, broader than Gregor. He was about the same age as them, at least the age they appeared to be. Short sleeves barely contained his bulging biceps. His wide shoulders tapered down into a narrow waist that led to a really nice, really firm, really round ass. Isabelle had to catch herself when her guard stopped. Running into her appointed brick wall would probably be frowned upon.

Isabelle was confused at first since she was still in the hallway behind the Hulk. He was standing sentry, legs spread, hands clasped behind his back. When

Isabelle didn't move, he looked back at her and jerked his head toward the doorway. Isabelle shrugged her shoulders at him. How the hell was she supposed to know what was going on? "Neanderthal," she muttered as she brushed past him, her elbow connecting with his rock-hard abs. She heard a quiet grunt and couldn't resist glancing back at him, cocking her eyebrow. His face held the same blank expression as before. Would Hulk tell on her for misbehaving? She would find out.

Isabelle was mesmerized as she entered the dining hall. And what a hall it was. She took in the high ceilings, the tall windows, and the tapestries and paintings adorning the walls. This was larger than any room she had ever been in. Even the dining room at Stavros's home was a closet compared to this. A man and woman waited at the table, obviously there to serve her. Neither one spoke as she walked to that end of the long table. Isabelle tried to mentally count the chairs before taking her own seat. The man placed her napkin in her lap, and the woman took the lid off her serving plate. Both made their way out of the room, not asking if she needed anything else, not caring if the food was to her liking. She noticed there was only water on the table for her to drink. The meat appeared to be prime rib. Asparagus, roasted new potatoes, and some type of mixed greens accompanied the meat. There was no bread, no dessert. No salt or pepper.

Isabelle picked up her fork and knife, cutting the beef then placing a small bite in her mouth. A small groan left her throat. She tried the vegetables. She looked behind her to where the man and woman disappeared. She would love to at least be able to nod

174

at the woman, showing her appreciation. If the food was poisoned, at least her last meal would be the best she ever put in her mouth.

She quickly devoured the delicious meal, remembering she only had twenty minutes to eat. Hulk approached the table without speaking and pointed at his watch. Since Isabelle didn't have on a watch of her own, she could only assume it meant her allotted time was up. Testing the waters again, she grabbed his wrist and turned the watch over so she could see the face. She let out a *hmph*, glad she hadn't been given dessert. It would have gone to waste. She stood from the table and gestured for Hulk to lead the way.

An hour later, Isabelle had seen every inch of the grounds available to her. She had pretended to be intrigued with the elaborate rooms. She also pretended to be bored with the grounds, especially those on the perimeter. Tessa would have already figured a way out of the compound. Isabelle would have to bide her time, look for anything that might allow her to escape. Her biggest obstacle would be the Hulk following her around. She had no way of knowing if he was a shifter except to really piss him off. Even then, he may be old and have a lot of self-control. If he wasn't, she still didn't know if she was strong enough to take him. Who was she kidding? She didn't know the first thing about *taking* someone. Not in that sense of the word.

Dante, please, please, please get me out of here. Isabelle would continue to snoop around and pretend to be the good sheep. She wasn't ready to go back to her room, but she couldn't remember the way to the library. She looked up at Hulk and mimed opening a book. He frowned at her. After several tries, she gave up.

"Where's the library?"

"Breaking the rules already?" A deep voice came from directly behind her.

Isabelle turned to see the same man who visited her room. She had to assume he was the one they referred to as the King. Knowing she should keep her mouth shut, she couldn't help herself anyway. "If you would hire guards with more brains than brawn, I might not have to break the rules. I'm trying to get to the library, and the Hulk here sucks at charades." If Isabelle wasn't a shifter, she would never have heard the sound coming from her guard. If she didn't know better, she'd think he was stifling a laugh. Not wanting to take her eyes away from the King, she said, "If you don't want anyone speaking, is it possible to get a map of this place?"

Something flashed quickly in the man's eyes. For a moment it looked like respect. She had to be mistaken, because in the next moment, he was in her space. Damn he was quick, sort of like… *Oh shit, he's a Gargoyle.*

"You would do well to remember who you are speaking to." The man was looking down at her, doing his best to be intimidating. It was working.

"I remember. I'll just search the premises until I find what I'm looking for. No more speaking to Bruce," Isabelle told him as she thumbed over her shoulder at her guard. She and the King both stood their ground. She would not give him the satisfaction of cowering.

Without taking his eyes off her, he told the guard, "Show Isabelle to her room. She can find the library tomorrow. Isabelle, I suggest you remember what I said about behaving. I'd hate to lose you so soon."

Without giving her time to respond, the King turned and walked away.

Isabelle let out her breath. She turned to her guard and gestured he lead the way. He didn't move so she looked up at his face. He wasn't smiling exactly, but one side of his mouth twitched. He gently placed a hand on her elbow, leading her back to her wing of the house.

NORMALLY, WAITING ON dental records took weeks, but Trevor was holding a manila envelope that contained the results in his hand. It was addressed to Dante since he was the Medical Examiner, so Trevor didn't dare open it. He texted Dante to let him know the results had arrived, and he would wait until his boss gave him permission to look at the contents of the envelope. Trevor had to wonder at the quickness in which these results had been obtained.

It had been a slow week in New Atlanta in regards to murders and unusual deaths, so Trevor had some free time on his hands. Time he didn't need, because with free time came a free mind. He needed to busy himself with something so his brain thought about anything but his new friend. Trevor should be studying. Or dissecting bodies. Or looking at blood cells under a microscope. Anything besides thinking about one hot detective.

Spending time with Jasper had been absolutely awesome. The detective was not like most cops Trevor met. Most of the men in blue ignored him at best. The

Chief even rolled her eyes at him for the most part. Not Jasper. When they were in the field, he treated Trevor with respect. He even heard Jasper take up for him with that nasty Quinn guy. Trevor had a bad feeling about him. He seemed like a bigger asshole than most other bigoted rednecks Trevor had run across in his twenty-eight years.

There's no way he or any of the other cops could know about Trevor's preferences. It was one reason he kept to himself. He was looked down upon enough without adding homophobia to the list of reasons people didn't care for him. Trevor dressed the part of assistant since he was required to, but his hair was a little long with a random purple streak running through his bangs. At least he was told it was purple. It could be pink for all he knew, but the girl at the hair salon was nice, and he didn't think she would fool him on purpose. He kept his tattoos covered while in the field. Dante never mentioned his hair or ink, never looked twice. Now that Trevor was studying to advance his career, maybe he should think about a more professional look. He decided to cut his hair and dye it back to its natural color.

He couldn't do anything about his ink unless he wanted to spend a lot of money to have them removed, which he didn't. Each piece told a story. Jasper asked about the various tattoos covering his arms and listened intently while Trevor told the meaning behind each one. He found it odd Jasper had no ink. Most badasses he came across had at least one tattoo. Jasper may be a detective with a goofy, geeky side, but Trevor knew a badass when he saw one. His boss was a badass, as was the warden. There was something about

178

the way they carried themselves that screamed "don't fuck with me". Maybe Trevor should join a gym, spend more time worrying about his appearance than playing video games. If he was going to be taken seriously, he needed to make some changes. He pulled out his laptop and set about starting on his new way of life. His cell phone pinged with a text message. It was Dante responding, telling Trevor to open the envelope.

Excitedly, Trevor did just that, removing the results of the dental records. He couldn't believe the name staring back at him. "No fucking way."

Chapter Twenty-One

DANTE WANTED TO kill the bastard. Claws out, fangs bared, rip the sonofabitch in two, dead. Keeping an eye on the ball cap, Dante followed Alexi. If his vision was correct, Connor had been in the same room with his father and grandfather. Scratch that. Dante wouldn't give them the privilege of those titles. Being a sperm donor did not a father make. The crowd was gathering on their side of the road as an open-air market came into view. Dante kept his eyes on the blue cap as it weaved through the throngs of tourists. The cap stopped moving. Dante continued closer, but not close enough Alexi would notice.

Alexi was looking at his phone and periodically glancing around. Dante scanned the crowd trying to determine who had Alexi's attention. When a large family moved, Alexi proceeded to move with them. *What are you up to?* The kids were seated at a table, and the parents left to purchase food. The oldest and youngest girls made their way to the restroom with Alexi slinking toward them. The smallest girl looked like the one in Connor's drawing. Had the picture been a foreshadowing of things to come? The older girl made her way back to the table, whispering to her other sister and pointing at some boys. Alexi left his spot by the door and purchased an ice cream cone, only to return to his out of the way place by the restroom. As the little girl emerged, Alexi dumped the ice cream cone at her feet. Dante reached out with his shifter hearing to listen in on their conversation.

"I'm so sorry! Did it get on your shoes?" Alexi asked as he squatted down, wiping at her shoes with a paper napkin.

"It's okay," the little girl answered, smiling shyly at Alexi.

"Would you like some ice cream? I'm going to buy myself another one." There was the bait.

The little girl didn't answer; instead, she looked around, obviously for her sister.

Alexi smiled and said, *"I told your sister I'd watch out for you while she went back to the table. I have a little sister your age. I was getting the ice cream for her. Do you want someone to play with?"* And there was the hook.

"Okay…" The little girl was sunk. Alexi didn't take her hand. He walked off toward the ice cream vendor, the little girl trailing behind him. Dante wanted to yell at the parents that their child was being lured away, but if his gut was right, Alexi would lead him to Connor. He would follow and make sure the girl was safe. Instead of stopping at the ice cream stand, they continued on. The little girl tugged at Alexi's shirt, informing him they had passed the ice cream. Alexi mentioned sprinkles and puppies, and the little girl was completely gone. Had her parents not told her of the dangers of strange people? Especially ones who lured children away with promises of sweet concoctions.

Dante's cell phone pinged with an incoming message. He pulled it out of his pocket as he kept his eye on Alexi and the girl. The text was from Trevor stating the dental records were back. Dante had called in a favor with another Gargoyle, one who worked for the government. Dante's gut told him the charred remains were those of Gordon Flanagan, and if his instincts were correct, he wanted to give Tessa the good news as soon as possible. Since Flanagan had served in the military, his records were easily available if you knew who to ask. He responded to his assistant to open the envelope and keep him posted. He hit send and looked up, just as Alexi was putting the girl in a car. Fuck! He took off running, trying to catch the car, but it was no use. He could chase him, but it was too risky for him to use his shifter speed in public. Instead, he memorized the license plate number.

The right thing to do would be to call the cops, tell them everything that transpired, but then the police would want to know why he didn't stop Alexi before he got that far. He would be detained and questioned himself. So instead of doing the right thing, he did the smart thing and called Julian.

Arriving back at the hotel, Dante was frazzled. Gargoyles didn't tire easily, but mentally he was frustrated. He reached out with his hearing to make sure Gregor and Tessa weren't doing anything he didn't care to see. He wasn't a voyeur or an exhibitionist. He didn't think those descriptions fit Gregor either, but he had walked in on Gregor once, and his brother had continued as if Dante wasn't in the room.

As he listened, he could hear Gregor singing to Tessa. It wasn't a song Dante was familiar with, but it was a slow, sweet, love song. His brother had a beautiful voice. He waited until the song was finished before entering the room. Dante immediately poured himself a drink, noticing the dining table was covered with maps and computers. "Let's take this to the patio, shall we?" Dante didn't wait for them to respond. He opened the sliding glass door leading outside. Instead of sitting in one of the wicker chairs surrounding the table, he leaned his hip against the railing and stared out into the cool Greek afternoon.

"I know who has Connor," he said without looking at them. His heart was warring with his brain in regards to who he should rescue first, mother or child.

"Is it Sarantos?" Gregor asked as he and Tessa took a seat at the table.

"Yes. I actually ran into the sonofabitch." Dante wearily pulled a chair out and sat down.

"What do you mean *ran into him*?" Tessa asked.

Dante recounted what happened earlier, from his lunchtime meditation to leaving the restaurant and literally running into Alexi. His phone rang with Julian's name showing on the screen. "Jules, you're on speaker."

"I was able to run the license plate. The car is registered to Jorge Kastinopolous. So either the car is stolen, or Alexi has borrowed a vehicle, possibly an employee's. It makes sense he wouldn't use his own car if he is kidnapping kids."

"We need more information. Dammit! Is this how he and his old man made their millions, as slavers?" Tessa stood and began pacing the small area.

Thankfully, Gregor pulled her into his lap as he asked Dante, "Did you tell Julian about your vision?"

"No. Julian, during meditation, I reached out to Connor. I connected with him after a fashion. He was coloring a picture. It was crude, unlike his other drawings, but it was evident who was in the picture. It was of Connor and both Alexi and Stavros. There was a blonde-haired girl in the picture as well. This happened before I watched Alexi take the child from the market. Either Connor has premonitions, or they already have another little girl."

"Fuck! This makes me sick." Tessa tried to stand, but Gregor kept a tight grip on her.

"It does me too, Red. That's why we have to stop them," Gregor said as his lips brushed against her forehead. "Julian, do you have an address on Kastinopolous?"

Julian was tapping away at his keyboard as usual. "Give me a minute, and I'll text it to you. Dante, I won't stop digging. Until we get a better handle on where Connor is being held, I think your best bet is to concentrate on Isabelle. At least you know where she is."

"Agreed. We are meeting up with some local Goyles who are loyal to Xavier. We'll check back later." Dante thumbed off his phone. He had a bad feeling about Alexi. If he was the type of man to kidnap and sell kids, how would he treat his own son? Would he accept him, or would he offer him up to the highest bidder? Gods, Dante felt nauseous. He couldn't even begin to imagine how Isabelle must be feeling. "I'm going to start calling names on the list. I want to meet as soon as possible. I feel like we are already losing so much time."

Gregor moved Tessa off his lap and walked over to where Dante was sitting. He squatted in front of his brother, placing his hands on Dante's knees. "We'll get them back, Brother. This I promise you." Gregor remained that way, offering his support, until Dante

184

nodded his acknowledgement. With the type of connection they shared, he didn't have to say the words aloud. The two of them had been through a lot together over their five hundred years. When one was ready to move to a new location, the other followed without question. He didn't worry about their future together; not really.

Tessa was a world traveler, having homes in several cities. Isabelle might be a little harder to convince. He didn't truly know the woman whom the fates had destined to be his. Having spent time with her over the past few weeks, he had noticed little things about her. The way she took her coffee. The fact she added extra mushrooms to her omelets then covered them in ketchup. How she tucked the same too-short strand of hair over her ear only to see it come loose again. How she pushed her non-existent glasses up her nose when she was nervous. The way her brown eyes lit up when he said something that made her smile. Isabelle may not want a relationship with him, but they were getting along well. He had waited over five centuries to find her; he could be patient a while longer and give her time to come to the conclusion they were meant to be together.

Dante went back inside the suite to begin calling the local Gargoyles. They would meet that evening and share as much intel as possible. Then they would set about getting his mate back. He was worried more about Isabelle than he was Connor. At least with the boy, he had their connection, as tenuous as it was. Having no idea what Isabelle was going through was going to drive him crazy.

185

JASPER COULDN'T STOP thinking about the kid. No, not a kid – Trevor. Yes, he was young, but he was a man, even if he had such a youthful energy about him. Rafael had assured Jasper the fates wouldn't be so cruel as to mate him with a female. What about a straight male? Would they play such a sick joke on him? He didn't even know if Trevor was his mate, but if the way his body reacted last night was any indication, he was fucked. Well and truly, just not in the good way.

With Gregor, Dante, Dane, and Nikolas all out of town, his Unholy patrol schedule had doubled. Frey was starting sword training as well. Between his Clan duties and his job, he didn't have much free time. He wanted to talk to Rafael before assuming Trevor was his mate. He also wanted to spend time with the... his friend. Gods, he had to stop thinking of him as a kid. Jasper wasn't slated for training until tomorrow, so he could slip away at lunch time and head to the hospital. Since Dante was out of town, Trevor would be manning the morgue and would more than likely be alone.

Kaya called Jasper into her office. Even though he had written a report on the charred remains that were now on a slab at the morgue, she would want to go over the details since she hadn't been around yesterday. Just as he got to her office, the dickhead Troy walked past and shoved his shoulder into Jasper's. "What the fuck, Quinn?" Troy just kept walking, giving Jasper the finger as he did. Shaking his head, Jasper stepped into Kaya's office and sat down.

"What was that about?" Kaya asked him.

"Quinn being Quinn. He didn't like the fact that I took up for Trevor yesterday. It's obviously still stuck in his ass."

"Why did you have to take up for Trevor?" Kaya leaned forward, propping her elbows on her desk.

"He called Trevor a weirdo. I didn't like it and told Quinn as much. He got his bigoted hackles up." Jasper slouched down in the chair a little, getting comfortable. When Kaya waited for him to continue, he asked, "How was the trip to Tennessee? Is Maria going to make it? Has Rafael heard from Dante and Gregor?"

Kaya arched an eyebrow but let his abrupt change of subject go. "Maria was still in a coma last I heard. We have round-the-clock protection at her door, but now that Connor is gone, we doubt the unsub will return to finish the job. We are going on the assumption he or she thinks Maria is dead. Still, we aren't taking any chances. This is Isabelle's family, and we protect our own. As far as the others, I haven't spoken to Rafael for a couple of hours, so I'm not sure what's happening across the pond." Kaya cocked her head to the side and squinted her eyes. "What's going on with you?"

"What do you mean?"

"You seem, I don't know, distracted. Do you want to talk about it?"

"I... maybe." Jasper sat up in his chair and reached back, shutting the door. He rested his elbows on his legs. "How did you know Rafael was your mate?"

"Do you think you've met yours?"

187

"I don't know. Rafael assured me the fates would choose the right type of person, but I'm not so sure. I… I get these feelings when I'm around a certain someone, but I honestly don't think he's gay."

"Jasper, if you've met your mate, you'll know it. At first, the feelings are so intense, you feel like you need your mate to breathe. You want to touch them constantly. If they are in the room, you know it without looking. The intensity lessens somewhat over time, but it doesn't go away. Your mate is part of you and you them."

Jasper nodded his head, thinking about what Kaya described. "Thank you, that helps. I think." His cell phone pinged with a text message, and he smiled when he saw who it was from. "Excuse me," he told Kaya as he glanced at the text.

Trevor: *Call me.*

Jasper stood up. "I need to go. Thanks for talking to me."

"Anytime Jasper. We're family now." Kaya smiled at him. Jasper opened the door, and before he could step out, Kaya told him, "Tell Trevor I said hello."

Chapter Twenty-Two

RAFAEL CALLED JONAS and set up a face-to-face. He would not tell the Gargoyle about his daughter over the phone. Jonas had shocked them all when he stayed in New Atlanta as Chief of Staff at the hospital. His cover as Joseph Mooneyham had been blown when he treated Tessa, but only with the Gargoyles. The workers at the hospital had no idea their leader was a full-blooded shifter or the famous scientist who created the first human clone.

Rafael called the meeting at his office. He had already shown himself in public too much as of late. It was time for him to go back to being anonymous. Willow, his administrative assistant, was sitting at her desk, early as usual. "Good morning, Willow. How are you today?"

"Fine, thank you. Welcome back." The young lady was a bit shy, but she was the best assistant Rafael ever had. He would hopefully be able to keep her around for many years to come. Of course, that meant trusting her with his secret since she would eventually look older than he did. When she didn't meet his gaze, he picked up the messages on the corner of her desk and took the pause in conversation to study her mood.

"It's good to be back. I am expecting a visitor, Joseph Mooneyham. When he arrives, please show him to my office."

"Yes, Sir. A package arrived for you yesterday. I put it on your desk."

"Thank you. I'll go see who it's from." Willow seemed a bit preoccupied, but other than that, she didn't seem upset, so he let it go. Rafael wasn't expecting a package. He pulled his suit jacket off and hung it up before picking up the thick padded envelope. There was no postmark, which was odd. He listened to make sure Willow was still at her desk. When he could hear her typing on her computer, he called forth a claw, using it to slice open the package. He retracted it before pulling out the contents of the envelope.

Sorting through the myriad of photos in his hand, Rafael declared, "Sonofamotherfucker."

"Is this a bad time?" Jonas Montague asked from the open doorway.

Sighing, Rafael shook his head. "No, this concerns you as well. Please, come in."

Jonas approached Rafael's desk but didn't sit. "What's going on?"

Rafael straightened the stack of photos in his hand and held them out to Jonas. "Might as well start with these." Rafe sat down in his leather chair while he kept his eyes on Jonas's face. The photos were of various people. Until he came across one showing Nikolas with lots of sand in the background, Rafael had been at a loss. He assumed the others were Sophia, her parents, and Ezekiel.

"I don't understand," Jonas murmured while shuffling through the pictures.

"Sophia's parents disappeared. She went after them. Nikolas is her mate, so he went after her. Tessa was going to go after them all until Elizabeth intervened and sent Ezekiel. Nikolas has had no luck in

190

finding Sophia, so Tessa put him and Ezekiel in touch with each other. Somebody, probably whoever is responsible for Sam and Monica's disappearance, knows all the key players. They obviously want me to know that they know."

"How do you know about Sam and Monica?" Jonas narrowed his eyes at Rafael.

"Tessa filled us in when she and Gregor made plans to go after them. Since Tessa is Gregor's mate, I am now her King. While you may have had a hand in raising her, her loyalty is to me and my Clan. This is something you would do well to get used to." Jonas started to say something but Rafe stopped him. "That's the least of it. You really might want to sit down for the rest."

Rafael rarely saw grown Gargoyles pale, but Jonas's color was a shade lighter. "Would you like a drink?" When the doctor shook his head, Rafael continued. "Gregor and Tessa's trip to Egypt has been postponed. We have a more pressing matter."

"What could be more pressing than my child, his wife, and my grandchild missing?" Jonas questioningly accused Rafael.

"How about your grandson is missing, and his mother offered herself up to the kidnappers?"

"What the hell are you talking about?" Jonas asked as he leaned forward in his chair.

"I'm talking about Isabelle. Do you remember Maria?"

"Of course I do, but what does she have to do with anything?"

"I probably shouldn't tell you this, but it's a dire situation, and we need your help. When Isabelle

191

returned from Greece, she was pregnant with Alexi's child. She turned to the only people she felt loved her, Rico and Maria. Isabelle was afraid if Stavros ever found out about the boy, he'd try to take him. Maria and Rico agreed to take in Connor as long as Isabelle remained a part of his life. Fast forward six years to the present. Rico has been murdered, Maria was left for dead, and Connor was taken." Rafael gave Jonas time to digest the information he'd thrown at him quickly.

"Where's Isabelle? And Maria, is she okay? Where is she? What do you mean Isabelle offered herself up? By the gods, Izzy. I should have cloned her, too. I need to call Caroline." Jonas rose from his chair.

"Sit down. You can call your mate later. And don't give me that holier-than-thou look. I've already been through this shit with Xavier. Do not forget I am King here. I have allowed you to remain in my territory for years. Now, more so than ever, it is important you claim your allegiance. Isabelle and Dante are mates; therefore, she and Connor are part of our Clan. Tessa is mated to Gregor, as you already know. Xavier has offered his Clan as backing against Alistair."

Jonas's head snapped up as if he had been physically slapped. Rafael didn't let up. "We know about your past with my uncle. While we cannot prove he is behind the kidnappings, it would make sense he is. His beef started with both you and me over two hundred years ago. Why he has waited until now to start trouble is a mystery. Whatever the reason, we need to work together."

Rafael waited while Jonas studied the photos again. If the older Gargoyle decided he wasn't going to play on the Stone Society team, Rafael would ask him to leave the States. He templed his fingers as he waited for a response.

Finally, Jonas looked up. "Tell me what you want me to do."

DANE WAS JUST stepping out of the shower when his phone rang. "Abbott. That's great news. I'm on my way." Quinten, the Gargoyle watching Maria, called to let him know she was awake. Dane hurried and dressed, making the short drive from the hotel to the hospital. When he arrived, Maria's doctor met him at the door to her room. "Mr. Abbott, your sister is awake, but she's extremely weak. I had to give her a sedative to calm her down. She's going on and on about Rico and Connor." The doctor already knew the circumstances that led to Maria being in the hospital.

Dane was almost glad to hear the woman had been sedated. It would give him a chance to talk to her while she was groggy, explaining who he was and why he was there. He noticed the doctor looking at him funny. "I was adopted, if that's what you're wondering." He hit the nail on the head, as the doctor nodded.

"She's probably not going to be awake for a while, but you're welcome to go in."

"Thank you," he told the doctor as they shook hands. He gave Quinten a knuckle bump before entering Maria's room. Dane should be used to full-bloods by now, but each one he met seemed larger than the last. Quinten could go toe to toe with Geoffrey in size. He wouldn't dare put money on who would win that fight.

Maria was hooked up to various monitors and machines. Dane felt bad for the woman who had done nothing other than help raise someone else's child. He thought back to his own mom. Not Caroline, but the one who raised him as if he were her own. In his opinion, someone who raised a child that wasn't biologically theirs was pretty special. He pulled the metal chair closer to her bed and sat. He knew Quinten would be able to hear his conversation, but if he was part of the Clan, Quinten would keep the information to himself.

Taking her hand carefully in his, Dane whispered, "Maria, my name is Dane. I'm a friend of Isabelle's. Actually, I'm more than a friend, but we'll get to that later. Isabelle wanted someone to be with you." Maria squeezed his hand so he stopped talking. Her eyelids fluttered open, and she smiled at him. Hmm, must be the drugs working. He continued, "Your doctor says you're going to be okay, but you need to rest."

"Connor?" she whispered, her voice scratchy. Dane poured a small amount of water in the cup on her bedside table and allowed her to sip a little through a straw.

"Isabelle has gone after him. She said not to worry, she will bring him home."

"Rico…" Her voice drifted off as the tears rolled from the corner of her eyes.

"I'm so sorry about Rico." What else could he say? Being a detective, he had to inform families of their loved one's death way too often. The words were never enough.

"Dane, please, tell your mother about Connor,

about Isabelle." Maria's eyelids drooped. She was trying to stay awake. "Tell… your… mo…" Her eyes closed before she could finish. Why would he tell his mom about Connor? Unless she was talking about Caroline. Dane set the cup of water on the table and leaned back in the chair. Did Maria know Caroline? If Jonas left Isabelle with Maria all those years ago, it was possible she knew of Caroline. Dane pulled his wallet out of his back pocket. On a folded piece of paper was a phone number and nothing else. Caroline had given it to him when he was going through his initial transition. She'd told him, "If you ever need me, for anything, at any time, just call."

Hopefully Rafael hadn't called Jonas yet. Dane didn't think two phone calls were necessary, and he wasn't ready to speak to Caroline. Making sure Maria was asleep, Dane thumbed through his contacts, dialed Rafe, and told him Maria was awake before filling him in on her short conversation.

Maria slept for the next few hours with nurses coming in to check her vitals. The woman was lucky to be alive. Dane wanted to get his claws on the bastards who left her for dead. He closed his eyes and thought of his sister and what she must be going through. When she was safely back in the States, he was going to let her have it for not trusting him, not trusting her mate. Thinking of mates brought a vision of Katherine Fox to mind. He had transitioned soon after meeting with her, but Julian was positive she belonged to him. What if he was right and Dane had no clue who his mate was? She could be anyone. The only people he was around on a regular basis were the people he worked with. After listening to the Gargoyles talk about how strong the bond was, he knew his mate wasn't someone on the force or a member of the Crime Scene Unit. He didn't feel anything out of the ordinary being around them.

Dane wasn't even sure he was ready for a mate. He was still getting a handle on controlling his phasing. He didn't need to add being spurred on by a sexual partner to the mix. He watched Dante lose his shit over something concerning Isabelle, and they hadn't completed the bond yet. If a five-hundred-year-old full-blood couldn't contain himself, Dane was afraid of what would happen when he figured out who tripped his trigger. He was better off being single for now.

Maria's monitors beeping erratically brought Dane back to the here and now. He jumped from his chair, sending it flying backwards. Nurses ran in with a crash cart, yelling for him to leave the room. He didn't want to comply, but he couldn't do anything to help. Before he could clear the door, Maria flatlined.

Chapter Twenty-Three

WHILE DANTE FINISHED calling all the local Gargoyles, Gregor and Tessa went in search of Jorge Kastinopolous's home. Julian had continued his search into the man and found out he was employed by Sarantos, Inc. Gregor wanted to find where he lived and follow him, hoping he would lead them to Alexi. Once they were out the door, Dante made his way to the patio. He was going to try to reach Connor again.

Dante allowed the constant breeze to soothe him while he worked to block out the everyday noises. He had never been more grateful to Geoffrey for teaching them all the art of meditation. Where Frey learned it, he wouldn't say. All Dante knew was it had saved Frey's mental health on more than one occasion. All the Gargoyles were badasses in their own right, but Frey was on a level all his own.

Dante was eager to get his woman and son and get back home. He had been complacent over the last hundred years or so, resigned to a life of being single. Now that the possibility of a family was within his grasp, he would stop at nothing to get Isabelle and Connor back to the States safely. He had to. Once they were home, he would be starting a new chapter of his life, just like Gregor was with Tessa. He and Isabelle may only be friends, but at least he would have her in his life. If that's what she wanted, he would settle for it. Temporarily. He would give her all the time she needed to fall for him.

Concentrating, Dante slowed his breathing, clearing his mind of everything except Connor. He pushed the prior vision out of his mind, wanting the connection to be fresh and true. As before, he reached out, calling for the child. This time, the connection was almost immediate. Maybe the boy was in tune with Dante and could feel when his mind was opening up to him. As with the previous connection, Dante was looking at a drawing. This time, however, it was more detailed. Connor must have found a pencil. The people in the picture had changed as well. The drawing was of two little girls instead of one. Even though the picture wasn't in color, Dante recognized one of them as the child he saw Alexi talking to earlier.

Before Dante could study the picture further, another drawing appeared. This one contained a woman and a man. The details weren't as distinct, but they were detailed enough Dante would recognize them if he saw them. He couldn't see Connor, but he could see a pencil moving over the paper. The words *they have momma* were faintly written. As quickly as the words appeared, they were erased. This picture, instead of being balled up and thrown away, was torn into shreds. Dante hoped beyond measure it was Connor who was doing the shredding. The child was risking a lot getting messages to Dante this way.

The connection was broken, and Dante felt a sense of loss. He knew, even without having met the boy, Connor was extraordinary, and he couldn't wait to be around him. Talk to him. Watch him grow. Dante's heart swelled with pride as if the boy were his own flesh and blood. Dante wished he was talented enough to recreate the drawing so he could pass it along to

198

Jules. The arts, however, were not his forte. He left that up to Rafael. Knowing it was a long shot, he called his brother.

Instead of greeting with *Hello*, Rafe asked, "Dante, Julian has kept me in the loop with what you have so far. Do you have anything new?"

"Maybe. I am able to connect with Connor during meditation as you suggested. Instead of speaking, he is showing me drawings. So far, there are two girls in the house with him; one of which is the child I watched Alexi take. Rafe, please tell me I wasn't wrong in allowing the girl to be abducted."

"Brother, I have faith in you. You will get Connor back, and in doing so, will save both girls. I would have done the same thing."

"There was another drawing, this one of a woman and a man. Right before the connection was lost, Connor wrote '*they have momma*' across the bottom of the page. The words were erased before the paper was shredded. Rafe, Connor knows who took Isabelle. If only I had the ability to draw, I could recreate what I saw, and Julian could do a facial recognition search. Do you think it's possible you could reach Connor?"

"I will try, but honestly, I doubt it will work. There is no connection between the boy and me, but I promise I will see if I can reach him. Now, I have some news for you. I spoke to Jonas, and let's just say the Goyle is beside himself. You should expect more help than you originally anticipated. Not only did he call Xavier, but he also reached out to our mother. I was skeptical she would help, but when Jonas explained about Isabelle and Connor, she was ready to go after Alistair herself. Dante, get ready. It seems our mother has her second wind now she is going to be a grandmother." Dante could hear something strained in Rafe's voice.

"Congratulations, by the way. Have you told any of the others? I assume this was what you were going to tell us all at breakfast on Sunday."

Rafael let out a short laugh. "Actually, I was referring to Connor. How did you know about Kaya? Never mind. You would think after all this time I would be accustomed to your abilities. Either you've been holding out, or they're getting stronger. Anyway, thank you. Sin is the only one I've told so far. I have been talking to him quite a bit more lately. With all the new revelations and threats, I want him to be as prepared as possible for what is coming our way. He and Finley are going to begin sword training on the West Coast. I have postponed my trips to meet with the Clan leaders until we get Isabelle and Connor home."

"Back to Mother. Do you really think she is going to help us against her brother?" Dante hoped it was true. If anyone had firsthand knowledge of Alistair, it was Athena. "As far as her being in our lives again, I will believe it when I see it, grandmother or not. Honestly, Rafe, I look to Priscilla to fill the role vacated by Athena. She has been more of a mother to us than our own ever thought about. I wonder if it's because she never had children of her own. And speaking of Priscilla, I am worried about Jonathan. Last time I spoke to him, something felt off. I want Isabelle to be his physician when we return, but I also think he needs to be checked out immediately. Please have Jonas run a full blood panel on him. Isabelle can take over once we return."

"What do you suspect, Brother?" Rafael asked, the fear evident in his voice. Not only was Priscilla a mother to all the Gargoyles, Jonathan had become a surrogate father figure to the men as well.

"I really don't want to speculate—"

"Speculate, dammit," Rafael cut him off. "What do you think it is?"

Dante ran a hand through his hair and sighed. "Cancer. I think he has cancer. What kind, I have no idea. And I pray to all that's holy I'm wrong."

"How often have your instincts let you down?" Rafael knew the answer, as did Dante.

"Rarely. That is why I want you to have him checked immediately. Now, I am going to concentrate on getting my woman and child home."

There was silence on the line for a few seconds before Rafael responded. "Dante, you do realize you are referring to Connor as yours?"

"Yes. You aren't the first to point that out. Rafe, I can't explain it, but I already feel a connection to him. If Isabelle decides she only wants to be friends, if she doesn't want to complete the mate bond, I will still ask to be part of the child's life. I have never met him, yet he has attached himself to my soul in a way even I can't comprehend. The love I feel for him already will only get stronger when we are together. He is going to need me, especially now Rico is gone."

"Truth, and there is no one better than you for the job. Now, go get your family and bring them home. Be well, my brother."

"And you, my King." Dante disconnected. He swiped at a wayward tear that was rolling down his cheek, vowing once again to rescue his family.

ISABELLE CONTINUED TO call her guard Bruce, at least in her mind. Before they reached her room, he stopped in the middle of a hallway. He put out his arm to stop Isabelle from proceeding farther. He cocked his head to the side as if listening for something. Turning his body towards hers, Bruce gently grabbed her biceps and leaned in close, his lips against her ears. "There are cameras and microphones scattered throughout the villa. This just happens to be a dead spot. I will draw you a map when I retire to my room, that way you can point to where you want to go. I like you, Isabelle. You have guts. I would hate to see something happen to you because you don't play well with the King."

Isabelle was stunned to say the least. She looked into his eyes and saw nothing but sincerity there. "Thank you…"

"Carter. My name's Carter, but I really don't mind the Hulk. He's a badass," he quietly informed her with a smirk on his lips. His head jerked around and the smirk was replaced with the blank look she was accustomed to. He continued on down the hall, so she followed. Using her shifter senses, she reached out and heard the footsteps coming behind them. Not wanting to give herself away, she kept her face forward until they reached her room. Carter opened her door without looking at her. Once she was tucked safely inside, he closed it behind her. There was no lock being turned. With someone the size of Carter standing guard, who needed a deadbolt?

She had already checked out everything in her bathroom and bedroom. Twice. Since she had been denied the library, Isabelle had nothing to occupy her mind, so she stepped out on her balcony. There were several balconies decorating the outside of the villa. Isabelle found it odd none of them were close to each other. The closest patio to hers was on a floor two stories up. The next one on the same floor she was on was at the other end of the building. Looking around the property, Isabelle noticed another woman walking along the sidewalk that led to the swimming pool. It wasn't Kallisto. This woman looked more like Isabelle with her long brown hair and her modest clothing. Was this one of the women she had heard talking earlier? And why were they allowed to speak when Isabelle wasn't?

The woman and her guard walked in silence until they reached the covered gazebo. Neither one spoke. The woman sat down on one of the wooden benches skirting the inside of the structure, pulling her feet under her. She opened a book and ignored her guard who sat on a bench across from her. Isabelle couldn't figure out the place she was being held captive. Thinking back to what the women were talking about, there was to be a choosing. Was it the women who were being chosen? Did this have anything to do with what the King mentioned, selling her to the highest bidder? It didn't make sense. The women had sounded like they were looking forward to it. Like Cinderella being sold off to the Prince. Which would be the lesser of two evils? Staying here under lock and key, or going to live with someone else as their personal slave? At least if she left this building, it might give her the opportunity to yell for help. Here, she could yell all she wanted, and the only thing it would do is make her hoarse. And piss off the King.

Chapter Twenty-Four

DANTE WAS ON his way to meet up with Gregor, Tessa, and the other Gargoyles. Gregor and Tessa had found the home that belonged to Jorge Kastinopolous. When they arrived, the house was empty. No sign of Alexi or the kids. Now they were on their way back to the meeting house in Athens. Dante was leery about meeting in a private residence, especially since they were gathering with other Gargoyles. He preferred to err on the side of caution. Dante still didn't trust Xavier one hundred percent, even if he was Tessa's father.

The taxi he was in arrived just minutes before Gregor and Tessa in their rental car. The three of them stood in the circular drive, looking at the house. Dante said, "I would have preferred to meet somewhere more neutral, but our subject matter is not such that we can discuss it in public."

Just then, the front door opened, and Dante could only stare. "Hello, my sons." Athena stood in the open door, looking no different than she had the last time Dante had seen her, two hundred years prior.

"Athena, what are you doing here?" Gregor asked as he wrapped an arm around Tessa's waist.

"Please, come inside and we'll get down to business." She motioned behind her through the open door. Dante knew they had a choice, but Rafael had warned him she was going to insinuate herself into their lives once more. He glanced at Gregor, giving him a small nod before walking up the steps. Dante didn't kiss his mother or offer any type of affection. As far as he was concerned, she lost that right when she left them all those years ago.

Gregor and Tessa followed him into the house. "Tessa, it's so nice to finally meet you." Athena held out her hand to the redhead. Tessa shook it without speaking. "Your father has told me so much about you over the years. I remember when you were —"

"Athena, we didn't come here to reminisce. Again, why are you here? Where are the Gargoyles?" Gregor had ceased calling her Mother a long time ago. Even when she was caring for them and their brothers, she hadn't seemed all that enthusiastic at playing the role of mom.

Dante didn't miss the hurt that flashed briefly in her eyes. "I am here because this is my home. As for the others, they are in the study. Follow me." Straightening her shoulders, Athena led them down a hallway into a large room. The study was more of a command center with a circular table in the middle of the room. In front of each seat was a monitor. Larger screens hung on each of the four walls. Eight Gargoyles were seated at the table. When Dante and the others entered the room, all eight stood.

Athena introduced Dante and Gregor to the other Gargoyles. When they had all shaken hands, she introduced Tessa. "I know you have all heard your King speak of his daughter. Gentlemen, please allow me to introduce your Princess, Andrea Montagnon." The men of Xavier's Clan fisted their heart and bowed their heads while declaring, "Our Princess."

Tessa was surprised, as were Dante and Gregor. Technically, they knew Tessa was a King's child, but since she had always lived in the States, she was in Rafael's Clan.

"Please, I prefer Tessa, but thank you." Tessa waved them off, and everyone took a seat.

Athena made her way to an empty chair on the far side of the room. "First of all, let me say thank you, Donovan, to you and each of your Clan. Xavier and I have been friends for centuries, and I appreciate his assistance in finding Dante's mate and her child. When Rafael reached out to me and told me what has been happening, I took the liberty of putting together a docket on my brother. If you will take a look at your monitors, you will see before you everything I know about Alistair, his properties, business ventures, and Clan. Since the tracking device has Isabelle on Poros, we have to assume he is behind her abduction."

Everyone was silent as they studied the information in front of them. Donovan was the first to break the silence. "Poros is the most private of Alistair's homes. It is a relatively small island and is heavily guarded. From what we've gathered, he normally goes there to conduct business a couple of times a year. However, he has been there more frequently in the past few months." Donovan stood and went to one of the computers and began typing. Within a few seconds, an image appeared on all four of the large computer screens. "This is Poros. There is only one road leading to the island. From our current location, it is a three-hour drive. We could helo in, but that would be more conspicuous than driving." The computer screen changed. "This is the main house on the island. One way in, one way out. It is basically a fortress. Impregnable unless you know the layout.

Fortunately for us, we do."

"That was one of our family homes when I was young." Athena now had everyone's attention. She stood and pointed at the screen nearest her. "There are tunnels running under the house. These were put in when the villa was built. It seems our father was not a well-respected King. The tunnels lead from a lower-level room to various parts of the island. Think of the passageways as spokes on a wheel. There are five of them, and I have the locations of them all." She sat back down and allowed Donovan to continue.

"If you look in your packets, there is a map of the island. The five exit points are clearly marked. We have scouts checking those areas daily to make sure the entrances aren't somehow covered."

Gregor spoke up. "If you don't mind my asking, why all the surveillance on Alistair and his holdings?"

Donovan opened his mouth to speak, but Athena interrupted. "My brother, much like our father, is not a good King. He is a hypocritical bigot who wants nothing more than to eradicate all human life from Greece. He has not found a way to do so without causing another Clan war, but the idea is front and center in his mind. Always. The other Clan leaders have watched Alistair for a long, long time. We all try to stay prepared in the event of an uprising."

Dante asked, "What do you mean hypocritical?"

Athena grimaced. "Alistair's mate died giving birth to their son. His only son. Alistair has treated him with the same disdain he does humans. Blames him for his mate's death. He has since taken many human women as lovers. There was one who did what none other has been able to do; she cracked his cold heart.

208

For a while, he was almost happy. At the least, he was less foul than usual. He even went so far as to adopt her young daughter. The human eventually died, throwing Alistair into a tailspin. He has never taken another human for a companion. The daughter is still with him to this day. Even though she's human, she is referred to as the Princess."

Dante didn't miss the look that crossed Donovan's face at the mention of the Princess. He turned to him and asked, "Are all the guards on Poros Gargoyles? If so, how many are we looking to go up against?"

"There are several Gargoyles on the island, but only two guards inside the villa. Believe it or not, Alistair uses mostly human guards. He hires them, trains them to be the type of employee he wants, and pays them well. When I say the type of employee he wants, I mean quiet. Loyal. Rarely do the employees return to their families. His turnover rate is pretty high, though."

"If he treats them well, why is there a high turnover?" Tessa asked.

"I didn't say he treats them well, Princess. I said he pays them well. Alistair molds the humans into robots. Quiet and obedient. If they don't comply, or when they're too old to be effective, the employees basically disappear. To where, we don't know. Look at your monitors. This is a list of all the employees on the island, whether or not they are Goyle, and where they are stationed."

Dante read over the list then asked, "And you know all of this how?"

Donovan grinned. "Because we have one of our own on the inside."

They studied and planned. Each had relevant ideas and valid concerns. When there was a lull in the conversation, Dante spoke to Athena. "We need to make sure Alistair is nowhere near the island. Xavier has already agreed to calling a Council meeting. Is that going to look suspicious?"

She thought on it before answering. "The last few times we have met were to convince your brother to take his rightful place on the Council. If Rafael were to finally entertain the idea, it would be a legitimate reason."

Gregor stood. "I will call Rafe and tell him what we are planning. Athena, you and Xavier please coordinate the Council meeting. Since we are planning on hitting Poros in the next couple of days, we will need to move quickly.

Tessa grinned at Gregor. "This is going to be exciting."

Athena frowned. If Dante wasn't a frowner himself, he would have found her expression humorous. She didn't know Tessa well enough not to ask, "How can going into a heavily guarded building, risking your life be exciting?"

Tessa smiled at her mate's mother. "Because that's my cousin in there, and I haven't been in a good fight in a while."

Jasper had ignored the knowing look on Kaya's face and exited the precinct. Trevor's text was short and to the point, giving Jasper no indication what he wanted.

It left him a little nervous. Thinking back to the previous night, had he done anything out of line? Did he somehow offend Trevor? Nothing came to mind other than the way they had easily fallen into a friendly camaraderie, eating pizza, drinking beer, and playing video games. Jasper couldn't remember ever having more fun just hanging out. Trevor was such a geek, but he was also smart. His wit had kept Jasper laughing all night. If the fates had deemed Trevor his mate, at least he would enjoy his company even if they weren't sexually compatible.

Jasper pulled his phone out of his pocket and stared at the text. *Call me.* He really hated text messages. They were so impersonal, and you couldn't tell what the sender's mood was unless they used one of those stupid smiley faces. Why couldn't Trevor have added one? *Because he's not a twelve-year-old girl?* Biting the bullet, he dialed the number, holding his breath.

"Dude! You're not going to believe this. We got the results back on the burn victim. Can you come over here? This is too incredible to share over the phone."

Jasper exhaled and did his best not to laugh at how excited Trevor was. "Yeah, I'm leaving now. I'll see you in a few." He hung up and shut his eyes, thanking the gods their friendship was still intact. The drive from the precinct to the hospital took longer than it should, which only gave Jasper more time to be nervous about seeing Trevor again. He parked his cruiser and slowly walked to the back door that led to the morgue. He could already hear the heavy metal music blasting from the speakers. If Dante had been there, it would have been classical.

Jasper stepped into the room and stopped dead in

211

his tracks. The man standing before him was not the same man he spent most of last night with. Trevor's hair was now styled shorter and there was no purple streak. He didn't know how he felt about it. He loved that purple stripe that fell into Trevor's eyes when he was being bashful. So many times, Jasper's hand had itched to push it off of his face so he could see his beautiful green eyes. And to touch his skin. Trevor reached up subconsciously to push the wayward hair back from his face, but it was no longer there.

Trevor finally noticed he had company and smiled his big goofy grin upon seeing Jasper. "Hey, man!" He turned the music down so they didn't have to yell at each other. "What's wrong?" Trevor asked him.

"Your hair. It's not purple," Jasper told him.

Trevor's face immediately fell. He ran a hand through the shorter locks and looked down. "Oh, yeah. Uh, you don't like it?" He wouldn't meet Jasper's eyes.

Jasper knew from talking with Trevor the previous evening how self-conscious the younger man was. After a few beers, Trevor had confided in him he was a clone and why he came into existence. Trevor never felt loved or wanted. His hands were itching to touch the beautiful man whose heart he could crush with one word. He closed the distance between them and, taking a big chance, he used his finger to lift Trevor's chin. "I love it." He let his finger drop and stepped back, giving Trevor space in case he wanted to take a swing at Jasper. Not that he thought Trevor actually would. He was more of a lover than a fighter type person. Still, touching a straight man in such a way was often cause for action.

Trevor didn't take a swing. His cheeks flushed and

his eyebrows climbed to his hairline. "You do?" he whispered. If Jasper hadn't been a shifter, he probably wouldn't have heard the words.

"I do indeed, but I miss the purple. It was so you." Jasper winked at him as he pointed to the documents spread out on the empty slab. "These the results you're so excited about?" He had to change the subject quickly before he did something stupid like run his hands through Trevor's short hair. Or kiss him. Or kiss him while running his hands through his hair. His body was humming from being so close to Trevor. He knew without a doubt he was looking at his mate.

"Yeah, man, you are not going to believe this! Look!" Trevor held out the paper that named the results.

"Holy shit, this is great. I need to tell Gregor," Jasper said before he thought about it.

"Why would you tell the warden first? Why not tell the chief?" Trevor asked then glanced down. This man was going to kill him with his insecurity. Even if they were nothing more than friends for the rest of their lives, Jasper was going to work on Trevor, make him understand how special he was.

"Because Gregor is Tessa's mate, and the man who has been gunning for her her whole life is finally dead. She can breathe a little easier. Of course, I'm going to tell Kaya first though." Trevor was still looking at him as if he'd said something wrong. "What is it?"

"You said mate. Not boyfriend, not fiancé, not man. Mate."

Shit. "Yeah, well, boyfriend sounds so high school, they aren't engaged as far as I know, and man, well..." Jasper just shrugged and focused on the paper in his hand. Trevor was smart. Too smart, and he would have to start thinking before he spoke. Unless Trevor turned out to be gay and truly his own mate, he had to keep the Clan's secrets.

Trevor didn't look convinced. "You know what I think? I think all you macho badasses have this club. Some secret society. Like the other night when you and Dante came in all bloodied up. I can see you being friends; you're all so full of testosterone. That brings me to the same question I had last night. Why are you hanging out with me?"

Jasper's heart shredded a little bit more. He laid the summary sheet down on top of the result analysis pages. He took another chance and stepped closer to Trevor. If he weren't over four hundred years old with a good handle on his phasing, his fangs and claws would be out. As strong as the pull to Trevor was, his wings were even itching to unfurl. He took a deep breath, calming himself, and pushed a stray strand of hair off Trevor's forehead. He could feel Trevor's heartbeat in his own chest. The younger man's pupils dilated, and his breathing raced. Jasper was crossing a line that couldn't be uncrossed. When Trevor didn't step away, Jasper rasped, "You have no idea how special you are."

Trevor opened his mouth to speak then closed it. He opened it again. "I... I have to go." He ran from the room as if he'd been stung.

Jasper hung his head. *Well, fuck.*

214

Chapter Twenty-Five

INSTEAD OF WAITING around for Trevor to come back from wherever he disappeared to, Jasper left, not wanting to see the look of disgust or rejection on his friend's face. Friend. He doubted they were friends any longer. With a heavy heart, he drove across town to the manor. He could tell Kaya the news over the phone, but right now, he didn't want to be alone in his big, empty house.

Jasper didn't bother knocking since Rafael and Kaya knew he was on his way. As per his usual greeting, he walked in the back door and announced, "Honey, I'm home." He was met by a spatula wielding Priscilla.

"There's my boy. I've missed you," she said as he bent down and kissed her on the cheek. Was she getting shorter?

"And there's my favorite girl. Priscilla, you're as beautiful as ever." He flashed her a cheeky grin.

"Ah, pfft. Come here and get yourself a cookie before Rafael eats them all," she whispered conspiratorially.

"Priscilla! You wound me," Rafe chastised his housekeeper as he, Kaya, and Dane came into the kitchen. They took a seat around the island while Priscilla poured milk for everyone.

Jasper cocked an eyebrow and gestured at the milk in front of Kaya. "What's up with that, Chief? I've never seen you drinking anything except wine at

215

night." He didn't miss the look that passed between her and Rafael.

"Oh, shit. I know that look. You're practically glowing," Jasper said, pointing a cookie at Kaya's belly. A loud clang sounded as Priscilla dropped the pan she was holding at the same time Dane gasped. Jasper dropped his head and sighed. "This just isn't my day. I take it you haven't told anyone?"

Rafe reached over and clapped him on the shoulder. "Don't sweat it, Jas. We were going to tell everyone Sunday, but then everything went to hell. Priscilla, come here." The older lady came to stand between Rafael and Kaya. He snaked his arm around her waist and told her softly, "You're going to be a grandmother." Rafael was glowing as much as his mate. Priscilla's eyes filled with tears as she hugged first Rafael, then Kaya. He kissed her cheek. "Why don't you go share the good news with Jonathan, yes?" She wiped her eyes on her apron and nodded, leaving them to their business.

Kaya, with her hand on her belly, asked Dane, "So, how do you feel about being Chief?"

"I should have known something was up when you stopped going to crime scenes," Dane said, not exactly smiling. He had an odd look on his face. If Jasper didn't know better, he'd say Dane was a little jealous. It would make sense; he and Kaya had worked together for a long time. "But to answer your question, yes. I'm ready."

"Excellent. It will take a while for the paperwork to go through. I have to submit my resignation along with my recommendation for you to take my place. I don't see why your approval wouldn't be unanimous. You are the senior detective," Kaya explained.

Jasper was happy for his partner. They hadn't been working together long, but he had already learned quite a bit from the seasoned detective.

"So Jas, what's the big news you wanted to share?" Rafael asked as he snagged another cookie.

"Trevor called with the results of the dental records from the burn victim who was discovered yesterday. If the results are legitimate, the victim was Gordon Flanagan."

"How the hell did he get the results so fast?" Kaya asked.

Rafael took a sip of milk and responded, "I have a feeling Dante called in a favor. If it truly is Flanagan, this would be great news for Tessa and Elizabeth. They would be free once and for all. It would also explain why the Unholy are so much more active. We've had to double up on our patrols."

Kaya wore a concerned look when she asked, "So, how *is* Trevor?"

Straight. Jasper could feel his cheeks redden. He shouldn't be embarrassed, but at times in the past, his sexuality had been cause for ridicule. The fact that he had feelings for an obviously straight man had his heart and head all twisted. "We're just friends, but I like him. He's funny, and smart, and plays a mean game of Gods of Chaos."

Dane perked up. "Gods of Chaos? I can't wait until Four comes out."

Jasper laughed. "It just so happens…" He couldn't help teasing Dane.

"You don't!"

"I do. If you wanted to come over sometime, you

know, before you become Chief and get too big for your Gargoyle pants, we could play. Hey, how's Maria? I guess she's going to be all right if you all are here."

Dane was almost solemn when he said, "Things were touch and go for a while. She actually flatlined while I was there, but they were able to revive her. I think the knowledge of Rico's death and Connor's disappearance was too much for her. Once she was stable, I reminded Maria that Isabelle and Connor would need her when they were returned safely. Then I made a promise I hope Dante and Gregor can keep for me. I told her they would definitely be back safely and soon."

Rafael leaned back and crossed his arms over his chest. "We all want that. Jonas is with Maria now. As soon as she's able, he's going to transfer her to New Atlanta so he can watch over her.

"I have some bad news. I know it's late, but I need to have a conference chat so I can fill everyone in on the latest. I received a package at my office. It was full of pictures from Egypt, and they weren't of the pyramids. I don't know who sent them, but I can only assume it's one of Alistair's people. Whoever has Sophia and her parents knows Nik and Ezekiel are there. They sent pictures of all of them. Sophia appeared to be unharmed as did Nik and Zeke. As for Sophia's parents, it was hard to tell if they were injured or not. The lighting was pretty dark. Things are escalating. Once Alistair figures out I lied about a meeting just to lure him away from Poros, it's only going to get worse. Take your sword training seriously, my brothers. I have a feeling war is upon us."

ISABELLE WAS ONCE again in the library. Last night, Carter escorted her to dinner, and as soon as she was finished eating, he had automatically taken her to the only room in the house she cared anything about seeing. She spent hours in there, at first just taking in the room itself. It was two-story and had a ladder on wheels she had only seen in movies. Next, she had looked at all the titles, amazed at how old some of the books were. There were no romance novels, no self-help books. Only the classics were allowed on these shelves. At the top of the ladder, she had come across an old journal that reminded her of one of her father's. That was the book she decided to take to her room and read.

Now, having finished breakfast, Isabelle was back in the large room, looking for more books like the one she had read last night. The ladder was where she left it, so she climbed to the top and replaced the journal. Carter was standing at the bottom, quietly holding the ladder in place. He hadn't said another word to her, but she didn't need him to. Isabelle knew there was something different about her guard, something good. She had taken time last night to really study his features. She would bet any amount of money he was a Gargoyle. Even though he was drop dead gorgeous, his presence didn't cause any stirrings within her core. She wondered if the mate bond took care of that. Now that she had met Dante, was he the only one she would ever feel a tingling for? Carter clearing his throat snapped Isabelle out of her musings. Seeing her hanging on to the top of a tall ladder, just standing there, was probably cause for alarm to her guard. She quickly chose another book before climbing down to the floor.

Isabelle glanced at Carter and nodded her head in a silent thank you. He inclined his head and moved out of her way. She wanted to get out of the house and pointed at the window. He must have understood her meaning since he led her to a door in the hallway that opened to the garden. Isabelle really needed sunscreen, but since she had neglected to use any before leaving her room, she found a bench that was mostly shaded. Carter sat on the ground under a small tree, stretching his long legs out in front of him. He crossed his beefy arms over his chest and closed his eyes. Isabelle knew he was alert even if he looked relaxed. She had been around Dante and all the guards at the Pen enough to know they were always aware of their surroundings.

Speaking of surroundings, Isabelle could feel something in the air. She didn't know what it was exactly, but the mood in the house was heavier. She had dined alone at breakfast, but had passed another woman on her way out. This was the same one she had seen the previous night; however, a different guard was following her. Isabelle wondered if she was here of her own accord, or had she been lured in under false pretenses as Isabelle had? She opened the book in her lap and began reading. She hadn't finished the first chapter when she heard a familiar voice.

Sergei appeared and spoke to Carter. "Isabelle is needed in the infirmary at once." He didn't wait for either one to respond before he retreated in the same direction he came from. Carter stood and silently waited on Isabelle to follow him. They made their way through the large house to a room somewhere in what she deemed the basement. She hadn't been aware there was another floor below them. Carter pushed open a door and waited for Isabelle to walk through. The woman she had seen the night before was sitting on a standard doctor's table with Kallisto standing beside her, holding her hand. The room she was in could have been in her own clinic.

Kallisto said, "We need you to stitch her up. She had an accident." Isabelle noticed they didn't use the woman's name.

"Let me see what we have," Isabelle said as she took the woman's hand from her captor.

"No talking," Kallisto chided.

Isabelle froze and glared at the blonde. "In this room, I am a doctor, and as such, I will behave as one. If you want a mute robot, you will need to find someone else to do your bidding." She heard the gasp from the woman sitting on the table. Isabelle ignored them all until Kallisto grabbed her hair and pulled her head backwards.

"You will do well to remember who you are speaking to." Her face was close enough for Isabelle to smell her breath.

Isabelle slowed her heart rate and responded calmly, "I know very well who you are, Princess." She said Princess as if it were a bad word. "But like I said, I am a doctor and will conduct this room as I see fit." Isabelle held Kallisto's eyes until the woman finally backed down, releasing her hair. Isabelle ignored everyone else in the room – Kallisto, Carter, the woman's guard – and concentrated on her patient. She unwrapped the bandage and looked at the wound she was supposed to stitch up. There was a cut on her wrist that looked similar to a self-inflicted suicide attempt. Not wanting to draw attention to the woman, she didn't pick up her other wrist, only glanced to see that it was undamaged.

Isabelle moved around the room, opening cabinets and drawers until she found everything she needed. She was washing her hands when Sergei came into the room. "Kallisto, you are needed upstairs."

"I'm busy, Sergei. Whatever it is will have to wait." Her voice was frustrated, but her face was soft as she spoke to the man.

"I'm sorry, but it was an order," Sergei said, almost apologetically, before he cast his eyes to the floor.

Kallisto sighed before telling Carter and the other guard, "I expect this to be handled quickly. Get her back to her room, and do not let her out of your sight." Kallisto was pointing to the woman on the table but speaking to the other guard. Had she tried to slit her own wrist, or had it been an accident as Kallisto alluded to earlier? Either way, Isabelle had a job to do.

She scrubbed her hands and laid out all the supplies she would need on a stainless table beside the woman. Isabelle wanted to ask her what happened, but the other guard did not have a patient look on his face. Would he get in trouble for allowing the woman to be damaged? She heard the woman crying and wanted to console her. Instead of speaking, Isabelle softly pushed the woman back so she was lying down. She grabbed a tissue and gently wiped the tears from the woman's eyes before pressing the tissue into her undamaged hand. Within a few minutes, the laceration was stitched and bandaged, and the woman was on her way out the door. This wasn't Isabelle's clinic, but she cleaned and sanitized it as if it were. She could feel Carter's eyes on her as she moved about the room. When she was finished, she finally looked at him. He nodded, a look of appraisal in his eyes, and gestured toward the hall.

When they topped the stairs, Isabelle faintly heard loud voices coming from somewhere down the hall. She continued walking as if she weren't eavesdropping, but she shut off all other noise and zoned in on the irate voice. "I do not have time to drop everything because King Rafael decides a meeting is in order. Fine, I'll be there, but he better be serious about this."

Rafael was calling a meeting? Did that mean he was here in Greece? He had told Isabelle she was family, and he would take care of her and Connor. Just hearing his name brought a sense of relief to Isabelle. For the first time since leaving the States, Isabelle felt a little bit of hope at being found. She had expected Carter to lead her back to her room. Instead, she found herself being led outside, back to the garden and her book.

A helicopter flew overhead, coming in low. Isabelle watched its decent as it landed on the roof of the house. Within a minute, the helicopter lifted off and eventually disappeared. She was curious about a lot of things. One of them was whether or not Carter was a Gargoyle. She decided to test that theory. Looking at her guard who was reclining under a tree she whispered, "Was that the King?"

If she didn't have exceptional hearing herself, she

wouldn't have heard him respond in his own whisper, "Yes."

One mystery solved. Isabelle thought of the King and shuddered. The man was pure evil. Was Rafael meeting with him and demanding Isabelle's release? That was preposterous, really. How could Rafael know where she was? What if Dante was with him? She knew from being around him and the other full-bloods they were badasses in their own right, but the King exuded badass in an evil way. His sort of alpha made her cringe. What if her stupidity got Dante hurt? Or worse.

She heard Carter mutter, "Oh, shit". Another guard, one Isabelle hadn't seen before, strode to stand beside the tree Carter was lounging under. He stood to face the other guard and asked, "What are you doing here? It's not your shift."

The guard responded, "It is now." Carter glanced her way, his face was almost sorrowful. He didn't linger, though. He left the garden and Isabelle. The replacement was a miniature version of the evil man. She could feel his intense gaze, so she looked at his face. His eyes were cold and calculating. Now that she thought about it, Carter couldn't watch her around the clock. He would have to sleep at some point. Her hands began to tremble as she read the next sentence in her book. Her mind couldn't focus on the words. The man standing fifteen feet away, doing nothing more than being in her vicinity, was instilling dread in her gut.

Chapter Twenty-Six

CONNOR SAT AT a patio table filled with more food than he had ever seen in his life. He was looking out over the water and remembering everything around him: the buildings in the distance, the beach below. He was storing it all in his brain so he could draw it later. The big man had visited him in his mind, and Connor knew he would come rescue him. The man who called himself Grandfather was sitting across from him reading a newspaper. He seemed nice enough, except when the Alexi man came in. Grandfather had said Alexi was Connor's father. He didn't believe him. Alexi was mean and said bad things about his momma. Connor wanted the big man to be his father. He knew his Papi and Mimi were dead. That made him sad. They had told him his father was dead, too, but Alexi was here, in this place. Maybe Papi and Mimi weren't really dead either.

Grandfather asked, "Do you not like the food, Connor? You aren't eating."

"It's fine." He bit off a piece of toast, thinking about the four girls who were somewhere in the house. "What are the girls eating? Why can't they help me eat all this?" Connor knew there was way too much food on the table, and it would go in the garbage. The door opened, and Alexi stuck his head in and scowled at Connor before stating, "One more then we need to move." He disappeared into the house.

"Don't you worry about them. They are eating in

225

their rooms, sort of like a tea party," Grandfather answered. "What would you like to do today? Do you like to fish? I can take you out on the boat. Would you like that?"

Connor had never been on a boat, never been out of his neighborhood really. "I want to draw. Can I have some pencils?"

"I gave you a pencil. Besides, you have the largest box of crayons there is," his grandfather said with a frown.

"Crayons are for babies. I prefer to draw with real pencils. Colored ones," he said, almost pleading.

The older man looked at him from around his newspaper. "Babies, huh? Is there anything else you would like?"

"I would like a pad of drawing paper, please. And some canvases and paints and brushes," Connor answered honestly. If he had to be stuck here, he wanted to be able to paint. He looked out at the blue water, and memorized the depth of the color.

"So, we have an artist in the family. I tell you what. I will take you shopping myself, and you can pick out whatever you would like. How does that sound?"

"I'd like that very much." Connor would get to see his surroundings. He would memorize them, too. Anything to help the big man find him. Connor knew he would find him. For the first time since being taken from his bedroom at home, Connor wasn't so scared.

AFTER A RESTLESS night's sleep, Dante was pouring over the map of Poros. The plan was solid. The Gargoyles' contact on the inside assured them Alistair was no longer at the compound. The only point they all hadn't agreed on was the timing. Dante and Gregor were used to patrolling at night when they could fly unseen. Donovan insisted it would be best to hit the compound during the day when his man on the inside was watching Isabelle.

Dante's heart skipped a beat. Tessa walked out of the bedroom she shared with Gregor, only she wasn't Tessa; she was Isabelle. Once again, she had applied the prosthetic and wig. How she got all her red hair tucked under the shorter brown wig was a mystery, but the look was flawless. "Good morning, Dante."

"Holy gods, you even sound like her." Dante had to sit down. For a five-hundred-year-old being who had seen a lot of changes over the years, he still couldn't wrap his head around the technology before him. "How did you accomplish that?"

"I was able to tap into her landline and copy a recording of Belle talking to Maria. I programmed it into my computer then transferred it into the micro transmitter at my throat. It's more about the vibrations than the actual tone really." Dante looked closely at Tessa's throat. Even knowing there was something there, he couldn't see it.

Gregor was leaning against the door post, arms crossed over his chest. Instead of freaking out over the fact that his mate was disguised as her cousin, getting ready to go into possible battle, Gregor was grinning at her, eyes full of love and admiration. "And here I thought you and Julian were the smart ones," he said to Dante.

"I really don't understand how you are so calm about this. She's *your* mate, yet I'm the one ready to call the whole thing off. Tessa, I appreciate you doing this. Honestly, you have no idea how much this means to me, but are you certain you want to go in there?" Dante would never forgive himself if something happened to Gregor's mate.

"She's my cousin, Dante. I have failed Belle enough. It's time she was shown her family, at least some of us, really have her back. Let's just say this is for my own selfish reasons." Tessa placed her hand over Gregor's heart while still looking at Dante. "This right here…" She patted Gregor's chest. "His heart is my heart. The beating within his chest is the same rhythm pounding through my body. I want that for her. For you. You both deserve happiness. Now, let's go get your woman." Tessa didn't hesitate. She grabbed her canvas bag off the table that contained transmitters, communicators, and other items she affectionately referred to as spy gear.

Gregor pushed off the door frame and stood before Dante. "She'll be fine, Brother."

Dante had been working on keeping the frown off his face, but he knew what he'd see if he looked in the mirror. "How can you be sure?" he whispered to Gregor.

"Because, you and I have her back." Gregor pulled Dante's head down, touching their foreheads together. "As Tessa said, let's go get your woman."

Before the sun rose in the sky, the three of them traveled to Athena's. Donovan and his Clan were already there. To say they were impressed with Tessa's transformation was an understatement. "Does the King know you are doing this, Princess?" one of the Gargoyles asked.

"No, but he knows the job I lead as watcher. I have plenty of experience in covert missions." Digging in the bag, she pulled out equipment and passed it around. "All coms are set to the same frequency as the transmitter at my throat. You will be able to hear everything I say as well as be able to talk to me and each other. The technology is such that the depth of the tunnels should not be an issue."

Donovan took point, going over the plan one more time. "Gregor and Dante will follow Tessa to the bank with the rest of us taking the other four tunnels. Team One will hit the tunnel by the pier. Team Two, you will take the postal center. Team Three, you will head to the cathedral, and Team Four, we will hit the arena. As previously discussed, the tranquilizer darts should be all we need this time of day. Shoot to disable, not to kill, unless it's absolutely necessary. Bloodshed will surely accelerate a Clan war. There should only be one Gargoyle on site, and that's our inside guy. You all have a picture of him, so if you see him, you'll know it. Any questions?" When nobody spoke up, Donovan said, "Let's do this."

Each team took a vehicle to their designated location. If they had executed the rescue during the night, they could have worn fatigues and camouflage. As it were, they were dressed much the same way as the other tourists. They all carried a backpack containing their equipment. The drive took a little less than three hours. Once on the island, the vehicles split up.

Gregor stopped the SUV and let Tessa out before he parked down the street. Dante and Gregor made their way down the sidewalk, keeping a good distance between them and Tessa. Gregor tested the equipment one more time. He softly whistled a short tune, and Tessa whistled back to him. That was the cue for the other teams to check in.

"Team One's in place."

"Two's here."

"Team Three is good."

Donovan came through with, "Team Four is set. Gregor, when your team is in place, let me know."

"Copy that," Gregor said as he walked beside his brother.

"Isabelle, what are you doing out here?" A male voice was loud and clear through Tessa's transmitter. She didn't respond. Dante could see Tessa stopped on the sidewalk less than ten feet in front of them. The man who stopped her was as large as Dante, but he didn't look menacing, only concerned. As a matter of fact, he looked like the Gargoyle who was supposed to be inside watching Isabelle.

"I needed some fresh air. What are you doing out here? You're supposed to be guarding my door."

"What? You know I'm not guarding your door right now. How the fuck did you get out of the compound?"

Donovan's voice broke through, "Tessa, is that Carter?"

"Yes," Tessa answered Donovan.

Carter replied, "Yes, what?" at the same time Donovan responded, "Son of a bitch. Tessa tell Carter I said to get his ass back to the compound. Stat."

Dante and Gregor closed the distance so they were standing close enough to help Tessa if she needed it.

"Donovan said to get back to the compound, stat," Tessa told him.

"Tell him our timeline moved up when the King left the building. Tell him you are her cousin."

"How do you know Donovan?" Carter eyed Tessa suspiciously.

"Because, I'm not Isabelle; I'm her cousin, Tessa. We're going in to get her." Tessa looked around, making sure they weren't causing a scene. Carter grabbed her upper arm, pulling her away from the foot traffic of pedestrians on the sidewalk. Dante heard the growl both through the earpiece and from his brother beside him. Tessa heard it as well. "Carter, my mate is about five feet behind me and about five seconds from removing your hand physically." Carter let go quickly. "Thank you. We don't have time to stand here and argue. If you don't believe what I'm saying is true, call Donovan. Or better yet, call your King and ask him who his daughter is."

Carter must have seen something in her eyes that caused him to believe her. "Where is your mate?"

"Here." Gregor and Dante made their presence known.

"Where is Donovan?" Carter asked, but Tessa was listening to her ear piece.

"We are wasting time. Bring Carter with you and tell him what's going on while you walk," Donovan instructed.

"Ten-four. Come on, Carter. I will take you to Donovan."

"Where are we going?"

231

"To the bank."

Dante had to give props to Tessa. She was on her game, and even the glitch of having an extra player thrown in the mix hadn't shaken her. She pulled her backpack off her shoulder as she walked. Unzipping a side pocket, she reached in and pulled out an extra communicator. "Here, put this on."

Carter did as Tessa instructed. "Donovan, Carter has you in his ear now. You can say hello to your little friend." Several laughs came through the transmitter.

Donovan came through their coms. "Carter, why are you out here and not inside?"

Carter explained how he was relieved of guard duty and left the villa to call Donovan. While they made their way to the tunnel entrance, Carter listened as Donovan went over their plan on getting Isabelle out. They reached the bank, but before showing them the entrance, Carter responded, "That would be a solid plan except for one thing."

"What's that?" Donovan asked.

"Theron is guarding Isabelle," Carter said as if they would know what that meant.

Dante asked, "Who is Theron?"

Carter pushed back the brush that was covering the opening to the tunnel. "The King's son." He stepped through the opening as Dante listened to the multitude of voices coming through his ear piece. All the words ran together, but they all said the same thing – trouble.

As they walked deeper underground, Carter explained how Theron unexpectedly showed up in the garden, and how he'd had no choice in leaving Isabelle.

"Is he a threat to Isabelle?" Dante asked, not liking

the implications.

"No. The King doesn't want her harmed. I honestly don't know why Theron pulled me away. The only reason I can think of is he likes Isabelle."

Dante growled low in his chest. The thought of another Gargoyle being around his mate had his shifter clawing at his insides. He calmed himself and paid attention as Carter explained Isabelle's schedule as well as where in the house her room was located. Tessa stated what Dante was thinking, "He's one Gargoyle."

"He's more than that. Theron is bigger than I am and has a tendency to kill anything that gets in his way."

"Kill? I thought full-bloods could only be killed with a sword," Tessa said, looking up at Gregor.

Carter responded, "That's true, mostly. I've never seen him go up against another Goyle, though. Nobody is crazy enough to stand up to him."

"Where's Frey when you need him?" Gregor asked, jokingly. Dante sized up Carter. If this Theron was larger, he would be a formidable foe. If fighting the larger shifter meant getting Isabelle out, Dante would take him on.

Donovan's voice came through. "The good news is there are no other Goyles on the premises. He can't take us all on and win. I had hoped we would get out without causing a riot, but it looks like that isn't going to happen. Princess, you are highest ranking here. Is your father going to have our necks when we start a Clan war?"

"Princess? Shit! You're Xavier's daughter?" Carter stopped walking, fisted his heart, and bowed.

"Yeah, yeah, yeah. Princess, that's me."

Dante inwardly grinned at Tessa for not taking her role as royalty too seriously. He answered Donovan's question. "No, Xavier won't have your heads. I was there when he pledged your Clan's allegiance to our King, Rafael."

As the teams reached the ends of their tunnels, they were trying to come up with the best way to handle Theron. It was Tessa who broke through. "Leave him to me. I have a plan."

Carter reminded her, "He's a Gargoyle. He will hear us coming."

"He's going to be confused, because he'll think I'm Isabelle. By the time he realizes what I've done, it'll be too late."

Gregor groaned and pulled Tessa to his chest. "Why do I have the feeling I'm about to have a heart attack?"

Tessa pulled her backpack off her shoulders and pulled something out of a pocket. Holding up a syringe, she grinned. "Like I said, I have a plan. Give me a chance to try it the easy way. If that doesn't work, then you can let the claws out."

"What is that exactly?" Carter asked, pointing at the syringe.

"Hellebore root."

Dante shouldn't be surprised Tessa was prepared to take down a full-size Gargoyle. Gregor took her face in his hands and placed a soft kiss on her lips. "I'll be right behind you."

Once it was settled Tessa would take point, Carter explained where Isabelle's room was in relation to the opening of the tunnel. They had gone over the maps several times, and everyone knew their jobs. The plan to tranquilize all the human guards was still in play. The only difference now was their primary target. Tessa had one shot to take Theron out with the tranquilizer.

Before he opened the door, Carter told Donovan, "Kallisto and her sidekick were in the house when I left." A loud groan was heard, and Dante assumed it was Donovan.

"I'll take care of them and head your way," Donovan said.

"Okay, Princess, you're up." Carter opened the door.

Tessa gave Gregor one last kiss and headed to take on the giant.

Chapter Twenty-Seven

SILENTLY, DANTE AND Gregor followed Tessa, tranquilizing any human guards they came upon. The zapping of guns and thunking of bodies hitting the floor came through the transmitters. As they neared the hallway where Isabelle's room was located, Tessa took point. She didn't look at Gregor. Dante knew from his own experience Tessa was in the zone. Her head was in the game, focused on the play ahead of her. She strolled along the hallway as if she didn't have a care in the world. Dante and Gregor stayed out of sight, listening through their coms.

As they waited, Dante felt the familiar pull of Isabelle. His heart clenched, and his lungs tightened. His body knew it was so close to its lifeline. He would have her in his arms soon. Tessa sniffed, her cue to the men that Theron was in her sight. Dante and Gregor looked around the corner, and true to the plan, Tessa walked past the guard causing him to turn his back to them. "What the fuck are you doing out here?" he yelled at Tessa. She pretended to turn a key on her lips.

"I don't give a godsdamn about my father's fucking rules. I asked you a question. How the fuck did you get out here?"

Tessa ran her left hand up the big Goyle's chest. "I went back to the library. I was so bored being stuck in my room." Her hand slid up the side of his neck and into his hair. She tugged him down closer and whispered in his ear, "You are so sexy when you're mad." Before he could register what was happening, she plunged the needle in his neck and released all the hellebore into his system.

Theron roared and backhanded Tessa with everything he had. She went flying down the hall, hitting the wall about ten feet away. Gregor let out a roar of his own and charged the larger Gargoyle. Dante was right behind him yelling, "Check on Tessa, I've got him."

Theron rounded on them both and phased. The large Goyle was pissed. As Gregor got closer, Theron took a swing. Gregor barely missed the sharp claws aimed at his face. Dante took advantage of the opening and punched him in the kidneys. Theron staggered, shook his head, and came at Dante. Dante took the fighter's stance, waiting for another opening. Theron was large, but he wasn't quick. His movements were being impaired by the poisonous herb in his system. Leading with his claws, Theron took a swipe at Dante, but he was too slow. Dante led with a left hook then followed up with a right uppercut. The larger Goyle went down to his knees, and Dante popped out a front kick to his jaw. Even without the drugs in his system, the kick would have taken him down. Dante was thankful for the late-night sparring sessions with Frey.

"Isabelle?" Dante yelled at the door.

"Dante? Dante, I'm here!" Isabelle was pounding on the door.

"Stand back, Beautiful. I'm going to kick the door in."

"I'm back. Dante, get me out of here!"

Dante planted his foot beside the knob, and the door splintered. Isabelle was on the far side of the room, but as soon as he pushed through the mangled wood, she was in his arms.

"I knew you'd come for me," she whispered into his neck.

"Always. I'll always be here for you, Beautiful." Dante ran his hands down her face. "Are you hurt?"

Isabelle shook her head. "I'm fine. Who was the creep yelling at?"

"Tessa. Oh fuck, Tessa." Dante grabbed Isabelle's hand and led her into the hall where Gregor was cradling an addled Tessa in his arms.

"What the hell?" Isabelle was staring at a version of herself lying in Gregor's arms.

"Hey, Belle." Tessa grinned at her cousin.

"That's amazing," Isabelle whispered. "Are you okay? What happened?" Isabelle bent down, studying her cousin.

"That happened," Tessa said, pointing at Theron. "Help me stand up," she said to Gregor, holding her hand out. Once she was on her feet, she said, "I'm good."

"Teams, check in," Donovan commanded through the transmitters.

When each team gave the all clear, Donovan asked, "Dante, is Isabelle safe? What about Tessa?"

"Yes, I have Isabelle. Tessa's a little shaken, but she's on her feet."

"Excellent. We need to clear out." The coms went silent as all the teams headed toward their respective tunnels and made their way toward the city.

Tessa pulled off the wig and prosthetic as she tried to walk. At the first stumble, Gregor picked her up. "Let's move out," he instructed.

Dante took another look at his mate and kissed her forehead before threading their fingers together. They followed Gregor to the entrance of their tunnel. Carter met them just outside of the doorway with a woman by his side. Dante knew this wasn't part of their plan and was going to question him until Isabelle held her hand out to the woman and pulled her into a tight embrace. "Are you okay?" Isabelle asked, concern shining in her eyes.

The woman nodded and whispered, "Thank you."

"Wait, there are two more women. Where are your friends?" Isabelle couldn't leave anyone behind.

"Huh? I haven't seen anyone else since I got here besides the Princess," she responded, obviously confused.

Isabelle was certain she had heard three women talking.

"She's right, Isabelle. There were no other women besides you two and the servants. Let's go," Carter urged them on.

Everyone was quiet as they travelled back the way they'd come earlier. Once they reached the end of the passageway, Carter said, "I need to get Eve to a safe house. Her leaving and my betrayal is going to cause as much chaos as Isabelle escaping." He glanced at Isabelle then turned to Dante and held out his hand. "You are a lucky man, Dante." They shook hands, and Carter turned to Tessa. Once again fisting his heart, he dipped his head quickly. "My Princess, it has been an honor. Gregor, likewise." They too shook hands, and Carter opened the doorway, allowing them all to exit before he and the woman did. Once the foliage was back in place hiding the entrance, they went their separate ways.

"Princess, huh?" Isabelle asked, smiling at Tessa, tears filling her eyes. "I can't believe you found me. How *did* you find me?" Isabelle asked looking from Tessa to Dante.

"I put a transmitter in your purse," Tessa told her, grinning.

"My purse! I left it in the room!" Isabelle turned toward the door, but Dante snagged her around the waist.

"I will buy you a new purse. I will buy you fifty purses, but you are not going back in that house. We need to get out of here and go get our son."

Isabelle's heart clenched. "Connor! Oh my god, Connor. Do you know where he is?" Isabelle's previously unshed tears rolled down her cheeks.

Dante pulled her into his body. "Shh, Beautiful, we will find him. I promise." Dante pushed her hair off her shoulder and cupped her face. "Isabelle, look at me." When she looked up, he said, "I made you a promise, and I don't make vows I cannot keep." He wiped the tears away with his thumbs and placed a soft kiss on her lips. Their tender moment was interrupted by a fussing Tessa.

"Put me down, Stone. I can walk."

"Red, you took a nasty hit."

"And it won't be the last one I take, either. As much as I love being in your arms, we are going to cause a scene walking down the streets of Greece with you carrying me. We are still not out of the woods yet. When Theron wakes up, he'll be on the hunt for us. We need to get to the condo. Now."

Dante knew exactly what Gregor was feeling. He
240

wanted to lift Isabelle in his arms and never let her go. His body was tight at the nearness of Isabelle, especially now she was safe. He couldn't wait to get her back to the condo and have some alone time with her.

The two couples walked the short distance to the SUV and piled in. When the doors closed, they all just sat there quietly. Gregor put his hand on the side of Tessa's face, assessing her bruise. Dante felt Isabelle slide over next to him. She laced their fingers together and looked up at him. "Have I said thank you?" Her eyes were again wet with unshed tears.

Dante gently traced the contour of her eyebrows, her cheekbones, her chin. He leaned in and touched their lips together. He had no idea what she had been through, and he wanted to take it easy on her. She obviously had different ideas when she pulled his head closer, carding her fingers through his hair. She opened her mouth, her tongue touching his lips. His body thrummed with electricity; his cock stirred to life. Moans were coming from all four throats. Tessa broke the moment when she rasped, "I wish we'd taken a helicopter. Get us back to the condo, and take me to bed." Gregor cranked the SUV and headed back toward Athens.

Dante touched his forehead to Isabelle's, needing the connection. As he thought of Gregor and Tessa going back to the condo to make love, his dick hardened even more. Not because he was thinking of them together, but because he knew he would be alone with Isabelle in just a few hours. He was not an aggressive Goyle. In fact, he was quite the opposite. However, with the adrenaline still flowing through his veins, he had no doubt he would have her naked and under him as soon as they were alone. He leaned back and searched her eyes. "Are you really okay? Did they hurt you?"

"Other than drugging me and scaring the crap out of me, they pretty much left me alone. How long until we get where we're going?"

"About three hours," Dante whispered in her ear.

Isabelle pulled Dante back down to her for another kiss. He didn't think he would last three long hours without getting her skin to skin. Thankfully, she stopped her tormenting kisses. She threaded their fingers together and leaned her head on his shoulder. For the rest of the drive, she filled them in on everything that happened from the time she got on the jet with Kallisto to right before they rescued her.

Finally arriving back at the condo, Gregor parked the SUV in the underground garage. As soon as the engine was off, he and Tessa were out of the vehicle and on their way upstairs. Dante reached out to open his door, but Isabelle stopped him. "Wait." She surprised him when she snaked a leg over his lap so she was straddling him. With her hands on his shoulders, Isabelle settled herself against his erection. Dante couldn't help the growl that escaped. His beast was trying to take over. He may be passive, but his beast was alpha all the way. Isabelle pulled his T-shirt up, running her hands along his skin. He slid down in the seat so she had better access to his cock, grabbing her hips and urging her on.

Isabelle rubbed back and forth over his erection, her arousal flooding his senses. "I want you, Dante," she husked, her voice pleading.

Dante's brain was half-way functioning. Most of his blood was in his other head. "Bed," he managed to choke out.

"I need you, now." Isabelle unbuttoned her blouse and let it slide down her arms. She reached between her breasts and unsnapped her bra, her milky skin on display. She grabbed Dante's head and pulled his face down where she wanted it. "Please," she begged.

While Dante would have preferred to be stretched out on the bed, he wouldn't deny his woman what she wanted. Couldn't deny her anything. His hands left her hips and cupped both breasts, pushing them together. Her nipples were hard peaks just waiting to be laved. She had the perfect breasts to slide a hard dick between. As Isabelle continued to grind against his cock, he licked and sucked, one nipple, then the other. Isabelle leaned her head back, eyes closed, her breathing ragged. He continued with his attention on her breasts, scraping his teeth across her nipples. She moaned at the rough treatment and bore down on his cock. If she didn't stop writhing against him, he was going to come in his pants.

"I need to be inside you, Beautiful. We can go up to the bedroom, if you like."

"No, I want you inside me now. I can't wait. Fuck me."

Dante was surprised and a little hurt at the crude words. Was that all she wanted from him? Just a fuck? His beast was on board with the idea, clawing at him to be unleashed.

"Dante, please…" When Isabelle reached between them and grabbed his dick, all hurt left his heart and was replaced with a savage need to take his woman.

243

Here. Now. Beast one, Dante zero. Not so gently he moved her off his lap so he could push his pants down his legs. If she wanted a fuck, a fuck she would get. Isabelle removed her clothes. Instead of straddling him, she leaned down and took his hard prick into her mouth. She grabbed the base of his shaft with her hand and licked the moisture off the swollen head. She took him to the back of her throat before sliding her tongue from the base to the tip. "You taste so good," she said, licking her lips.

If Dante didn't get inside her soon, he was going to come in her mouth. The idea of fucking her face definitely turned him on, but the first time he came, he wanted to be inside her heat. "Isabelle, I am too close." He grabbed her gently, pulling her body over his. Rising up on her knees, she grabbed his cock and directed it to her opening. With one quick thrust, he was seated as far as he could go. As much as it was killing him, he stayed still, allowing her body time to acclimate to his size. Isabelle had other ideas. She clutched his shoulders, using his body for leverage, as she rode him. The sight of his woman writhing in pleasure, the sound of her moaning, was too much.

His fangs popped out against his will. She was his woman. His mate. He needed to mark her, make her his in the true sense. But she didn't want that. He pushed the thought out of his mind and just enjoyed being in her, being one with her. Dante filled his hands with her ample breasts, rolling and tugging on her nipples. Isabelle let out a growl of her own, her fangs elongating. He could feel her heat tightening, her release close. He was barely hanging on, but he wanted her to come first. The sight of her fangs had his beast howling. Isabelle squeezed her eyes tight. Her body shuddered around his hard cock, right before she sank her fangs into his shoulder.

Dante's own orgasm roiled through his body and shot into hers. The fact that she had marked him intensified his release almost to the point of painful. Isabelle licked the place on his shoulder where she had bitten him before collapsing against his chest. To say he was shocked was an understatement. She had marked him. Was it the bond she was looking for, or was it just something that happened in the heat of the moment? His heart was conflicted. She told him she wanted to fuck, not make love. Then she bit him. Yes, she had to have been caught up in the moment. There's no way she could want to be mated to him. Not him.

Chapter Twenty-Eight

ISABELLE HAD NEVER felt so complete in her life. She should feel like a wanton slut, attacking Dante in the middle of the day in a vehicle. She didn't. There was no way she could have waited one more second to feel the connection. And she had bitten him. Holy crap, did that mean they were mates? Wouldn't he have to bite her too? What if he had changed his mind? She leaned away from his body, searching his eyes. She didn't like what she found there. Sadness.

"I'm… Dante, I'm sorry." She couldn't look at him. He was going to reject her, and she had thrown herself at him. She tried to get off his lap, but he tightened his hold around her waist.

"What are you sorry for? Biting me? It's okay if you didn't mean to. I understand if you got caught up in the moment. We can forget it happened." His voice was filled with regret.

At that, she looked back into his eyes. "I meant to," she whispered. "I wanted to, but you…you didn't bite me back. If you've changed your mind..." She couldn't help the tears. How could she have been so stupid? She had decided to open her heart, one last time. When would she learn?

"What?" He was once again wearing the old frown. "Isabelle, I didn't change my mind. I want you now, still. I will always want you. Always."

"But you didn't bite me back. I just thought…" He interrupted her with his lips pressing against hers. He kissed her softly, moving his mouth from hers to her cheek, down her neck to her shoulder. He sucked at the skin hard enough to leave a mark.

"I was so close to marking you, Beautiful, but the last conversation we had, well you weren't sure you wanted me. Not forever anyway. What made you change your mind?" He searched her eyes.

She gave him what he was looking for, the truth. "You said *our son.*"

Dante's frown was immediately replaced with a warmth she had never seen on her Gargoyle. How was that possible? Dante didn't know Connor. "Isabelle, I need to show you something. Where's my phone?" He tried to dig his cell out of his pants pocket. Maneuvering was a little awkward since they were both practically naked. "Maybe we should take this inside, after all," Dante said.

Isabelle kissed him quickly and gently eased off his still semi-hard cock. Come trickled down the inside of her thigh. She looked around for something to wipe her leg with. "I need a towel," she said more to herself than Dante. Coming up short, she decided to tough it out. She slid one leg in her pants, but before she could insert the other leg, Dante's big body was angled between the seats, pushing her legs apart. He grabbed her left leg and lifted it higher so it was resting on the back of the seat. He licked a trail from her knee up her thigh, cleaning their mixed essence off her leg as he went. That was the single most erotic thing she had ever seen in her life. When he had lapped up all the come, he slid up her body and teased her lips. She immediately opened for him, allowing him to share their mingled taste with her.

His cock was hard again, rubbing against her inner thigh. If she slid down in the seat, just a little, he would be inside her. God how she wanted him. "Dante," she moaned into his mouth, pushing her core towards the intended target. Dante sat back, his eyes filled with lust. "I want you too, Beautiful. But this time, you're going to be spread out beneath me. Get dressed. Please."

Isabelle wasted no time in finding her clothes. She walked with Dante up to the condo he had been sharing with Tessa and Gregor. Hopefully, the walls were soundproof, because she planned on letting go. Her cousin and her mate were nowhere to be seen. Dante led her to the far end of the room to his bedroom. He shut the door and leaned against it. Isabelle knew what she wanted. What she craved. And he had too many clothes on. "I need to see you. All of you," she said as she began undressing him. Dante stood still, allowing Isabelle to have her way with him. Remembering what Tessa said about him possibly being submissive, she tested the waters.

She stepped back from his body, admiring the ripped abs and chiseled chest. He wasn't bulky like a lot of the Gargoyles, and for that she was grateful. Dante was sheer perfection. His long cock was pointing up, the tip glistening with precome. Isabelle licked her lips as she slowly began undressing. Dante's eyes followed her every move. When she was bare before him, she dipped her finger between her legs. Instead of licking the moisture, she stepped closer to Dante and held her finger up to his mouth. He opened up, sucking her finger clean. She looked at him under hooded eyes, breathily describing what she wanted. "I want you to make love to me. I want you to show me how much you want me. Can you do that?"

As soon as the words left her mouth, Dante picked her up and not so gently laid her out on the bed. She spread her thighs, offering herself to him. His eyes scanned her body, almost clinically. He paused as he gazed at her glistening core, glanced at her breasts then took in her eyes. She held her breath as he lazily stroked his cock, looking her over one more time before stretching his long body over hers. He nestled his erection in the wet juncture of her legs. Propping himself up on his elbows, he gazed into her eyes as he rocked himself back and forth, his dick brushing against her clit with every pass.

"Dante, please." Her body was on fire. She was going to come from the friction alone. "I need you inside me," she urged him on. Dante placed another soft kiss on her lips as the wide head of his shaft found what it was looking for. Dante raised one of her legs up and thrust in to the hilt. Slowly, sensually, he moved in and out of her body, never taking his eyes off hers. In that moment, she knew. Isabelle knew without a doubt Dante was her other half, the missing part of her soul. Whether it was the mate bond or love or something else altogether, she didn't care. She only knew she had to have it. Have him. Forever. "Bite me."

The change that came over Dante in that instant was almost frightening. The green of his eyes gave way to black, his fangs burst forth from his gums. His wings unfurled behind him. "Are you sure, Beautiful?"

She nodded. "Yes. I'm positive." Her eyes widened at the beautiful sight on top of her. She had seen wings from afar, but to have them this close, close enough to touch, it made her body burn. What began as slow, steady lovemaking quickly turned into a hard pounding. Dante's breath was ragged, and he rumbled deep in his chest. The beast had taken over. "Oh god, Dante. Harder." Her claws itched to tear at his skin. Not in a way that would hurt bad but hurt good. She couldn't help herself. "Oh, god. Oh fuck…"

As Dante moved in and out of her core, she ran her hands down his shoulders, stopping only when they met with his wings. She ran her fingertips along the rigid, leathery edges, causing Dante to growl. She knew in her soul the sound he emitted was one of passion, not anger. His growl was a call to her shifter. Both her fangs and claws released with the latter scraping down his back. Isabelle's orgasm was building, her spine arching, needing him closer. "Isabelle," he hissed. His pupils were blown, no green to be seen anywhere. His breathing was coming in short pants, words coming from his mouth in a language she didn't understand. God, that was hot.

"Deeper. I need you…" she panted and dug in with both her claws and her heels. As soon as her claws found purchase in his skin, Dante let out a roar and thrust his cock as far as was physically possible into her pussy. His fangs found her neck, puncturing the skin at the juncture of her shoulder. She yelled out his name as her climax shredded her. Dante's come mixed with her release as he continued to pump inside, milking his still-hard cock. She couldn't breathe. The bite of his fangs intensified her orgasm to the nth degree. Isabelle couldn't stop thrusting up, needing more contact as her body shuddered with small aftershocks. Dante circled his hips, rubbing against her clit until her release subsided.

When they both stilled, Isabelle blinked away the stars, willing her brain to function properly. She had been mistaken before. *Now*, she felt complete. With a rush of air, Dante's wings retreated. He lifted his body off hers just enough to allow her to breathe. *Mine*. Isabelle snapped her eyes to meet his. Had she heard his voice in her head, or was it just her imagination?

Dante's face gave nothing away as his fangs slid back into his gums. He rolled to the side, bringing Isabelle's body with him. She was wrapped in Dante's arms, her leg draped across his thighs. She phased back and relaxed into him, drawing swirls on his chest with her fingertips.

"My beautiful Isabelle," he whispered against her hair. "As much as I would love to stay here forever, we need to talk."

Isabelle stiffened. Had she done something wrong? Already? Dante pulled her up his body so she was lying on top of him. "Look at me. What's wrong? Why did you tense up just now?"

She closed her eyes, finding the strength to tell him the truth. "I… I'm scared."

"Isabelle, look at me." When she looked into his beautiful eyes that were once again green, he continued, "You have no reason to be scared. Never again. You are mine, and I will cherish you until our time together is no more. However many centuries that is, you will never have to be afraid of anything. I will love you, honor you, and protect you with everything I am. I cannot wait to be a father to Connor, and when the time is right, be a father to our other children." He stopped talking long enough to kiss her on the forehead.

She had to be dreaming. "You really want to have children? With me?" She still didn't understand why a badass Gargoyle would want someone as plain as she was.

"Of course, with you. Unless you don't want children with me." The scared feeling she had was reflected in his eyes.

She couldn't help the laugh that escaped. "What a pair we make. Yes, I want to have your babies. But first, we need to work on getting Connor back."

Dante rolled Isabelle off his chest and stroked her cheek. "And *that* is what we need to talk about. Come on, let's get dressed. There's something I want to show you." She couldn't help but drink in his beautiful body as he stood. "Isabelle, stop it. If you keep looking at me that way, we will never get anything accomplished. Let us get our boy back and then we will have the rest of our lives for this," he said as he pointed between their naked bodies.

As difficult as it was, they showered together without having sex. Isabelle kept reminding herself they needed to find Connor. Wrapped in a fat, white towel, she remembered she didn't have any clean clothes. Just then, there was a knock on the door, and Tessa yelled, "Belle, I put some of my clothes on the bed for you."

She was glad to see Tessa chose the more conservative clothes for her to wear. Dante was getting dressed beside her. It should have felt awkward, but it didn't. It felt right, as if they had been together many years. This was the first time she had seen him in casual clothing. He had been wearing shorts and a T-shirt when he rescued her, but her mind had been preoccupied with other things. She took a good look at her Gargoyle who was now dressed in blue jeans and a polo shirt. His bare feet were sexy. Once they were both dressed, Dante kissed her softly then led her to the living area. The sliding glass door was open, allowing the sea air to flow inside. Gregor was sitting in one of the patio chairs with Tessa in his lap.

Dante took a chair and pulled Isabelle down onto his lap, something he'd never done before with a woman. The way their bodies naturally fit together was like the last two puzzle pieces being snapped into place. The worry Dante would turn out like Alexi was completely gone. He wrapped one arm around her waist as he opened his phone with his free hand. "Isabelle, I want to show you something." He held his phone out, and she took it, looking at a drawing.

"Oh my god, that's us. Where did you get this?"

"Rafael found it in Connor's bedroom along with various other drawings."

"But... that's you. That's all of us. How?" Isabelle knew Connor was talented, special even. But this was an exact likeness of a man he had never before met in his life.

"That's what I wanted to ask you. I know my photograph is available on the internet. Is it possible Connor could have seen it? Have you mentioned me to him at all?"

"No, he isn't allowed on the internet. He's only six. And I haven't mentioned you because I wasn't certain of our future before now. How can this be?" She looked at the picture on the phone again, using her fingers to widen the shot.

"He and I have a connection of sorts. Remember when you and I discussed how my abilities are a little more advanced than most Gargoyles, and I am able to sense things others cannot?" Dante waited for her to respond, so she nodded. "I think Connor has those same abilities. If I concentrate hard enough, I can see Connor. The first time, I sensed the room he was being held in. Since then, it has been like looking through his eyes. I see what he sees. I'm pretty sure Connor is with Stavros. Connor showed me a drawing of himself with a little girl, Alexi and Stavros."

"Alexi? Why would he be drawing Alexi?" Unless his grandfather had shown him a picture of Alexi, there's no way he could know what his father looked like.

"Oh shit, you haven't told her?" Tessa sat up straighter in Gregor's lap.

"Told me what?" Isabelle's heart sank. The way the three of them were looking at each other, they were hiding something. "Told me what, Dante?"

"Alexi. He's alive."

Chapter Twenty-Nine

ISABELLE JUMPED OUT of Dante's lap, backing up against the balcony railing.

"No, that's impossible," she whispered. "I saw him go overboard. They never found the body."

Dante stood and came toward her, but she held out her hands. "No, stay away from me. How do you know this?"

"First, we saw his picture in the newspaper, but then I ran into him. When I was coming out of a restaurant down by the pier, I literally ran into him."

"I'm married. I'm still married, and you knew it. You marked me knowing Alexi is alive. Why would you do that?" Not that Isabelle wanted anything to do with the monster, but if she were in fact still married, she couldn't be mated to Dante. Could she?

"I'm sorry. I didn't realize you would want to stay married to him. I'll go call Julian." Dante left the balcony, a defeated look on his face.

"Belle, please tell me you don't want that douche bag for a husband! He's kidnapping kids!"

"What? No! I don't want him. Jesus H. What do you mean he's kidnapping kids?" Isabelle's heart was torn. Shredded in a million pieces. She was still married to Alexi, and she didn't want to be.

"Dante followed him and watched him abduct a second blonde girl from the boardwalk. Connor has been drawing pictures, hopefully trying to give Dante clues as to where he is." Gregor gently pushed Tessa out of his lap. "If you'll excuse me, I need to check on my brother."

Isabelle couldn't believe it. Her body was shaking; her fangs and claws popped out. Blood was running down her chin, down her hands, but she couldn't stop it. That monster had her baby. The thunder of her heartbeat was pounding in her skull. She couldn't shut it off. Someone was shaking her, trying to bring her back to her senses. It was no use. She was married to the monster, and he had her son.

Tessa left the patio and returned with a wet towel. "Belle, stop it, right now. Get a hold of yourself. Do you honestly think we are going to sit by and let Alexi have anything to do with Connor? And Dante, holy mother of Zeus, you should have seen him when he found out Alexi's alive. And not just because you're still married to him, but because he has Connor. I don't know what's going on with your mate and your son, but somehow they have a connection, and it's a beautiful thing. The first thing Dante did was call Julian. No, I take that back. The first thing he did was lose his shit. The second thing he did, after he gathered said shit back, was to call Julian to see if you can have your marriage annulled. Belle, you mated with Dante for a reason. I heard you say the words, so I know you wanted it. I saw the smile on your face when you and Dante sat down. Don't let Alexi take your happiness away from you. Don't let him win."

Isabelle should have been mortified that Tessa and Gregor heard her having sex. She took in everything Tessa just said, really took it to heart. She had wanted Dante for her mate, still did. Was it possible she could get an annulment? That would be too easy. While

Tessa continued to clean her up, she asked, "Did I tell you thank you?"

Tessa looked up from wiping her hands. "You don't have to thank me, Belle. We're family."

"Oh, god. Dante…"

"Shh, Gregor's gone to get him. He'll bring him back. I promise."

"What if he changed his mind?" Isabelle was so tired of screwing up.

"Isabelle, Dante is crazy about you. He wouldn't phase with no thought if he didn't love you. That isn't something he can just turn off."

"Dante loves me?"

DANTE COULDN'T BREATHE. He would give anything to be home where he could fly and hunt Unholy. Tessa had been spot-on when she accused him of targeting the creatures purely for sport. He couldn't fly, but he could run. He didn't care he was wearing blue jeans. He needed to go, get away from the condo, from Isabelle. No matter how far or how fast he ran, he couldn't leave behind the memory of what happened earlier. How she had given herself to him freely.

"Dante, hold up! Dante!" He should have known Gregor wouldn't let him go alone. He slowed his legs and eventually came to a stop. If he were human, he would be winded. Since he had Gargoyle metabolism, he wasn't even breathing hard. Dante didn't speak, just looked out over the water. Gregor was silent as well, a hand on his shoulder for support. Neither one moved for what seemed like an eternity until Gregor's phone rang, breaking through the silence. "It's Rafe."

"Hello, Brother. I'm with Dante. I'm putting you on speaker. Go ahead."

"I wanted to update you on what's happening Stateside, but first, how are things on your end?"

"We have Isabelle. She's safe," Gregor told Rafael. "We have to thank you for your diversion with Alistair." Gregor explained their plan and how they worked with Xavier's Clan. "Now, we are going to focus our efforts on Connor."

"Dante, I'm sorry. I haven't been able to reach him during meditation. You are his best bet at this point."

"I appreciate you trying. I have reached him three times so far. Hopefully, I can continue."

"I have faith in you, Brother. As far as Alistair, he's going to be pissed when he finds out my jet happened to malfunction. I have a feeling our uncle has just begun to target us. I received a package in the mail. The postmark was from New Atlanta and not Greece, but I know in my gut he sent it. The envelope contained photographs from Egypt. The pictures were of Nikolas, Sophia, her parents, and Ezekiel. Whoever sent the pictures knows we are helping in the search. Julian hasn't been able to reach Nikolas since we sent Ezekiel to him. Jonas is working with Elizabeth to contact Ezekiel. I didn't call so you would worry about Nikolas. I wanted you to be made aware of the situation, especially you Gregor, since you and Tessa are planning on joining the search.

"Now, for the good news. I wanted to let Isabelle know Maria is awake. Jonas pulled some strings and is taking over her care. As soon as she is able to be moved, he is bringing her to New Atlanta. From what he told me, Maria's and Rico's families have been friends of Jonas for many years. It was why he felt comfortable leaving Isabelle with them. There's more to the story than we all know, but that is something he will have to talk to Isabelle about. Speaking of Isabelle, why aren't you with her?"

Dante groaned. "It's a long story, but let me shorten it by saying I fucked up. Royally."

Gregor squeezed his shoulder. "We need to get back to the women and make plans to get Connor. Rafe, do you have anything else for us?"

"As a matter of fact, I do. Dante, have you spoken to Trevor?"

"Not since yesterday. Why?"

"He has the results of the burn victim. I thought he would have called you immediately."

Dante frowned. "I texted him, telling him to open the results. How do you know who was named?"

"Fuck, I feel like I'm in a soap opera here. Jasper was sitting in Kaya's office when Trevor texted Jasper. Jasper went to see Trevor who showed him the results. Jasper, in turn, came to the manor and told Kaya and me. I know that isn't protocol, but Dante, the victim is Gordon Flanagan."

Gregor let out a whoop. "Is he sure? Oh gods, this is wonderful!"

Dante couldn't help but be glad for his brother. This would be a great load off Tessa's shoulders and, in turn, Gregor's.

"Jasper saw the results with his own eyes. Unless someone fabricated the papers, it's true. Gregor, I know you'll tell Tessa. Now, go get Connor and come

259

home so we can all celebrate. Be well, my brothers."

"And you, our King," they said in unison.

"Brother, this is great news. You should get back to Tessa and share it with her."

"Not without you. Dante, Isabelle chose you. She mated with you of her own free will. You've heard her talk about how badly Alexi treated her. Put yourself in her place. She thought her husband was dead, and she was free to love whomever she chooses. Now, after six years, she finds out he's alive. It's not bad enough Stavros has his hands on Connor, but Alexi as well? Come on, don't give up on her so soon. She chose you. After you walked out, Tessa asked her point blank if she still wanted Alexi, and she adamantly said she does not. She's in shock and confused."

"She doesn't want him? He's..."

"He's a fucking loser who kidnaps little girls, for the gods' sake! Give her a little credit, Brother."

Dante nodded. "Okay. Yes, let's get back. I need to apologize for keeping that from her."

Gregor clapped him on the shoulder. "Did you have to run so fuckin' far?"

Dante gave a hint of a smile, and his heart loosened a little. He could always count on Gregor to make him feel better. "Have I said thank you?"

"For what?" Gregor asked as they jogged along the pier.

"For coming with me, helping me get Isabelle back."

"I wouldn't be anywhere else. You know that."

"I know." And he did know. Dante was grateful for his brother.

They made it back to the condo in twice the time it

260

took them to get to the pier. When they reached the door, Gregor reminded Dante, "Be patient with her. If I know my mate, Tessa's already laid it out for Isabelle, including how Julian is working on getting the marriage annulled."

"You go ahead in. I need a second." Dante wanted to pull himself together. He leaned against the wall and closed his eyes. Visions of Isabelle spread out in the car, laid out naked beneath him on the bed, claws digging into his back, it all came to mind. Gregor was right; she wanted him. At least, she had before she found out she was still married. Dante took in a deep breath. He knew he was being a coward, hanging out in the hallway, but he couldn't face her rejection again. Not yet.

He wanted to attempt to reach Connor. Considering they had the top floor to themselves, he shouldn't be bothered by any other guests. He slid down the wall until he was sitting, legs crossed in the lotus position. Closing his eyes, he put Isabelle out of his mind and replaced her beautiful face with the sweet face of Connor.

Connor, can you hear me? Connor, it's Dante. Come on, Buddy, help me. Help me find you. I have your momma here with me.

The door opened, and a shaky, unsure voice whispered, "Dante?" Isabelle called his name, breaking his concentration. She shut the door behind her but didn't come closer. "Are you okay?"

He probably looked out of sorts, sitting in the hall meditating. "Yes, I was trying to reach Connor," he said as he stood.

"Did you? Reach him?" Isabelle wrapped her arms

261

around herself. Dante wanted his arms around her, but she needed to come to him. He had marked her, and in his heart, she was his. If she didn't want him though, he would do his best to forget what happened less than an hour ago. He took a step toward her but stopped.

"I had just closed my eyes, so no." He looked at his feet instead of into her eyes. He was afraid of what he would see there.

"I'm sorry," they both said at the same time. He did look up then. "You don't have to apologize. I should have told you about your husband." He lowered his eyes to his shoes.

"He's not my husband," Isabelle huffed as she took a step closer. "At least, not in my mind. Or my heart. Dante, please."

He couldn't resist the pleading in her voice. He closed the gap between them, pulling her chin up so he could search her eyes, seek for the truth of her heart. The shimmer there was his undoing. He pulled her into his embrace, and she circled her arms around his waist, laying her head on his chest. "I'm so sorry I freaked on you. It… It was just a really big shock," Isabelle whispered into his shirt. "I don't want him, don't want to be married to him. Please tell me you didn't call Julian to stop the annulment."

"I didn't call Julian. I couldn't." Dante kissed her hair. They stayed quiet for several minutes, just holding each other.

"How do you reach Connor? Do you just think about him?" Isabelle asked, looking up at him.

Dante didn't answer immediately. Her chocolate eyes were so beautiful. He kissed her forehead and her cheek, squeezing a little tighter. With his lips against her hair, he answered, "Something like that. I calm myself and block out everything around me. I call to him. It took a while the first time, but now we have the connection, it gets easier each time, almost like he's waiting for me."

"Okay, then I'll leave you alone so you can try." Isabelle tried to pull out of his arms, but he held her tighter. He wanted her to be there with him this time. Her presence was a dichotomy. On one hand, it was torturous. Being near her like this had him wanting to throw her over his shoulder and take her back to bed. On the other, it was the most peaceful feeling he'd ever felt in his life. A feeling of being complete. Whole. She was part of him now, just as Connor was.

"No, please. I want you to stay." He kissed her temple, and Isabelle settled against his chest. Standing in the middle of the hallway, Dante focused his mind on their son. *Connor, are you there?* The connection was immediate. Connor must have felt him before Isabelle interrupted. As with the other vision, a drawing appeared. Connor must have found colored pencils, because this drawing was much more detailed. Four little girls huddled together. One was the same blonde Dante saw Alexi take. The artistic ability of this child absolutely amazed Dante. His work was good enough to be in art galleries around the world.

The picture slid behind another, this one depicting a street corner complete with road signs. Signs written in Greek. *Fuck.* Dante concentrated on the symbols hoping to recreate them later. He studied the sidewalk in the background. Some type of purple flower was canopied over the roadway. Next was a beautiful drawing of the sea complete with buildings on either side of where Connor had been drawing from. Connor began sketching a boat on the sea. It was a rough drawing so he must not be looking at a real boat. Quickly, he scribbled the letters *MAGD* before madly erasing. The connection was severed quickly. "Fuck!" Dante hoped that didn't mean Connor was in trouble.

"What? Dante, what's wrong?" Isabelle was holding on to his forearms, eyes pleading.

"I lost the connection quicker than I wanted, that's all. I need a pencil and paper before I forget the symbols." Dante grabbed her hand and pulled her into the condo. He quickly found what he was looking for and began drawing the shapes as he remembered them.

Tessa was on the phone with Elizabeth, sharing the news Gordon Flanagan was dead. Dante was trying to concentrate on the conversation as well as remember the drawings. Tessa eventually hung up, and she and Gregor gathered beside him, watching quietly. He explained what he was doing. "Connor showed me several pictures. This one is of a street sign. Unfortunately, it was in Greek. Why couldn't he have been taken to Italy?"

When he finished, Isabelle studied his sketch. "May I?" she asked, holding her hand out for the pencil. He passed it to her and watched as she erased a couple of the lines, redrawing them slightly different.

"That's it. How did you know?" Dante smiled at her proudly.

"It's a street corner not far from one of the Sarantos's villas. What else did he show you?"

"There was another drawing of the girls, only this time there were four of them. Then there was a street

264

that had purple flowers in a type of canopy."

"Wisteria," Isabelle confirmed.

"The last drawing was of the sea. The odd part was he had drawn this beautiful picture, rich with detail. Then I saw the pencil moving over the paper. He was quickly sketching a boat. It was a rough likeness, so I'm pretty sure he wasn't looking at a real boat, but drawing one from memory. Right before I lost the connection, he wrote four letters. M, A, G, and D. Does that mean anything to you?"

"Oh, god. I know where they've taken him. Dante, I know where Connor is!"

Chapter Thirty

ISABELLE WAS SHAKING. Whether it was the adrenaline crash, the fact she was mated to Dante, the knowledge Connor was possibly with Alexi, or all of the above, she didn't know. What she did know was she was ready to get her son back. *Their* son, as Dante called him. If she had any doubts before at accepting the mate bond with her Gargoyle, they flew out the window when he claimed a child he'd never met as his own. And the picture Connor had drawn of all three of them together? How could she deny there was something greater, something unexplainable, pulling them together? If her beautiful, smart, sweet boy could accept someone he had never met, how could she turn her back on that? She couldn't. She didn't want to.

She and Dante stood behind Tessa as she pulled various maps of Greece up on the computer monitors. The need to touch Dante now they were truly mates was far stronger than before. When they had worked closely for the last few weeks, the need had been palpable, tangible. Now, there was an urgency to the pull. If she didn't have him near her, skin to skin, she was going to suffocate. She wanted sex with him, yes. This went so far beyond sex. There was an invisible line tethering their souls together, winding around her heart, pulling her toward Dante. As if he could read her thoughts, he pulled her to stand in front of him, wrapping his arms around her, blanketing her in comfort. She placed her arms on top of his, allowing the bond to meld them into one being.

"There, that one," Isabelle told Tessa, indicating the map currently on the screen was the correct one according to Connor's drawings. "Zoom in to the south. Now east just a bit. There it is. That's the street the villa is on. This is located on Pochi. The homes on either side also belonged to Stavros. They used them as servant quarters."

Tessa whistled. "Damn, it pays well to be a slave to the rich."

Gregor hung up his cell phone. "That was Donovan. Alistair returned to the villa. He was furious when he found out his two prisoners were gone. Surprisingly, the only one he took his anger out on was Theron. Donovan's hidden cameras are few and far between, so when they took the fight outside, he didn't get to see the outcome."

"What about Eve? Did he mention her and Carter?" Isabelle asked Gregor.

"Yes, they are headed to Italy where she will be taken care of. Carter seems to think her being abducted has affected her mind. She talks to herself quite a bit."

"It makes sense now."

"What does, Beautiful?" Dante asked, placing a soft kiss on her temple.

"I was sure that I heard three women speaking to each other. According to Carter, there were no others in the villa. She must have been talking to herself. Gregor, please have Donovan get in touch with Carter. I feel she may be schizophrenic." Gregor nodded and left the room to make the call.

Dante hugged her a little tighter. "I want to move out first thing in the morning. Let's look at the maps and get ready."

"Something doesn't make sense. If Connor was talking about *The Magdalena*, it should be in Zakynthos. They have boats on every island where they own a home, and that's where it was."

"Maybe they moved the boat after what happened. It has been six years since you were here, Belle," Tessa reminded her.

Dante added, "Or, maybe Connor had a premonition. The drawing wasn't as detailed as the others."

"Maybe." Isabelle bit her lip between her teeth. She was anxious to get Connor back. She was also ready to be rid of Alexi once and for all. Julian was still working on the annulment.

Room service was ordered, and they ate while they planned. They spent the next few hours deciding the best way to go after Stavros and Alexi. Eventually, Isabelle could no longer hold her eyes open. Dante, noticing her yawns getting closer together, told Gregor and Tessa good night. Isabelle didn't protest. It had been an exhausting couple of days, and she wanted to be fresh in the morning when they went after her son. Even though she and Dante had completed the bond, she was nervous about sleeping with him. The sex earlier had been brought on by adrenaline. Would every time be as powerful, or would they be able to slow down and make love?

Dante shut the door behind them and headed straight to the large bathroom. Instead of turning on the shower, he opened the spigots on the huge jetted tub and began filling it with hot water. Taking his time, he slowly removed her clothes before undressing himself. She took in the amazing sight before her. Dante's lean body was beautiful. She let her gaze lower to his cock. It was long and hard, ready for her. He was taking in her body as well. His eyes drank her in from her face, down to her toes. When he lingered on her breasts, her nipples hardened, wanting his mouth there.

Dante closed the distance between them, but instead of touching her, he reached around her body and grabbed one of the fragrant oils lined up on the vanity. He poured the contents of the small bottle into the water. When the water was deep, he turned the handles off and stepped into the tub, holding his hand out for her. She stepped in, and they sat down. Dante leaned against the back of the tub, allowing Isabelle to settle against his chest. He gathered her hair into a ponytail and twisted it up behind her head so it wouldn't get wet. Using one of his large hands as a cup, he poured the scented water over her skin. Isabelle was amazed at the tenderness he was showing her. Even on his best day, Alexi had never tended to her needs. Dante continued to pet her. Contrary to the erection poking her in the back, he gave no indication he wanted anything from her. He was content in making her feel safe, cherished.

Isabelle couldn't stop her hands from touching him. She stroked his legs, enjoying the feel of the curls under her fingers. His arms held the same dark hair as his legs. The friction she felt when she rubbed his skin wasn't enough. Being naked in his arms was nice, but she wanted more. She turned her head so she could see his face. The look in his eyes was surprising. His pupils were dilated, his eyes hooded. She should have known by his hard cock he wanted her. He had to be using his shifter abilities to keep his breathing calm. "Kiss me," she breathed into his lips. Dante leaned closer and pressed their lips together. He touched his tongue to her mouth, and she opened for him. He took advantage, sliding his tongue along hers. The kiss was a slow, sensuous dance. One that told of things to come.

Isabelle arched her back and turned a little more, giving her better access. She wrapped one arm behind his head, pulling him closer. Dante's hands that had been gently caressing her skin moved from her toned stomach; one slid up to cup a breast, while the other delved between her thighs. He stroked her core with one finger, then two, causing her to push toward his hand. She wanted more. Isabelle couldn't stop the moan that left her mouth and entered his. She felt more than heard the rumble in his chest. Eventually she broke the kiss. "Make love to me." Dante's eyes flashed and with a quickness only a Gargoyle could manage, he stood, picking her up as he did. Cradling her close, he didn't bother drying them off. Instead, he carried her to the bedroom and laid her in the middle of the bed, stretching out over her.

Dante kissed her mouth as he rocked his hard cock against her clit. He teased her body, tormenting her in the best way. She wanted him with a fierceness she didn't understand. "Dante, please," she whimpered when he broke the kiss. His dark eyes indicated how badly he wanted her. In one slick movement, he was buried to the hilt inside her body. Isabelle's heart caught at the conflicted look in her mate's eyes. "Dante," she whispered, her voice catching.

"I'm right here, Beautiful. Always right here." Dante continued stroking her core, slow and steady. He rarely took his eyes off hers, only when he leaned in and touched their lips together. Her body was burning up from his thick erection, stretching her, filling her. He reached between them, using his thumb on her clit. Moving a little faster, a little harder, his breathing changed. His fangs slid out of his gums, his eyes dark with desire. "I'm close. I want you to come with me. Can you do that for me, Beautiful?"

His thumb was circling her clit, her own orgasm close. "Yes. Oh, god Dante. So close. Move. Faster." Isabelle was so close to coming. She had asked for love making, but she needed more. "Harder, baby, I… harder… please." Her mate gave her what she asked for. Rising on his knees, he wrapped his strong arms under her legs and gave it to her hard. His grunts were in sync with the slapping of their bodies. Isabelle's claws were unsheathed. She cried out incoherently as her orgasm hit, her clit pulsing. She grabbed hold of the bedding so she wouldn't rip into Dante's skin again. As soon as her core clamped down on Dante's cock, he shuddered hard inside her body, his grip on her legs almost to the point of painful. She watched his face as he came. It was a beautiful sight. As he came down from his high, he graced her with a look that said she was the sole reason for his existence. If she could see that look on his face every time they made love, she would withstand any amount of pain. She would give that to him.

Isabelle cupped his cheek in her hand. "Dante, I…" She what? She never felt that way before. She never wanted the night to end. She lov… No, it was too soon.

271

Dante rolled, tucking her in close. "I know, Beautiful. Me, too."

TREVOR WALKED INTO Lion Hart Gym, taking in the numerous men and few women working out. He was glad to see not everyone was built like the mammoth standing in front of him, talking to a teenager. Their conversation seemed tense, and Trevor tried his best not to eavesdrop. The name Troy floated across the teenager's lips as he clenched his fists at his sides. The large man finally noticed Trevor and whispered something to the kid who glanced back at Trevor before walking to the back of the building. The kid's face was a bruised mess. When the man approached Trevor, he had to look up. Way up.

"Can I help you?"

Trevor swallowed hard and cleared his throat. Where Dante and the warden were badasses, this man made them look like pansies. "I'd like to work out," Trevor told him, shuffling from one foot to the other.

Instead of laughing at Trevor, his face softened as he said, "My name's Geoffrey Hartley. I own the place. You are?"

"Trevor. Trevor McKenzie." He held his hand out, and surprisingly, the big man didn't squeeze it to the point of breaking.

"You look familiar, Trevor. Have I seen you around here before?"

"I don't think so. I work and go home. That's it."

"Come on, let me show you around. So, what kind

of work do you do?" Geoffrey asked him as they walked. The man seemed genuinely interested.

"I'm the M.E.'s assistant over at the hospital." They stopped walking when they came to the first machine.

"That's right, you work for Dante. I thought I recognized you. So, what are you looking for in a workout? You want to build muscle? Bulk up? Get ready for bikini season?"

Trevor gaped at the huge man standing before him. Was he seriously cracking jokes? "I, uh, just want to get in shape. Maybe build a little more muscle."

Geoffrey smiled and let out a small laugh. When he did, Trevor noticed how beautiful the man was. Not beautiful in a girly way, but off the-charts good-looking. It was crazy how a smile could transform someone from looking like they were about to rip your head off to something you knew you could never get enough of seeing. His size and ruggedness only made him that much more beautiful. The way he smiled and the tender way he talked to the teenager, this giant had a heart in his chest. Someone behind him cleared his throat. Geoffrey said, "Hey, Brother. I'll be with you in a minute."

Trevor felt a chill. Not a cold chill, just a zing running over his body. He was there. Jasper was there, and he was standing behind him. Trevor turned around, and sure enough, there he was. Instead of the ever-present smile, the confident grin, the badassedness, Trevor saw sadness in Jasper's eyes. "Hi, Trevor," he said, almost shyly.

"Hi." Trevor didn't know how to act. He was the one who'd run like a scared kid instead of a grown man. "I was thinking about joining the gym." *Real smooth, Mr. Obvious.*

"Jas, I need to take care of something really quick. Can you show Trevor around until I get back?" Geoffrey and Jasper were obviously more than friends. He called him brother. The same way Dante had called Gregor brother. He was further convinced there was indeed a club of badasses in New Atlanta. A club he would never be a part of.

"If it's okay with Trevor, sure." Jasper looked to Trevor for his consent.

"Yeah, it's fine." Trevor felt his face heating with embarrassment.

"Trevor, I'm sorry. You know, about yesterday," Jasper said after the owner walked away.

Jasper was dressed in his work clothes, and Trevor couldn't help but take in his appearance. It was a look he should be used to, but the way Jasper's arms filled the sleeves to almost bursting, it was just too sexy. Too much for Trevor to handle, especially in public. When they worked crime scenes together, Trevor had a dead body to concentrate on. Now, here in this testosterone-laden building, the bodies were anything except dead. As a matter of fact, his was coming to life more and more the longer he stood next to Jasper.

"You have nothing to be sorry for. I get it," Trevor said, even though he didn't really get it. He didn't understand why Jasper would have touched his face unless he felt sorry for him.

"You do?" Jasper sounded surprised.

"Yep. Just forget it. Do you want to show me around before the big guy gets back?"

Jasper cocked his head to the side, studying Trevor. He looked like he wanted to say something else, but what else was there to say? "Sure. I didn't know you were interested in working out. Let's start over here."

Jasper showed him all the machines and explained what each one was for. Afterwards, he pointed out other parts of the facility such as the boxing ring and the showers. "So, are we okay?" Jasper asked him when they were alone in the changing room.

He wasn't sure how to answer. Trevor really liked Jasper, but he didn't want him to be his friend out of pity. "I guess. I just…" He was interrupted when Geoffrey and the teenager from earlier came in the room.

"There you are. So, Trevor, what do you think?"

"I would like to take advantage of the trial offer. See how it works into my schedule and all that."

"Sounds good. Jasper, would you please take Matt here into the office? I'll get Trevor signed up, and then I'll be right in."

"Of course. Trevor, maybe we could work out together?" The insecure tone of Jasper's voice surprised Trevor. Maybe he was reading the situation all wrong.

"If you promise not to make fun of my non-badass form," Trevor said, seriously.

Jasper laughed, and the sound did strange things to Trevor's insides. Geoffrey's laugh had been beautiful, but Jasper's hit Trevor deep within his soul. "I promise," Jasper said, a tentative smile on his face. "Matt, let's go find some water. I need to cool off." He gave Trevor one more glance before leaving the room.

Geoffrey was looking at him with an odd expression. Instead of saying what was on his mind, the big man took him to the front of the building so he could get signed up. After he filled out the paperwork, he told the owner he'd be back the next day to get started.

He left the building, excited to be starting on his new body, but terrified he'd be working out with Jasper. He didn't think his heart could stand it. He knew his body couldn't. He would need to invest in really long, oversized T-shirts to hide the hard-on he'd no doubt get around Jasper.

Trevor walked down the sidewalk and turned the corner to the parking lot. A man was peering in the side window of the gym, his hands cupping his eyes to shade the sun. Using the key fob, Trevor beeped the locks on his car, letting the man know he wasn't alone. The stranger jumped when Trevor approached. He was a big man, not as big as the badass society, but not far off either. With a scowl, the man stalked off. *Creep.*

Chapter Thirty-One

DANTE RETURNED TO the condo after a quick trip to the pier. Thankfully, being a major tourist location, the shops opened early to attract the visitors disembarking the ships. Everyone was awake and at the breakfast table, but his eyes found Isabelle first who was dressed in Tessa's clothes. They looked good on her, but they weren't what she would normally wear.

"Good morning. I hope you saved some for me; I'm starving." He quickly went into the bedroom, deposited the packages filled with clothes on the bed, and returned to the dining area. "I took the liberty of doing a little shopping for you this morning," he told Isabelle as he placed a kiss on her cheek. He sat in the open chair next to her and picked up an English muffin, slathering it with butter and raspberry jelly. The quiet was almost deafening as he noticed everyone staring at him. "What?"

Isabelle placed a hand on his thigh and said, "Thank you. Your note was a little on the vague side."

He hadn't wanted her to panic when he left so early. His note had simply stated he would be back soon. Isabelle poured his coffee, leaving it black, the way he liked it. While they finished eating, Gregor filled them in on his conversation with Donovan. "Stavros still has most of the government in his pocket, but there are a few of the higher officials we can trust. I have the names of the detectives in their police department we can call once we know where the girls are."

Their plan was to find the kids and turn Stavros and Alexi over to the authorities. While they didn't know Stavros and Alexi were trafficking the abducted girls, they assumed that was the reason behind taking four girls who were so similar in characteristics. "Look," Tessa said, pointing to the television. She rose and grabbed the remote, turning the volume up on the local news channel.

The news anchor was saying, "Another child has gone missing from Piraeus Port. The fifth child, seven-year-old Lauren Chapman, has blonde hair and blue eyes." A picture of the girl popped up on the screen. Tessa turned the volume back down as her phone rang. When she saw who it was, she announced to the room, "It's Xavier." She ran her thumb across the phone and answered. "Dad, I'm putting you on speaker."

"Good morning, Sweetheart. Donovan filled me in on the rescue. Isabelle, it's good to have you back where you belong. Tessa, I promised I would call as soon as I knew something more on Stavros. It's not good. I want to take out the bastard myself. It took a lot of digging and calling in some favors, but I found out he has been abducting women for years. He takes them into his home, trains them to be the perfect mistress, and then releases them to the person who placed the order. It's like a mail-order bride service, only the women aren't brides. He kidnaps destitute women. He takes them in, giving them every amenity available: nice clothes, three meals a day, an extravagant villa to live in. By the time they figure out they are being given to someone else, they are so sucked into his game they don't object to being traded off."

"Gods, Dad, that's horrible. How did you find this out?"

"From one of the women he did this to. Once the woman is older and no longer attractive to whomever purchased her, she is traded for a younger model, shall we say. The older women are passed along to someone wanting a servant who has learned how to be a good and loyal employee. This particular woman wasn't wanted by anyone, so she was cast out into the street again. Since she had no employer, she didn't feel the confidentiality agreement she signed twenty years ago was still valid. One of my businesses in Italy is an employment agency. When this woman came in seeking a job, she listed her former employers and Stavros was one of them. Long story short, we pulled her aside and after a little coaxing, she told us her story. She is now a housekeeper for one of my Clan."

Dante pulled Isabelle into his lap. Her face had gone pale as she listened to Xavier talk about her father-in-law. Julian assured them he could get Isabelle's marriage to Alexi annulled. Dante wanted it done now. He didn't want Isabelle to feel connected to those monsters any longer than she had to be.

Tessa told her father, "That is disgusting, but if they can do that to women, it makes sense they would branch out to children. Gods, that makes me want to puke. We've got to get those girls back."

Gregor grabbed Tessa's hand. "We will, Red. We won't stop until all five of those girls are safe from the clutches of the Sarantos."

Dante felt Isabelle stiffen, so he tightened his arms around her, pouring every ounce of love he had into her through his touch.

279

"Good luck, and be careful. Donovan is on standby in case you need his assistance. Gregor, I don't have to tell you to take care of my girl. Tessa, I love you, Sweetheart."

"I love you too, Dad. Thanks." Tessa thumbed off the phone. "Those are some sick motherfuckers," she said, shaking her head in disgust.

The emotions swirling inside Isabelle were becoming stronger with each passing second. Her pain was reaching out and taking hold inside Dante's body. His heart was breaking as he felt the torment within her.

"How could I have been so stupid? I saw these women. I saw them but didn't know. I thought they were just random mistresses Stavros had at each of his villas. They never spoke, but they seemed happy enough. Oh god, I should have changed my name. Why didn't I change my name when I came back?"

Dante reached for the cloth napkin he hadn't used and gently wiped her tears. "You didn't know, Beautiful. How could you? This is obviously something Stavros has been doing a long time and is very good at. If the women had let on they were anything but happy, he wouldn't have been doing his job very well. Besides, from what you told me, you weren't in a good relationship at the time. You had your own life to worry about, am I correct?"

Isabelle nodded. "I don't want to be a Sarantos. I don't want anything to do with the name or the monsters who carry that name."

"We will take care of that as soon as the girls are safe and we get our son back. Speaking of which, I'm ready. Why don't you go take a shower and get
280

changed? Gregor and I will finalize plans, and when you're ready, we'll all move out." Dante pulled her face around and softly kissed her lips. The only thing he wanted more than to deepen the kiss and carry her to the shower was to get Connor back. She stood and walked to the bedroom, closing the door.

"Godsdamn bastards. She won't be a Sarantos after today." His fangs were cutting into his lip. His beast was ready to rid the world of two vile men so they couldn't hurt anyone else ever again, especially his family. He was going to have to be stronger today than he'd ever been in his life. The right thing to do was to find and detain Alexi and Stavros and let the police handle them. Dante didn't know if he could do the right thing.

Gregor placed his hand on Dante's neck, effectively calming him. "Truth, Brother. Let's get packed and go get your boy."

STAVROS SHOULD HAVE taken Connor to another villa. After his first run-in with Alexi, he planned to do just that, but he found Connor had a calming effect on the girls. After watching Alexi drug the first child into submission, he felt something he thought was lost a long time ago: compassion. When Stavros found Connor in the girls' room, talking to them comfortingly, he decided to stay where they were. As soon as Alexi had all five girls, the transactions would be completed, and they could get on with their new lives having Connor around. Of course, they would have to keep Connor hidden away from almost everyone. He didn't need his grandson telling the wrong person about the girls.

Alexi strode into the kitchen and poured a cup of coffee. Stavros stared at his son. Alexi's easy, infectious personality had disappeared into the sea six years ago. He hadn't wanted to marry Isabelle but did it anyway out of duty for the family. Stavros knew all about the whores Alexi had scattered across Greece. Alexi didn't make a move his father wasn't aware of. He had been overjoyed when Alexi miraculously reappeared after a month of thinking his only son was dead. That joy was short-lived when Stavros began to see the changes taking place. Alexi was cold and distant. Cruel and calculating. That was the look he currently had on his face. His son was up to something, and that worried him.

Stavros hadn't bothered to wake Connor. The boy was obviously scared of Alexi, so whenever they were at the villa at the same time, Stavros allowed Connor to stay quietly tucked in his room, drawing. Five little girls were all sound asleep in the other rooms, no doubt having been drugged the night before. Alexi walked over to the table and grabbed a piece of bacon. "The girls are all yours. I'm taking my kid and going fishing," he announced as if he were talking about the weather.

"I beg your pardon?" Stavros had seen the way Alexi acted around Connor. Stavros wasn't scared of his son, but something in his gut nagged at the thought of Alexi being alone with Connor. "I don't think that's a good idea. Besides, we need to get the girls to the meeting. The buyers will be there this afternoon."

"That's not my problem, old man. My job was to get the girls. Your job is to conclude the transactions. That's the way it's always been. No need to change now. Besides, I'm ready for some down time, and that includes taking the boat out for a few days. You don't need the kid getting in your way while you are conducting business. It's time I get to know my son." If the tone of Alexi's voice wasn't warning enough, the darkened look in his eyes was. Stavros knew better than to argue, though. This Alexi wasn't one to be ordered around or bargained with. Somewhere along the line, their roles had reversed.

He couldn't sit still and allow Alexi to take Connor without him speaking to the boy first. He followed his son to Connor's room. Alexi threw open the door. "Let's go kid. Get up."

"I'm up." And he was. As usual, Connor had the pad of paper in his lap, the colored pencils lined up neatly in front of him. There was no disorder, no chaos where the child was concerned. Stavros had no idea how Isabelle raised him, but he was almost appreciative. Stavros stepped around Alexi who was leaned against the door frame, arms folded across his massive chest.

"Connor, I have some business to attend today. Your father is going to take you out on the boat for a while. Let's get your things together so you can get going."

"He's not my father," Connor muttered as he did as he was told. If the boy insisted on being difficult with Alexi, the outcome would not be good.

"I know it's all a little new for you, but you and Alexi need this time to get to know one another. I will

283

take care of business and check on you later today. If you don't like the boat, you can come back home."

"Why the fuck are you coddling him? What's happening to you, old man? You're turning into a sap all because of the kid." Alexi didn't wait for an answer. He turned and headed back toward the kitchen.

"He is not my father," Connor said again, this time louder.

"If you continue to insist, I will have a paternity test done. Do you know what that is?" Connor shook his head no. "It's a test where it shows you and Alexi have the same DNA in your bodies. He is your father, so you might as well get used to the fact."

"My father's coming to save me," Connor stated with such finality that Stavros took a step back. He stood speechless as the boy gathered the few clothes they had purchased and neatly placed them in his backpack. He tore the top sheet out of his sketchpad, crumpling it up and tossing it in the garbage. He placed the pad and pencils inside the bag with his clothing. He was already dressed save his shoes. Once he placed those on his feet and tied the strings, he placed the backpack over his shoulders. "I'm ready."

Stavros didn't know what to make of the boy. He was only six, but carried himself with the maturity of a teen. He motioned for Connor to precede him out the door. As they were walking down the hall, Connor stopped for a few seconds, cocking his head to the side as if listening for something. As quickly as he stopped, he started again. Stavros felt a shift in the air. Something about that moment scared the shit out of him.

Chapter Thirty-Two

ISABELLE WAS ONCE again sitting in the back seat of the SUV beside Dante. She was wearing comfortable clothes he had picked out for her. Clothes she herself would have chosen. She liked that the bra and panties he picked were matching lace numbers. Everything he bought her fit perfectly. She had to wonder how he knew her sizes, unless he had looked at the tags on her dirty clothes. No matter how he knew, it warmed her heart he had taken the time to go shopping for her. These gifts were so much more intimate than the chocolate diamond bracelet sitting at home on her dresser.

After her mini melt down, she had showered quickly. She was ready to get her son back. If Dante's visions were accurate, Connor could be in Zakynthos on *The Magdalena*. She really hoped not. If she never set foot on a boat again, it would be too soon. At least this time she would have Dante by her side. She had no desire to come face to face with either Alexi or his father, but she would do whatever necessary to get her son away from them.

When they arrived at the villa Connor had drawn, Gregor slowly drove past. This particular villa wasn't as secluded as most of the ones Stavros owned. This one was just off a main thoroughfare and easily accessible from the road. Isabelle had told them as much about the layout of the grounds as she could remember. She had only visited this particular home a couple of times, and it had been six years ago. They had decided searching for the girls and Connor in the daytime would be less conspicuous. If they happened to get caught, they could claim to be tourists looking for their rental home.

Gregor parked a few blocks down from the home in a public lot which led to a small pier. Tessa grabbed her backpack out of the rear of the SUV and placed the straps over her shoulders. Tessa's bag was filled with all sorts of gadgets. After they had explained how Tessa supplied the Gargoyles with the tech toys used in her rescue, Isabelle had a new appreciation for how much of a genius her father was. The couples walked down the sidewalk, holding hands, taking in the scenery. To anyone passing them, they looked like any other tourists with their sunglasses and casual clothing.

When they approached the first house that was used as a servant's quarters, they all stopped under the guise of Gregor tying his shoelace. All four of them reached out with their shifter senses. The men, being Gargoyles, had keener hearing, but the women listened anyway. After it was determined the house was empty, they continued on, walking past the main house. Each shifter listened as they passed, not hearing anyone inside. Standing in front of the second servant's home, the women took pictures of the other couple with their phones. Finding that house empty as well, they circled back to the main house.

They walked around the house to a side door leading into the garage. Tessa pulled a small black kit out of her backpack along with a small electronic looking box. She placed the box over the alarm and after a few seconds, the alarm was disabled. With a quickness Isabelle admired, Tessa picked the lock on the door. She used her shirt to turn the doorknob, careful not to leave fingerprints. They all entered the garage that was empty of vehicles. Gregor stepped into the house first, listening again for any sign of life inside. "Clear," he said, and the others followed him inside. Isabelle led the way up the stairs to the kitchen.

Leftover breakfast dishes were still on the table. Isabelle noticed only one place setting. The food had barely been touched. Tessa picked up the coffee cup. "It's cold." She walked to the coffee pot and placed her hand on the carafe. "It's still warm. Whoever was here hasn't been gone long." Other than the table, the room was immaculate.

Isabelle, remembering the layout of the house, headed for the bedrooms. The first door she came to showed a made up bed that looked like it had been sat upon. A box of crayons sat atop the dresser. Her heart clenched. "Connor," she whispered as she stepped farther into the room. Dante came up behind her and picked the crayons up, closing his eyes. She didn't know how his special abilities worked. "Are you getting something?" she asked, holding her breath.

"No, Beautiful, it doesn't work that way. I just wanted to feel close to him for a moment."

That could possibly be the sweetest thing she had ever heard in her life. Dante picked up the garbage can and pulled out the crumpled-up piece of paper. He unfolded the paper, placing it on the dresser, using his large hands to carefully smooth it out. "This is the same picture as before; he's added to it though. This little girl is the fifth, the same one from the news broadcast. And those two are new." Dante pointed at

287

the men. "He has Stavros standing with the girls. Alexi is off to the side with himself. If this isn't a clue, I'll streak my hair purple like Trevor's."

Gregor and Tessa were somewhere down the hall. "In here, Brother," Gregor called to them. Dante folded the paper neatly and put it in the side pocket of his cargo shorts. He and Isabelle took in the sight of the next two rooms. Both beds were still unmade, and a stuffed penguin was lying on the floor. There was a jar on one of the beds containing a dead lizard. "The girls were here," Tessa said, peeking into the last room on the hall. "We must have just missed them. We need to figure out where they would go."

Isabelle said, "I know where the office is. Follow me." She led them to the office on the far end of the villa.

As they were walking, Dante said, "We found a drawing Connor left. I'm pretty sure he was letting us know Stavros has taken the girls, and he is with Alexi."

Gregor nodded. "If that's the case, we may need to split up. First we need to figure out where they've gone."

The office was immaculate, like the rest of the house. There were no papers strewn about the desk, no stray coffee cups marring the surface. The only article on the desk was a laptop. Tessa pulled latex gloves out of her backpack and opened the computer. As soon as it powered up, she began typing away, various files flashing quickly as she opened several folders. Isabelle watched in amazement as Tessa expertly searched. "There. What a fuckin' idiot. Even though his files are encrypted, he didn't have a password." She pulled a thumb drive out of a small pocket on her backpack and inserted it in the side of the computer. She began typing codes into the laptop until the encryption was broken, copying the files from Stavros's hard drive. "We can't use this as evidence with the police, but if he somehow gets away from us today, I want to have the evidence we need to at least confront him."

As the information was copying, Tessa opened Stavros calendar. In pencil, he had scribbled noon. "Look, something's going down today, in just a few hours. I bet he's offloading the girls. Question is, where? Belle, do you have any idea of properties they own that would be off the grid?"

Isabelle was thinking when Gregor's phone rang. "Stone. Hey, Donovan. That's great news. Text me the address and we'll head that way. Yeah, thanks." Gregor hung up and relayed the information, "One of Donovan's men is a computer genius, much like Julian. He spent all night hacking into Stavros's system. He found one email between a buyer and Stavros regarding the purchase of one of the girls and the meeting place. Stavros responded telling him to never email him again. Obviously, he didn't want the electronic trail, but the damage had been done. Lucky for us. The meeting is today at noon, and Donovan's sending us the address. He's meeting us there, just in case we need back up."

Tessa pulled the thumb drive out of the computer and closed it back down. They retraced their steps, making sure they didn't leave fingerprints or any evidence they'd been there. Isabelle's stomach was in knots. She took a couple of deep breaths, calming herself. It would do no good to lose her breakfast. Once they were seated in the vehicle, Dante laced their fingers together. Her body immediately calmed even further. She would never yell at him again for helping her gain control of her emotions.

The address led them to another villa. This one was secluded and gated. The property was surrounded by a beautiful, ornate fence. Olive trees lined the driveway. The road leading to the villa was void of traffic as this was one of the few properties on the street. Even though it was secluded, they couldn't sit and wait without being seen. "Isabelle, are you familiar with this place?" Gregor asked as he pulled over to the side of the street.

She didn't answer. Couldn't. Her throat was closing up, and she wasn't able to breathe. The one and only time she had been here had been when she was sick. She had taken off from work because she had the flu, and Alexi insisted they get away from Zakynthos for a while. He thought a change of scenery would do her good. All the change did was make Alexi even more intolerable than usual. She was sick, and he was drinking. He didn't care how bad she felt, only that she had neglected his sexual needs for too long. Isabelle had come downstairs to get a drink of water and her antibiotics. Before she could make it to the sink, Alexi grabbed her, pushing her face first over the arm of the sofa. Her fever kept her from wearing too many clothes. Dressed only in a sheer nightie and panties, she was easy prey for her husband.

He dragged the panties down her thighs and forced her legs apart. She fought back as best she could, but her body was weak. He was so much larger than her anyway, she had no choice but to let him take her. And he did. Alexi took her, bare. That's the thing that always stuck out most in Isabelle's mind. Alexi never had sex with her without a condom. Even though she was on the pill, he made it perfectly clear he wasn't ready for kids. Between him spilling his seed without the use of protection and Isabelle's contraceptives being made ineffective by the medicine, Alexi got exactly what he didn't want that night. A child.

"Isabelle. Izzy, look at me." She was no longer the wife being raped. She was now a little girl, bouncing on someone's knee. She was giggling and clapping her hands. "Izzy's my girl, aren't you? The only one who loves me. Promise you'll never leave me, Izzy. Promise Gabriel." There was that name again, the same one Vincent mentioned.

"Belle!" Tessa's voice was like ice water. Isabelle's eyes focused, and all three of them were staring at her. She was sitting on Dante's lap.

"Beautiful, what happened? Where did you go just then?" Dante was frowning, not his usual somber look. Dante was scared.

"I..." She cleared her throat and wiped her hands down her face. "Yes, I know this place. It doesn't have happy memories. What do you want to know?" Isabelle would think on her vision of herself as a child later.

"Belle, are you sure you're okay? You look like you saw a ghost." Tessa was turned in her seat, looking at her much the same way Dante was.

"You could say that. But yes, I'm fine. Just... Gregor, you're going to need to park somewhere on the main road. There is nowhere to park here without being seen. The fence surrounds the property completely. The house sits on a couple acres that slopes down to the beach. There is a private gate we can probably get in. After that, we'll need to climb the steep path leading up to the house."

"Probably?" Tessa asked.

Isabelle nodded and remembered who she was talking to. "I guess since it's you, definitely. I haven't seen a lock you couldn't pick." She felt Dante tense up beneath her. Turning from Tessa, she asked, "Dante, what is it?"

"Connor…" Dante shut his eyes and held still. Isabelle held her breath, not wanting to disturb him. When he opened his eyes, he sighed. "That's a first. I felt the tug at my brain. Either he just figured out how to open the connection himself, or…"

"Or what?" Isabelle asked.

Dante shook his head. "He's on an airplane."

"Oh god, he's taking him to the boat. I just know it." Isabelle couldn't stop the tears from rolling down her cheeks.

"Dante, we need to split up. Call ahead and have the jet readied. You and Isabelle go to Zakynthos, and Tessa and I will handle things here," Gregor said as he pulled back onto the road, heading toward the airport. Isabelle moved off Dante's lap and put her seatbelt back on. Dante placed the call to the pilot who was on standby.

"We need a taxi." Isabelle was anxious to get to Connor, but she also didn't want them to miss rescuing those five little girls, too. "If you drive us to the airport, you won't have time to get back here before the meeting."

"Dammit, you're right," Gregor said as he kept his

eyes on the road.

"Head back toward town. The farmer's market brings in tourists. We'll be able to find a cab there." Isabelle couldn't admire the beautiful scenery floating by. If she had been paying attention earlier, she would have been prepared when arriving at that particular location. Having had six years to suppress the memory of Connor's conception, she had learned to look at it as a blessing. Dante's strong hand pulled her smaller one to his lips.

"I'm not going to pry, but if you ever want to tell me what happened, just know I'm here for you. I'm here for you in every way you need me to be. I will not judge you or abandon you for anything you tell me." He kissed her knuckles again before threading their fingers together. She leaned her head against his shoulder. It seemed to be her favorite spot on his body.

The drive into town was quick. Gregor found a parking spot out of the way, and they all exited the SUV. Gregor pulled out his phone to call Donovan while Dante opened the back hatch and pulled his suitcase out. Isabelle had added her new clothes to his since they only had the one piece of luggage.

Isabelle was surprised when Tessa pulled her in for a hug. "I'm so proud of you, Belle. You may not realize this, but you are the strongest woman I know. Let us get the girls out of there safely, and Gregor and I will come help you." Tessa leaned back and smiled at Isabelle, tears in both their eyes. Isabelle had been mad at Tessa for a while. Now she was glad they were getting closer. Isabelle had never had a real friend before. They had their arms around each other when Isabelle felt Tessa tense up. "Tessa, what is it?"

293

Tessa was staring hard in the direction of the market. "I thought I saw…"

"Who? Gordon's dead. You don't have to worry about him any longer."

Tessa shook her head. "No. I thought it was Tamian."

Isabelle squeezed her a little tighter. Tessa had to be missing her brother. The bond they shared was as strong as any she'd had ever seen. Speaking of bonds, Isabelle hadn't missed the closeness between Dante and Gregor. She had been a bit jealous at first. Envious they could finish each other's sentences. Could know what the other was thinking without speaking. Isabelle knew it was something deeper than just Dante's special abilities. Theirs was a closeness that defied any relationship Isabelle had ever encountered. Now, she wasn't jealous. She was happy for Dante as well as for Gregor. She longed for a connection that deep. Gregor and Tessa had it. Now that she and Dante were true mates, she felt it in her soul they would have it, too.

The men touched their foreheads together, whispered their farewells, and broke apart. Both their eyes were shining with unshed tears. It did something to Isabelle's heart, seeing these two alpha Gargoyles openly showing their emotions for each other. These were the type of men who would be raising her son, and maybe someday soon, her other children. She knew as close as the Clan was, all the Gargoyles would have an influence over Connor. Taking him under their wings, figuratively and literally. She didn't know if her child would remain human or if he would become a shifter. Either way, he would be taught and nurtured by these alpha males who weren't afraid to openly love

294

with everything they had. How had she gotten so lucky?

Chapter Thirty-Three

DANTE HAILED A taxi, tossing their suitcase in the trunk. He and Isabelle settled into the back seat for the hour-long drive to the airport. Gregor and Tessa were going to search the villa. If there was any evidence Stavros was there with the girls, Gregor was going to alert the authorities and let them handle the situation. Gregor and Tessa would remain until that happened. If he wasn't there, they would switch to plan B. Donovan's computer hacker had sent them a list of every known, as well as a few unknown, properties the Sarantos family owned. If Stavros didn't arrive by noon, Donovan and some of his Clan would split the list with Gregor and Tessa. They would search each one until the girls were found.

Dante had no idea what would happen once they arrived on Zakynthos. He didn't want to worry Isabelle any more than she already was. Connor had surprised him when he sought their connection. What he kept from Isabelle was Connor was scared. He believed the boy had been able to reach him out of fear. Neither one said much on the drive. Isabelle was lost in thought, and Dante wanted to keep his mind clear in case Connor tried to reach him again.

Once they arrived at the airport, Dante paid the driver and took their suitcase. The plane was prepped and ready. When they were seated, the pilot put them in line for take-off. The airport was busy, but they were soon in the air. The flight from Athens to Zakynthos would take less than an hour. Once on the island, they had a rental car waiting. They were going directly to the boat and prayed it was still docked.

Dante led Isabelle to the bedroom in the back of the jet. "Let's relax, Beautiful." Dante stretched out on the bed, and Isabelle snuggled in next to him. With her head on his shoulder and an arm around his waist, Dante wrapped her up tightly, pouring every bit of peace into her he could. His beast understood his need to just *be* with his mate. The bond pull was there, but it wasn't a sexual need.

The silence was disrupted when Isabelle whispered, "He raped me."

Dante's body tensed, his beast howling inside. His mind was murderous. He was going to kill the motherfucker as soon as he saw him. "Isabelle, you don't have to…"

"Yes, I do. The villa back there, when I freaked out? I was remembering. I was sick with the flu. For some reason, he wanted to get away from his father, so we went to that particular villa. He accused me of ignoring his needs because I was sick. I was too weak to fight him off. I kept telling him no, that I didn't want it, but he was too strong. That's the night I conceived Connor. I never thought about an abortion, even though my baby was the product of anger, not love."

"You are so precious, Isabelle. I admire you. You kept your baby even though he served as a reminder of a tremendous wrong that had been done to you. How strong you are. I haven't seen you with Connor, but I'm sure he loves you as much as you love him. I cannot wait to get you both home and start our lives together. I've always wanted a son." He kissed her hair, stroked

297

her arm, continuing to allow his energy to flow from his fingertips into her skin.

"He does love me. I hate everything that's happened, but just like his conception, all the bad is leading up to the good. I have a feeling he already loves you. I don't understand how he knows about you though. I know he's special, with his artistic abilities, and his intelligence is off the charts. I had no idea he had any kind of other gifts. I wish I knew if he was going to be a shifter. I don't think we can hide that part of you from him."

"I don't want to hide what we are from him. Remember, you're a shifter, too. He is going to be around Gargoyles the rest of his life. Whether he transitions or not, he needs to be aware of us, learn about our ways. I want to train him as if he will be a shifter, if that's okay with you."

"What type of training?" Isabelle leaned up on an elbow, looking down into his face.

He couldn't help the smile forming at his lips. He could see Connor with his small sword running among the large Gargoyles. "Frey has begun sword training. I am letting him use my property since it is secluded yet open. I hope that won't be a problem."

"You want Connor to learn to use a sword?" she asked incredulously.

"I want you to learn as well. I will have Uri make you a special sword, a lighter version of the one we use so you will be able to wield it. If a war is coming, we all need to be prepared. Unless you plan on poisoning our foes, you will need to be able to protect yourself should I happen to be elsewhere."

"You and I both know I'm much better with a

syringe than I would be with a weapon, but I think it would be interesting to learn."

"Will it bother you to have Gargoyles coming and going on a regular basis?"

"Why would it bother me? It's your home." Isabelle's words cut him. Deep. Did she not want to be together?

"We are mates now. I want you in my home. Our home. If you don't like the house I have, we can build one together, more to your liking. But regardless, I don't want you and Connor living anywhere but with me. I've been thinking." He continued before she could say no, "Jonas is looking after Maria, and she's expected to make a full recovery. I think it wise for her to move in with us as well. Connor is used to having her around, and she is going to need her family now Rico is gone."

"How did I get so lucky?" Isabelle asked before she pressed their lips together.

"Is that a yes?"

Isabelle kissed him again and breathed "yes" into his mouth. Before they could turn the kiss into something heated, the pilot alerted them they would be landing soon. Dante's heart was nearly full. One small hurdle, getting Connor back, and it would be overflowing.

As soon as the plane landed, Dante and Isabelle got in the waiting SUV and headed toward the marina. He could feel the nervous energy rolling off his mate as they closed in on their destination. The two sides to his psyche were warring against the other. The side that contained his special abilities was fighting hard to remain calm, keep his mind open in case Connor reached out. The other side, the beast, was tearing at his insides to be let loose. As soon as Isabelle had confessed what Alexi had done to her, the beast within had ravaged to get revenge for his mate. The closer to Alexi and Connor they got, the stronger the beast was.

The marina came into view, and Isabelle began shaking. Dante couldn't imagine the strength needed to live her life as she had. Thinking back to all the bad she had been through, Dante wanted to give her the good. The best. After finding a parking spot, he grabbed her hand, squeezing it. "Let's go get our son."

WHAT THE FUCK kind of kid didn't like fishing? Stavros had insisted the kid had a name. Connor. Where the hell had she gotten the name? After someone she fucked, probably. He refused to call him by his stupid name. Why he thought taking the bitch's spawn out on the boat was a good idea was beyond reason. All the brat wanted to do was draw. Sure, he had some talent, but sitting with your head down had to get boring.

The waters were calm, unlike Alexi's mood. He had dropped anchor half an hour ago. From the time they had left the villa to now, the kid had yet to say a word. Fine by him. Silence made for better fishing anyway. Alexi was now rethinking sending the crew away. When he did it, he had been thinking he didn't need an audience if he lost his temper. Had he let the crew remain on board, he would have had a babysitter. Now he was stuck taking care of the kid by himself.

As he walked by where the kid was sitting, he

noticed what he was drawing. *Fuck.* Alexi couldn't believe his eyes. Even a bastard like him could appreciate the talent it took to draw an exact replica of *The Magdalena.* Not only were the boat's details precise, but the kid had captured the blue of the sea, the depth of the water, the horizon, everything. Alexi didn't need to look around to know the picture could have been taken with a camera. The kid was adding something else to the picture, but he didn't stick around to find out what.

ISABELLE LED DANTE to the slip where *The Magdalena* used to be docked. Her heart caught when she found the space was empty. "Here, this is the spot," she told him, gesturing with her hand.

"That's quite a large slip. Just exactly how big is their boat?" Dante asked.

"It's not their biggest, but probably around one hundred feet?" All she knew was it wasn't big enough. Had it been larger, she may have been able to hide from Alexi that night.

"We need a boat of our own. Let's go see if there are any rentals available." Dante gently took her hand and was headed for the office when a familiar face came toward them.

"Carter, what are you doing here?" Isabelle asked. The closer he got, though, she realized something was off.

"Dante, Isabelle?" he asked as if he didn't know who they were. Isabelle found herself behind Dante.

Obviously, he felt something was off as well.

The man held his hands up defensively. "My name's Hunter. I'm Carter's brother. Donovan called and told me to be on the lookout for you. I'm here to assist, should you need my services."

Isabelle stepped from around Dante and took in Hunter's features as the two males shook hands. She could see no physical differences in Hunter and his brother; only his voice was different. Deeper. Their looks were identical, yet Hunter carried himself differently. Where Carter had been serious yet relaxed, there was something cautious, more rigid about his brother. His eyes weren't soft. Hunter's eyes held the look of someone battle-scarred, hardened. "Are you and Carter twins?" She couldn't help her curiosity. Why she was surprised there were Gargoyle twins, she didn't know.

"Yes, he and I are an anomaly. As far as we know, we are the only twins of our kind." Hunter barely looked at Isabelle. Instead, he kept his eyes on Dante when speaking.

"Hunter and Carter aren't your average Greek names," Isabelle said, more as a thought than expecting a response.

"My brother and I have reinvented ourselves several times over the years. Our given names are Castor and Hector. We wanted modern names to fit in with our modern lives." Hunter's attention was still on Dante when he spoke. "Donovan filled me in as much as he could on your situation. Is there anything I can do to help?"

Dante pulled Isabelle close to his side, wrapping his arm around her shoulder. "We believe our son is on

The Magdalena. Isabelle hasn't been here in six years, so they may have moved the boat from this marina. The slip it was kept in back then is now empty."

"Let's go back to the office, and I will look that up." Hunter walked away from the empty slip, and she and Dante followed.

"So you work here, Hunter?" Isabelle knew Gargoyle's had all kinds of jobs; it just seemed a little menial for someone with his temperament.

"You could say that. I own the marina." He didn't elaborate. He said nothing else until they reached his office. Isabelle had been in the office before, a long time ago. She didn't remember seeing Hunter there. She would definitely have remembered someone like him. "Please, have a seat. Can I get you anything, coffee or water perhaps?" Both she and Dante asked for water. Hunter produced two bottles out of a refrigerator and passed them out. He poured himself a cup of coffee and sat behind his computer. He tapped on the computer keys.

Isabelle felt Dante tense beside her. She looked at his face and saw his eyes were closed. *Connor.* She caught Hunter's attention and put her finger to her lips, motioning for him to remain quiet. She sat still, waiting while her son contacted Dante. Hunter arched an eyebrow, questioning what was happening in front of him but quickly looked away. Isabelle found it odd a Gargoyle of his size would be shy around a female.

Dante opened his eyes and found hers. He squeezed her hand and smiled. "I know where they are. Hunter, I trust you to keep what I'm about to tell you between us." Dante waited until Hunter gave his word. "Isabelle's son and I have a connection of sorts.

He contacts me mentally and shows me pictures. Isabelle, this time he drew an exact replica of *The Magdalena*. He has seen the boat, not just what he thinks a large boat should look like. He also drew another picture. In this one he was looking off the deck into the water. The calm water. Connor drew himself into the picture, his feet propped against the rail, his pad in his lap. He drew a picture of himself sitting on the boat drawing. He's okay."

Hunter cocked his head to the side. "That's some connection. I understand it, though. Carter and I communicate in much the same way." Hunter looked off as if he were thinking of his brother. "Anyway, I checked our records. Sarantos still uses that slip, so Alexi and your son are out on the water. You said the water was calm. That means they have anchored somewhere. Alexi is an avid fisherman. If we're lucky, he will have found a good spot and will stay put." He went back to work on his computer. "There are approximately fifty boats on the water, twenty of which are larger vessels. Ten are anchored. I will contact a few of my men and we will head out. Give me a few minutes."

Hunter made several phone calls, giving orders to look for *The Magdalena*. Once the boat was spotted, Hunter would take over. He stood and said, "Let's go for a little ride."

As they walked, Isabelle asked, "If you are in Greece, do you not have to declare your loyalty to the Greek King?"

Hunter's face was blank when he responded. "Who says I haven't? Carter and I are of Greek decent. Our families have been loyal to Alistair for centuries.

Let's just say my brother and I don't agree with the way things have been deteriorating for a while now. We aren't the only ones. By some twist of the fates, we met Donovan. After a while, we figured out he felt the same way. For several years, we have secretly been forming alliances with others who aren't happy with our King. While we live and serve in Greece, our true loyalties lie with King Xavier."

"That's good to hear. Alistair is causing trouble for our King in the Americas. We feel a war is on the horizon, and it's a relief to know we will have allies on several fronts," Dante said.

They boarded a small boat, one perfect for a family of four. If anyone saw them on the water, they would look like any other couple taking a rental boat out for the day. They sat on the upper deck close to Hunter. He and Dante talked strategy while Isabelle found herself taking in the sea. It had been six years since she had been on a boat. Before the incident with Alexi, Isabelle had loved the water. Most of the time when they went out, Alexi would fish and leave Isabelle to her books. She would stretch out on a lounge chair on the large front deck and relax. The servants made sure her beverage of choice never ran out.

Looking back, she had enjoyed life on the water, even if the trips were few and far between. Her schedule at the hospital had been grueling. When she had the day off, she actually looked forward to their boat outings. The peacefulness of the water allowed her a day of relaxation. Those were the only days she could remember Alexi being somewhat pleasant. If they were stuck at home together, he was typically in a foul mood. The water had a calming effect on him as well.

"Isabelle. Izzy!" Dante was calling her name, bringing her out of her memories. *Izzy.* Why did he keep calling her that? She shook off her mental sluggishness and looked at him. His face was serious. "We found them."

Chapter Thirty-Four

DANTE'S BEAST WAS begging for a fight. He explained his feelings to Hunter, needing to know how the other Gargoyle felt about the situation. Hunter remembered the accident years ago. He had just bought the marina and was part of the search for Alexi. He had been pissed when Alexi showed up out of the blue after so many man hours had been spent searching for him. Hunter knew both Sarantos men by reputation, and he would not feel bad if either one of them disappeared for good.

One of Hunter's men spotted *The Magdalena* and called the location in. Hunter found the larger vessel and stopped a few hundred yards away. They were close enough to use their shifter eyesight and far enough the crew of the yacht wouldn't think anything about another boat being out on the water. They couldn't pull alongside without the crew of the larger boat's assistance, thus taking any element of surprise away.

"I'll swim," Dante said his thoughts aloud. "You stay here, and I'll swim. I will disarm any of the crew members who get in my way and still be able to surprise Alexi. If he should put up a fight, let's just say he won't win. I will flag you down when I have Connor safe, and you can pull alongside."

Isabelle protested, "Dante, this is my fight. I can't let you do this."

He appreciated the sentiment, but did she really

307

think he was going to let her fight her husb…Alexi alone? "Beautiful, if you think for one second I'm going to let him anywhere near you, then you don't know me very well." He pulled her body to his, brushing the loose strands of her hair out of her eyes. "This is what Gargoyles do. We take care of our families. You and Connor are my family, and I'll be damned if I allow Alexi to harm either one of you." He kissed her forehead. "This is settled. I'm going to get our son back."

He removed his shirt and shoes. "Hunter, I trust you to keep my mate safe while I'm gone." Dante knew the threatening tone wasn't necessary, but his mate was a beautiful woman.

"On my honor," Hunter responded, fisting his heart and bowing his head. The solemn oath spoken by a Gargoyle indicated he would lay down his life for the mate of another.

Dante pulled Isabelle to him. This time the kiss wasn't gentle. He crashed their mouths together, pouring all his love from his body into hers. He ended the kiss abruptly and whispered, "I love you." He gave her no time to respond as he dove into the waters of the Ionian Sea.

He thought about trying to contact Connor, but decided it was better if the boy wasn't expecting him. Connor was a bright child, but he was only six. Dante glided through the sea until he was close enough to get a good look at the boat. Treading water, he searched for signs of life other than Connor and Alexi. Surprisingly, Dante couldn't detect any others on board. This was going to be too easy. He swam closer and saw Connor was no longer sitting on the deck. He was standing with his little fists clenched. Alexi was holding the sketchpad, flipping through the pages. Dante didn't bother diving under the water. Instead he used his Gargoyle strength and swam on top of the water, long stroke after long stroke pulling him closer to his son.

Dante reached the back of the boat and pulled himself out of the water. He quietly climbed the stairs of the transom and paused. He listened once again for crew members. When he found none he headed to the bow where the arguing continued. The scene before him had his beast roaring. Not wanting to scare Connor, Dante tamped down his anger, kept himself from phasing. Connor didn't need a crash course in all things Gargoyle.

"You little shit. I'm your father, and you will do as I say," Alexi yelled.

"You are not my father. He is," Connor yelled back, pointing at Dante as he approached. His heart caught in his throat as Connor claimed him. Alexi whirled around, dropping the sketchpad on the wet deck. Connor scrambled to pick it up, clutching it to his chest.

"Who the fuck are you, and how did you get on-board?" Alexi looked at the water, searching for another boat.

"As he said, I'm his father, and I've come for my son." Dante stepped toward Connor, but Alexi got there first. He grabbed the boy around the neck and pulled a knife out of nowhere. Dante froze.

"Alexi, let the boy go. No matter what happens here, you are finished. You're going to jail for kidnapping." Dante didn't like the cruel glint he saw in

Alexi's eyes. The knife was precariously close to Connor's throat.

"You can't kidnap your own kid," Alexi said with a smirk.

"Da, please," Connor whispered.

Dante made the mistake of looking at Connor's face. His boy was scared. His beast was furious. "As I stated previously, Connor is my son. I have the papers to prove it. Besides, he is not the only child you have taken. Those five little girls you abducted are now safe with the authorities, and your father is in custody. You will rot alongside him in prison." Dante was bluffing. They hadn't heard from Gregor since parting ways.

Alexi flushed, and he yelled at Dante, "You can't prove anything."

"Oh, but I can. I followed you at the pier when you tricked the second child into going for ice cream."

Recognition registered on Alexi's face. "You were the motherfucker who ran into me."

"Like I said, it's over. Let the boy go, and—"

Alexi yelled, "No!" pulling Connor backwards until their backs were against the railing. The knife was now cutting into Connor's skin. As soon as Dante saw the blood, he couldn't contain the beast any longer. With his shifter quickness, he lunged at Alexi, praying the knife didn't do any more damage to Connor than it already had. Dante held onto Alexi as they both landed in the water. He let the beast loose and clung to Alexi as he pulled him under the water. Alexi slashed at him with the knife, but it did no damage against his Gargoyle skin. Dante swam deeper and farther from the boat, knowing all along he was committing murder. Humans could claim self-defense, but being a shifter, Dante had an advantage over Alexi. The human had no chance of surviving. Dante searched his conscience and knew this was something he would have no trouble living with. The man had threatened his son, held a knife to his throat. There was no question about his decision.

Dante knew as soon as the life left Alexi's body. He let go and kicked hard to the surface. Gargoyles couldn't drown, but they could run out of air, eventually causing unconsciousness. He couldn't have that; he had to get back to Connor. He broke the surface of the water, gasping air into his lungs. Dante swam hard and fast back toward the boat. Hunter's smaller boat was already alongside with both he and Isabelle aboard the yacht. He pulled himself up and held his breath as he noticed the blood on Isabelle's hands.

"No!" he yelled as he neared the boy. Isabelle was cradling him in her lap, rocking him back and forth. She looked up at Dante smiling. Why in the gods' names was she smiling? He heard a small voice, "Da, I knew you'd come for me."

Dante dropped to his knees. The blood was coming from Connor's cheek. The knife had sliced a gash down his angelic face, barely missing his left eye. Hunter appeared from somewhere inside with a towel. Isabelle took the cloth and pressed it gently to Connor's now smiling face. He reached a tentative hand out to his son's shoulder and let the tears fall. The absolute, pure, unconditional love Dante felt for this small being was so much more than he would have ever fathomed.

"Don't cry, Da. I'm fine." Connor looked from Dante to Isabelle. "Momma, you don't cry either."

Dante put his arm around Isabelle's shoulder and pulled them both close. His son was going to be okay, and now their family was complete.

Dante took Connor from Isabelle's lap and carried him below deck so Isabelle could search for a first aid kit. She wouldn't be able to stitch his wound, but she could clean it and bandage it for now. Hunter's phone rang. He answered it and passed it to Dante. "It's for you. Gregor."

"Hello?" Dante asked, not taking his eyes off Connor.

"Brother! What's going on? I've been calling, and neither you nor Isabelle was answering."

"We have him, Connor's safe. I'll fill you in later. How are things on your end? Are the girls okay?"

"Yes, Stavros showed up at the villa along with the buyers. The girls are safe and being returned to their families. Stavros and the others are in custody. Where's Alexi?"

"Swimming," was the only reply Dante could give in the presence of Connor. Isabelle looked at him. If she was listening in on their conversation, she would know what he meant. Her eyes met his, and he saw no judgment there. No sadness, no disdain. Only relief. She gave him a small smile and returned her attention to her son. Their son. One day he would have to talk to Connor about Alexi. Just not this day.

"I understand. We'll talk about it later. What happens now?" Gregor asked with Tessa fussing in the background. "Hush, Red."

Dante let out a chuckle. He didn't envy his brother at all. Tessa was a handful. Now, Dante had his own hands full with his woman and their son, and he wouldn't have it any other way. "We are taking Connor to get stitched up. He has a small cut on his cheek, but it will heal. Once we return home, I'll have the scar removed. We haven't decided if we are heading back immediately or if we're staying a while."

"Tessa and I really need to get to Egypt. I'm going to call Xavier and ask to use his jet. We'll leave the Society jet for you and Isabelle."

"Gregor..." Dante couldn't find the words to tell his brother what he was feeling. They had rarely been apart in five hundred years.

"I know, Brother. Me too." Gregor hung up without saying goodbye. Dante knew Gregor would do everything within his power to come home safely, bringing Nikolas and his mate with him.

Hunter pulled Dante outside the cabin, away from Connor. "I have some of my Clan coming to wipe the boat down. Nobody will ever know there was anyone else here besides Alexi. Lucky for us, he dismissed his crew today." Hunter paused and looked through the door at Isabelle. "Your mate is a trooper. She remained calm until we saw you and Alexi go overboard. Then she pretty much threatened my malehood if I didn't get her to her son," he said, grinning.

Dante smiled, thinking of Isabelle threatening a Gargoyle as large as Hunter. "I appreciate your help today. If you ever need anything, I am indebted to you." Dante fisted his heart, bowing his head.

Hunter clapped him on the shoulder. "Eh, I'm a sucker for a happy ending. Let's get you all to land."

Dante found Isabelle and Conner chatting. "Are you two ready to get off this boat?" he asked. Isabelle nodded, but Connor jumped off his seat and ran at

313

Dante, flinging himself into his arms. Dante caught him and stood, wrapping his large arms around his small boy.

Connor touched his forehead to Dante's. In his mind, Dante could hear Connor say, "I knew you'd come for me."

Dante responded silently, "Always."

ISABELLE WAS AMAZED at her two men. They were practically inseparable. When she thought of how close she came to losing Connor, her heart seized and she could barely breathe. When her thoughts turned to Dante, her Gargoyle, her mate, her heart unclenched and felt as if it would burst with so much love. She loved him. Looking back, the feelings she'd felt for Alexi hadn't been love. Infatuation possibly. The way Dante's soul entwined with hers, that was love. She welcomed it, embraced it, and vowed to hold on to it for as long as she was of this earth.

Hunter drove them to a Gargoyle doctor who took care of Connor's cut. The gash wasn't as deep as they first feared. Once the blood was cleaned off, they could see it could have been much worse. Dante held Connor in his lap as the doctor tended to their son. Once the cut was taken care of, Dante asked if they wanted to stay at the Clan villa, or if they wanted to go home. Isabelle was ready to get home, but she would stay if that's what Connor wanted. He was the one who had been through hell and back. "What do you want, Connor?"

"I have a question." His face became sad all of a sudden.

"What is it, Buddy?" Dante asked, still holding him close.

"Where will I live now? Mimi and Papi are gone."

Isabelle squatted down in front of her boy. "Yes, Papi is gone, but Mimi is still with us. She's in the hospital, but she's going to be just fine." Isabelle looked from her son to her mate. When Dante nodded, she asked Connor, "How would you like to move in with Dante? You, Mimi, and I could live in his big house where we'd all be together."

Connor looked up at Dante and asked, "Really?"

Dante's face lit up, and he nodded. "Really. You are my family, and I want you with me."

"Oh, Momma! Can we?" Connor jumped down from Dante's lap and wrapped his little arms around her neck. His smile was infectious.

"Yes, we can," she gladly told her son.

Dante stood so they could make their way to the airport. Connor grabbed Dante's hand before taking Isabelle's. As they were walking to the SUV, Connor asked, "Can I have a puppy?"

Isabelle laughed. Boy did they have a lot of explaining to do. She smiled up at her mate. "Let's go home."

Dante leaned down and softly kissed her lips. "Yes, let's."

The ride to the airport was mostly quiet as Connor sat in the backseat of the SUV, intent on the sketchpad in his lap. Dante's hand was resting on Isabelle's thigh, his thumb lazily rubbing back and forth. The view out her window was beautiful. Greece truly was a breathtaking world with the unique artistic designs and the pristine waters. Had her past experience in this place not been sullied with such ugliness, she would have longed to stay and enjoy what the islands had to offer. Maybe someday they could come back and make happy memories. Now, she wanted to close the book on her past, and start the next chapter of her life with a blank page, filling it only with love and goodness.

Chapter Thirty-Five

WITH GREGOR AND Tessa flying directly to Egypt, Gregor had given Dante the keys to his Hummer. The Aston Martin was a great car, but it wasn't suitable for a family. Dante wouldn't fit in Isabelle's small hybrid, so they would need to purchase something larger. Preferably something that would seat several children. Dante planned to give Isabelle time to adjust to her new surroundings, but he wanted to work on giving Connor a sibling very soon. With Kaya being pregnant, the Di Pietro line was already being continued. Dante wanted to add to it.

They arrived at Dante's home, their home, in the early morning hours. Even though he had slept most of the flight, Connor was asleep in the back seat. Dante hated the fact that Isabelle was seeing her new home for the first time in the dark, but it couldn't be helped. She could have a tour of the outside when daylight broke. He gently pulled Connor from the backseat trying his best not to wake the boy. It worked until they were inside. Connor raised his head from Dante's shoulder, his eyes growing wide as he noticed where they were. "Is this our house?"

It amazed Dante how one minute Connor had the mannerisms of a teenager, and the next, he acted like the six-year-old he was. "Yes, this is our home." Connor wiggled so he put him down, allowing him to look around. Dante stood silently as both Isabelle and Connor checked out the first floor. It was an open floor plan with the living area, dining and kitchen forming one large room. The lower level also held an office, a media room, laundry, and small gym. The second story held a master suite as well as five bedrooms and bathrooms.

"Can I see my bedroom?" Connor asked when he got bored with the first floor.

"This way," Dante said and motioned to the staircase. Clasping Isabelle's hand, he led his family upstairs. The master suite was separated from the other rooms. He turned in the opposite direction when they reached the top of the stairs. "There are five bedrooms. You may choose whichever one you like." Dante pulled Isabelle into his arms as Connor explored the rooms. "Welcome home, Beautiful," he whispered in her ear. She pulled his head down and brought their mouths together. He opened to her, their tongues dancing. The kiss deepened as Dante pulled her body closer to his. His beast knew its mate was home, and it wanted to welcome her properly. Dante did his best to keep his shifter at bay – for the time being.

"We've got a swimming pool!" Connor's excitement broke through their passion. "I want this one," he told them, exiting the room he'd chosen.

Laughing, Dante released Isabelle's mouth. "Then it's yours. Now, let's get you settled in bed," Dante said with a full heart.

Connor didn't argue, didn't ask any questions. Isabelle pulled the covers down, and after kicking his shoes off, he climbed into the bed. Isabelle hugged him and kissed him on the forehead, telling him goodnight. "Goodnight, Momma."

Dante didn't hesitate to go to his son. The little boy

held his arms open, and Dante wrapped him up tightly. "Goodnight, Da," he said with a sleepy smile.

Dante's soul was singing. "Goodnight, my son."

Isabelle took Dante's hand and pulled him from the room. "Can I see my bedroom?" she asked, grinning. His beast clawed at his insides, begging to be loosened. Without a word, Dante picked Isabelle off her feet and strode to the other end of the house. He gently placed her body on the bed before turning on the lamp. He shut the door just in case Connor decided to get up later. Isabelle was on her knees undressing by the time he got back to the bed. Her voice was husky as she demanded, "Come here to me."

Dante wasted no time in losing his own clothes. When he stretched out on the bed beside her, Isabelle pushed at his shoulders, rolling him to his back. "Have I thanked you?" she breathed into his ear before nipping at his earlobe. "Properly thanked you?" she asked as she licked a nipple. Dante's cock was throbbing, needing to be touched, but his mate obviously had an agenda. One he would gladly see played out. She bit the other nipple.

"No, I don't think you have," he hissed as he placed his hands behind his head, giving Isabelle complete control.

Isabelle's naked body was a beautiful sight. As she licked and teased his nipples, he drank her in. Her long hair was in a ponytail, loose strands falling around her face. Her nipples were teasing as they grazed his stomach. Her round ass was perfect, enticing, waiting to be bitten. Isabelle's strong hands massaged his thighs as her pretty mouth found his cock. He was more than happy to let her have her way, but he

319

wanted more than her mouth. He needed to be buried balls deep in her core. Isabelle took him to the back of her throat, swallowing. She licked his length, following her tongue with her hand, twisting the leaking head. Dante had Isabelle flipped onto her back with his cock slamming home before she knew what was happening. "Hey," she protested. "I was thanking you properly," she said, wiping the saliva off her chin.

"Yes, you were, and now I'm thanking you. How do you want me?" Dante would give her the option, but he really hoped she wasn't in the mood for making love. He needed to pound her into the mattress.

"Hard, Baby. I want to feel you." Isabelle wrapped her legs around his waist and grabbed his shoulders.

Dante didn't hold back. Couldn't hold back. He had already marked her, making her his. Now that he had her home, he needed to claim her again, here. He closed his eyes and let the beast loose. Isabelle's fingers were now clutching his skin, and her heels were digging into his thighs. His mate was meeting him thrust for thrust, her moans a symphony with his grunts. "Harder," she gasped as he drove in and out with everything he had. It amazed him how in tune their bodies were. He knew when her orgasm was closing in. Her breathing stopped as she anticipated her release. He lowered his body so he could capture her screams in his mouth.

Dante's cock shot his release into her body as her pussy pulsed around him. They swallowed each other's pants and gasps, their breath mingling. With his cock now spent, he moved off to her side, propping on an elbow so he could look at her. His mate. His beautiful female. With her face flush, she was the most gorgeous creature he'd ever seen. After a few minutes of quietly looking at his woman, he rolled off the bed and went into the bathroom, wetting a washcloth. He cleaned their combined come off his cock. After rinsing the cloth and rewetting it, he returned to the bed and wiped between Isabelle's legs. When he was satisfied she was clean, he tossed the wash cloth in the direction of the bathroom.

He pulled the covers down, and they both crawled underneath. He drew Isabelle close, wrapping her in his arms. "That was amazing," she whispered into his neck. He gave her a squeeze, letting her know he agreed.

Closing his eyes, he thanked the gods both his mate and their son were safely back where they belonged. His body was nearing sleep when Isabelle groggily murmured, "I love you, too."

The next few weeks were a whirlwind. Dante went back to the morgue, and Isabelle returned to the Pen. She was dedicated to undoing the harm the previous doctor had inflicted. She was also obsessed with Vincent. She confided in Dante she was having flashbacks to her childhood, memories triggered from being around the albino-looking shifter. She promised to be careful around him and to talk to Dante if she remembered anything.

Quinten had overseen packing up the old house and delivering Maria and Connor's things. They would wait until Maria was in a better place to deal with Rico's stuff.

Gargoyles came and went about their home as training was in full swing. Connor was in awe of all the new *uncles* who were thrust into his life. The Goyles

321

were just as awestruck as he was. Uri, Jasper, Frey, Mason, and Rafael were scheduled for today's session. They all arrived with Kaya accompanying them. Instead of heading to the area they used for sparring, they made their way into the kitchen. Isabelle was cooking breakfast, and Connor was at the island, drawing. Dante was just standing with his hands in his pockets, watching them both as he often did. When Connor noticed the men, he jumped down from his stool and ran to them. Dante grinned at his son as he knuckle bumped each one. Uri squatted down. "I have a surprise for you."

"For me? Is it a puppy?" he asked, his eyes wide. Everyone laughed. Connor had been asking for a puppy every day since they returned. Dante was going to have to explain why they couldn't get a dog.

"No, it's something else." Uri pulled a child-sized sword from behind his back. He had asked Dante's permission before crafting it. While it wasn't a wooden toy, it wasn't as sharp as a real weapon either. Connor carefully touched the tip of the blade. Before Uri gave it to him, he explained, "Connor, you are now a member of our family. When you are old enough, you will train with us, as one of us. Until then, we want you to have your own sword. This isn't a toy. It is a real weapon. This signifies you are a Di Pietro and are worthy of the blade. Practice with it, become one with it. When the day comes, it will serve you well."

What happened next had everyone in shock. Connor turned to Rafael, fisted his heart and bowed his head stating, "My King." He turned to Uri and asked, "May I?" Urijah placed the hilt in Connor's small hand. As he tested the weight and balance of the weapon, he nodded. "Feels good, thank you." Connor carefully placed the sword on the table and looked at Dante. "Now, about that puppy." The room erupted in laughter as everyone wiped their eyes.

ISABELLE AND KAYA sat on the back deck, enjoying coffee and small talk while the men were training. Connor, with his sword, was watching the Gargoyles, mimicking their movements. It was Thanksgiving break at school, and Dante and Isabelle were going to enroll him in the local elementary. Kaya said, "I'm glad I have a few years before I have to worry about schools." She placed her hand on her stomach. Kaya wouldn't be showing for a few more months, but Isabelle remembered well the feeling of having life growing in her stomach. She had often put her hand there, talking to Connor.

Isabelle grinned. "I hate to burst your bubble, but it'll be here before you know it. It seems like just yesterday I found out I was pregnant. Now look at him." Connor was carefully swinging the sword overhead. "I want to thank you for going to see Maria. She means a lot to Connor and to me, too. She is like a mother to me."

"You don't have to thank me, Isabelle. We are family now. I have to be honest with you. I'm still getting used to all this. I never had a big family. It was just my parents and me. Then when my father was killed, my mom sort of drifted away, even though we lived in the same house. After I joined the Academy, she moved out of town, leaving me alone. Said she couldn't handle me being a cop. It was just me for a long time. Until Rafael, and just like that, instant family." Kaya's face lit up with the smile of a contented woman.

"I was basically alone, too, even though I have sixteen siblings out there. Talk about a big family. One day…" She didn't finish her thought out loud, but one day, she would find them all.

Once the men left, Isabelle and Dante took Connor to see Maria. They visited her every day. She was doing exceptionally well and was ready to get home. Dante and Isabelle were standing beside the bed. Isabelle placed her back to his front, and he wrapped his arms around her waist. Connor was sitting beside Maria on her bed telling about the latest visit by his uncles when the door opened. He looked up and smiled. "Hello, Miss Caroline."

Isabelle tensed, and Dante squeezed her tighter in his arms. It was obvious Connor had been around Caroline since he knew her instantly.

"Hello, Connor. I came to check on your Mimi, but I see she has plenty of company. I can come back."

"No, don't go," Maria pleaded. "Dante, will you please take Con and find me a candy bar? I've suddenly got the urge for some chocolate."

Dante had vowed to protect Isabelle. If she said no, he would stay even though it would hurt Maria's feelings. She relaxed and turned in his arms. Placing her hand on his cheek, she told him, "It's okay. I've got this." Isabelle turned and plucked Connor off the bed. "Go with your father." She didn't miss the gasp that came from Caroline.

Connor held onto Dante's hand as they left the room. Isabelle continued looking at the door her two men exited, putting off the conversation as long as possible. Maria had other ideas. "Life is too short to continue with the lies. Isabelle, I have a confession to make." Caroline tried to interrupt, but Maria wasn't having it. "No, Caroline. She deserves the truth. After the harrowing few weeks we've all had, I'm done with the secrets. Isabelle, my family has been serving your father's family for many, many years. We know all about Jonas, who he is, what he is. While I don't agree with your parents leaving you to be raised by Enrico and myself, I understood why they did it. I'm not making excuses for them or taking sides."

Isabelle couldn't believe her ears. Maria knew?

"You and your mother have a lot to talk about, whether you believe it or not. Caroline, Isabelle needs to know about her siblings. It's time she learned about her family. *All* her family. No more secrets. Isabelle, if you don't want me in your life now, I understand. I am no better than your parents having kept secrets from you for so long, but know this. I love you. I have loved you since the day you set foot in my home, and I love Connor as if he were my own grandchild. You gave us so much when you were with us. You might not realize how much you meant to me and Rico. Thank you."

Isabelle stepped closer to the bed and gently raised Maria's hand. "No, thank *you*. You were always there for me when I needed someone. Of course I still want you in my life. Connor's already picked out your bedroom. It's right next to his." She leaned over and kissed her old friend on the cheek before turning to Caroline.

"Maria's right. The least you can do is tell me about my brothers and sisters. Until my latest ordeal in Greece, I didn't realize just how important family is. Dante and his family stuck by me when I thought I was alone. They had my back whether I asked for it or not. I want to be there for my own family, but I can't do that if I don't know who and where they are. So I would greatly appreciate if you would provide a list for me."

Caroline nodded, tears streaming down her face. "I can do that. Maybe one day you'll forgive me. I've watched over both you and Connor all these years. You didn't know it, but I was right there, always watching. I know I've lost you, but please, don't take Connor away from me."

Isabelle nodded, afraid to speak. For Connor's sake, she would do her best to find forgiveness for her parents. There was a small knock on the door, and Connor and Dante peeked in. "I found chocolate," Connor whispered. Isabelle couldn't help the laugh that escaped. Her son was something else.

"Come on in and give Mimi her candy." Isabelle ruffled his brown hair as he walked by. Dante was immediately behind her, wrapping her in the safety of his arms. Caroline looked wistfully at the three of them. She told Maria she would come back later and quietly left the room.

"Why is Miss Caroline so sad?" Connor asked Maria.

Maria took the candy bar from him as she said, "She misses her family."

"We can be her family," he said to his Mimi. Leave it to a six-year-old.

Chapter Thirty-Six

ISABELLE PLACED HER purse in her desk drawer as she did every morning. As soon as she sat down, she noticed an envelope – a plain white envelope with only her name written on it. The last time that happened, her world was upended. There was something familiar about the handwriting. Unlike the other letter where her name was written in block letters, this was a beautiful, artistic script. This letter was from her mother.

Carefully she opened the flap and removed the contents. True to her word, Caroline had listed the names of her brothers and sisters, as well as their last known whereabouts. Isabelle began reading.

My dearest Isabelle,

Here are the names of your siblings as well as their last known addresses. I've listed their names as they are now. Some of the adopted parents chose to keep their original names, though very few.

I know you would prefer to speak to Tessa about this, but since she isn't available, I'm here should you have any questions. I'm giving you both my home and cell phone numbers should you wish to talk. I hope this brings you some sense of peace. Please know I was only trying to protect you.

All my love,

Mother

Isabelle sat in stunned silence as she scanned quickly over the list of names. When she could focus more clearly, she started over. There towards the middle… Surely it was a coincidence. Or was it? Her memories from her childhood had continued to plague her in the form of flashbacks. She picked up her phone and dialed the number at the bottom of the letter.

"Hello?"

"Caroline, it's Isabelle. I received your letter, thank you."

"Hello, Darling. I'm really glad you call—"

"Tell me about Gabriel," Isabelle cut her off. She needed information, and she needed it now.

Caroline's voice was sad. "He was beautiful and brilliant. You were just a baby when…" Caroline's voice trailed off, sniffles coming over the line.

"When what? Mother, I need to know." Isabelle realized too late she called her *mother*.

"He was walking home one day when he began his transition. Unfortunately, some of Gordon Flanagan's men saw what was happening and took him. We didn't know what had happened to him for a long time. We searched; gods did we search. And his girlfriend, she never gave up on him." Caroline paused to blow her nose. Isabelle could sympathize, having gone through the last few days with her own child missing.

"One day he showed up. Out of the blue, he walked into the house. We barely recognized him. He had been beaten badly, and he was so pale. For weeks, he wouldn't speak. He would sit in the garden with his face toward the sun, eyes closed. Rebekah tried to reach him, but eventually he pushed her away."

Isabelle froze. *Rebekah.* Gabriel was remembering his girlfriend, his love.

Caroline continued, "You would crawl up into his lap and sit with him. Often you would fall asleep in his arms, and he'd just sit there, rocking you for hours. He knew I was there, in the background watching, but he ignored me for the most part. One day, while he was rocking you, he spoke to you, sharing his story. I'm pretty sure he was telling me what happened in a roundabout way, but I think the pain was too much for him to share with me. So he whispered his secrets to a toddler, asleep in his arms.

"For a while he seemed to get better. You and he were inseparable. Even at night when I'd put you in your crib, I'd often get up to check on you, and there he'd be, sitting quietly in the dark, just watching you. Upon a hope, I contacted Rebekah and asked her to visit with him. She agreed, but it wasn't the happy reunion we hoped for. Gabriel went on a rant, muttering about someone named Vincent and how the monster stole Rebekah. To say it broke my heart is an understatement. But poor Rebekah, that girl's soul was shattered again. I haven't seen her since that day, and it's been over thirty years. That night, I got up to check on you, expecting Gabriel to be in your room, but he wasn't. I checked the house, the garden, everywhere. He was gone. I haven't seen him since."

Isabelle couldn't breathe. It was true. Vincent… *Gabriel…* was here, in the Pen. He had recognized her on some level, and he was here. "I have to go." She hung up and ran out in the hallway. She had to find Deacon. "Deacon," she yelled, not caring if she sounded uncivilized or not. With his shifter hearing, it would be faster than a telephone.

She took off for the door that led to the lower level. As she rounded the corner, Deacon was jogging her way. "Isabelle, are you all right? What is it?"

"I have to see Vincent. Now." Isabelle's heart was speeding, but she didn't bother slowing it. She had to see her brother.

"I was just on my way to take you to see him. What's this about?" Deacon asked as he escorted her to the solitary cells.

"I just need to talk to him. I'll explain later." Isabelle wanted to be one hundred percent correct before she stated out loud what her heart already knew. As she did every morning, Isabelle approached Vincent's cell and looked in. Today was no different than any other; he was lying on his bed, eyes closed. She wasn't a psychologist, and she wasn't sure if what she was about to do would do more harm than good, but the sister in her won out over the doctor.

"Gabriel, it's me, Izzy." She placed her hand on the glass, nervous of what his response would be. She didn't have to wait long to find out. Gabriel flipped off his bed, and in a couple of steps was at the door. His large hand mirrored hers as he looked at her through the window. Tears wet his beautiful eyes.

"Izzy? Is it really you? I… my mind is so fucked sometimes. I remember a little girl, and I see… Fuck!" Gabriel leaned his head against the window, closing his eyes. "Rebekah. Are you… do you…?" Gabriel turned from the window, pacing the small cell.

"Gabriel, it's really me. I just grew up. Please look at me," she pleaded.

330

When he turned her way, she softly said, "It is me, I promise. I don't know where Rebekah is. Do you want me to find her for you?" Isabelle had no idea if she could find Gabriel's girlfriend. *Holy crap. Rebekah has to be his mate. They were dating, and he transitioned.*

Gabriel looked at his bare feet, his chest no longer heaving. He was calming himself. For her. "No, it's better she not see me this way. I'm not the man she fell in love with. I'm a monster."

Isabelle's heart broke for her brother. Knowing it was Gordon Flanagan who did this to him had her seeing red. If the man weren't already dead, she'd find him and kill him herself. "You are not a monster. The real monster is the man who did this to you. Gabriel, Gordon Flanagan is dead."

Gabriel's head snapped up, surprise covering his pale face. "Good," he whispered. "I'm tired. I don't want to talk anymore." He returned to his bed, putting his back to her. The one thing Isabelle couldn't understand was why Gabriel would return to the man who made him what he'd become. Maybe one day he would be able to explain it.

She knew there would be no more discussion this day, but her heart swelled with hope. Hope that she would be able to help her brother overcome what had been done to him so long ago. Hope that he would one day soon see the sunshine, whether it be the orb in the sky, or the girl who still had his heart.

Wiping the tears from her face, Isabelle turned to leave. Instead of finding Deacon, Dante was waiting quietly for her. She didn't hesitate to walk into his open arms, welcoming the love she felt pouring from her mate.

Epilogue

DANTE WALKED INTO the kitchen of the manor with his three-year-old son, Deklan, on his shoulders. Thanksgiving was always a big deal at Rafael's home, but now that their family was growing, it was important they all gather together at least once a year. Priscilla and Maria were busy preparing food as they chatted away. The two had grown quite close over the past five years, both having so much in common.

Rafael's four-year-old, Sebastian, was patiently sitting on the floor, playing with Gregor's twins, Anthony and Tabitha. When Deklan saw his cousins, he politely asked his Da to put him down by patting him on the head. Deklan didn't talk much, but when he did, he articulated his words as well as a much older child. He was well on his way to being as smart as Connor. Thinking of his oldest son, Dante's heart swelled with pride as it did every time he thought of the boy. At eleven, Connor was giving Julian a run for his money in the IQ department. Isabelle allowed Connor to spend time with his grandfather who was certain Connor would surpass even his greatness in the sciences. Even if Connor hadn't been a genius, Dante would have loved him just as much.

Dante took a long look around the room at his brothers, cousins, mates, family, and all the children present. Isabelle and Kaya were both pregnant and both due in July. Neither one was showing, but they instinctively held their stomachs, protecting the small beings inside. Isabelle had found most of her siblings with the help of Caroline. Their relationship was still a bit strained, but at least Isabelle was trying to forgive her mother.

"You are *not* cloning the twins!" Tessa screeched at Jonas as he followed her through the large house, trying to make her see reason. Dante glanced at Gregor who was laughing. Tessa Stone was the most stubborn woman he'd ever seen, as well as one of the strongest. His admiration for her had grown over the past few years as she continuously put her own life on the line to save others. In the two years since the twins were born, she had slowed down in the risk-taking department.

As usual, Connor had his sketchpad and pencils. He may look lost in concentration, but he was well aware of everything going on around him. Dante didn't understand the deep connection he had with his adopted son, but he wouldn't trade it for anything. It had come in handy more than once. It wasn't such that they could constantly hear the other's thoughts, and for that Dante was glad. He'd hate to scar his son with the sordid ideas he had for Isabelle, or those she had for him.

Dante was pretty sure Deklan had been conceived while they were acting out a mutual fantasy that had to do with Dante dressed in a suit and Isabelle spread out over the hood of the Aston Martin. Dante would never get rid of that car.

Priscilla and Maria announced dinner was ready. Everyone took their places around the table and began dishing out food, passing rolls, and generally enjoying their time together. Kaya and Isabelle were talking about pregnancies and baby names. Kaya and Rafael had chosen the name Stefania. Sebastian, also being gifted, had informed his parents there was a baby girl in his Momma's tummy, and her name was Seven. It was cute to watch Bas talk to Kaya's stomach, something he did often.

When Deklan was born, Isabelle agreed Dante could name the boys they had if she could name the girls. He already knew the babe inside her was a girl, but they agreed not to tell anyone just yet. Isabelle said, "I was thinking about Alyssa if we have a girl."

Dante thought it was a good name until Connor told his mother, "You can't."

Everyone stopped what they were doing and looked at him. Dante asked, "Son, what's wrong with Alyssa?"

"Nothing's wrong with it, Da. It's just we will have an Alyssa in the family one day. We don't need two." Everyone knew Connor was special; they just had no idea of the extent of his abilities.

"Do I even want to ask?" Isabelle asked anyway.

"She will be my mate." Connor slid his chair away from the table and collected his sketchpad. He flipped to the back and turned the pad around for everyone to see a blonde-haired little girl holding a jar containing a lizard.

"Is that *the* lizard?" Tessa asked.

"Yes. I don't know when we will meet again, but we will. Until then, I will wait for her." Connor put the pad back and sat down. He looked at his mother. "Please pass the potatoes."

And pass the potatoes she did.

A Note from the Author

Dear Reader: I hope you enjoyed Dante and Isabelle's story. Connor wormed his little way into my heart, and he is going to be something special. If you enjoyed the book, please leave a review. It doesn't have to be long, just honest and heartfelt. Frey and Abbi are next, and their story has all the feels. It will be hard for some to read, and it was equally hard for me to write as it deals with abuse.

About the Author

Faith Gibson is a multi-genre author who lives outside Nashville, Tennessee with the love of her life, and her four-legged best friend. She strongly believes that love is love, and there's not enough love in the world.

She began writing in high school and over the years, penned many stories and poems. When her dreams continued to get crazier than the one before, she decided to keep a dream journal. Many of these night-time escapades have led to a line, a chapter, and even a complete story. You won't find her books in only one genre, but they will all have one thing in common: a happy ending.

When asked what her purpose in life is, she will say to entertain the masses. Even if it's one person at a time. When Faith isn't hard at work on her next story, she can be found playing trivia while enjoying craft beer, listing to hard rock music (preferably live), reading, or playing with her pit bull pup.